The Scottish Duke, the Rules of Time Travel, and Me

THE RULES OF TIME TRAVEL

DIANA KNIGHTLEY

D1707435

To my husband for listening to me go on and on and on and on and so so much on and on about these new characters... I love you.

Chapter 1 - The Duke

1670

KILCHURN CASTLE

There was a rap on m'door. "Enter!"

M'brother Aenghus entered. "Nor, ye busy?"

"Nae." I placed my quill on the cloth beside the paper. "I was finishing these letters. What can I help ye with?"

He settled intae the chair and grinned. "Auld Lahn was askin' if I were busy and he had the look of someone who needed a hand in the cellars and tis a thankless job, he reeks as ye ken, and has that horrible flatulence. Sometimes I can bear it, but I was in nae mood, so I told him I was needed here in yer chamber. I am ready tae do yer bidding."

"Yet, ye are unbidden."

"I will do anything at the opposite end of the castle away from the cellars."

I chuckled and said, "Now I am left wonderin' whether tae be a good brother and keep ye here as company or whether I ought tae be a proper laird and tell ye tae head tae the cellars or ye will be whipped?"

"Verra funny, ye winna whip me, ye are too soft. Ye remember what it was like when Da beat ye and ye canna do it, tis why I kent yer office would be a safe harbor, else I would be hidin' in a corner somewhere." His grin went even wider. "I remind ye, he reeks, but also ye needed someone tae visit ye and bring yer spirits up."

Twas my turn tae laugh. "My spirits are low? How did ye ken? I was alone in m'office!"

"Today is the anniversary of yer Mary passin' away, may God rest her soul."

"Aye, tis that..." I took a deep breath. "But it has been two years — am I tae be a man in mournin' for long years? Tae be treated as someone who needs their spirits raised up?"

Aenghus shrugged. "If yer spirits are low, and they are low, yer brother ought tae try tae raise them, tis my fraternal duty. Our other brother, Malcolm inna here—"

"He returns in two months."

"Aye, so tis my duty tae raise yer spirits. I daena ken if ye hae been in mournin' for too long or nae, I daena begrudge it, or pretend tae ken how it must go. I am recently married, so I'm probably not the best judge, but I ken ye lack spirit and I wish I could find a way tae lift them."

I grunted, lookin' down at my inkwell.

He changed the subject. "Ailsa tells me the women of the castle are wavin' their tongues that ye are plannin' tae marry off Claray tae the future Earl of Dunfermline. He is yer choice for her? Truly? Ailsa witnessed Dunfermline eyin' Claray's bosom at the last feast, but I am surprised ye would consider it because of his..."

"His terrible temperament?"

"Aye, I daena want tae be impolite, but aye, his terrible temperament: his rude manners, his auld age, and his disagreeable appearance."

"What a relief ye were nae impolite!" I shook my head. "A match between Claray and Dunfermline is verra advantageous, he is a younger brother, the title is without heirs, he is desperate. The negotiations would all be in m'favor. Claray is young, she would likely bear him a son, and an alliance with the family would be verra advantageous for us—"

CHAPTER 1 - THE DUKE

"But—"

"*But,* he is auld and an arse. What do the ladies of the castle believe are Claray's thoughts on it?"

"I am nae sure, I can ask Ailsa if ye like? This is how I am useful tae ye, I ken ye would think of—"

I raised my brow. "Ye come tae lift my spirits, but at the first moment ye want tae return tae yer wife? I see how ye are useless — ye come with these rumors but ye daena ken the most important part! Even I, in all m'terrible low humor, ken Claray's thoughts."

"Do ye, how?"

"I asked her directly, as soon as I saw Dunfermline 'eye her bosom' as ye so aptly put it. When I was given the title I made her a promise that I would ask her afore I had her married. I suspected she would be verra upset by the idea of Dunfermline, as he is an onion-breath'd blusterer." I scowled.

"'Tis verra modern of ye tae give a maiden any say in the matter. I think makin' that promise will only lead tae unhappiness."

"Says a young man who is adored by his young wife, who sees in him *everythin'* that is good in the world. Somethin' ye ought tae keep in mind, Aenghus, our sister is a fair bit of trouble tae mind. Poorly matched she would likely make her husband miserable. One might say I am lookin' out for the men of the kingdom by askin' her thoughts on it. Our sister Claray inna as agreeable as yer young wife."

Aenghus chuckled. "Ailsa is verra fine tae me."

His words, *Ailsa is verra fine tae me...* echoed through m'head as I looked around at my chamber. The walls were built of stone, hung with tapestries for warmth. The wooden planks of the floor were fitted well, and covered in fine rugs, I sat at a good heavy desk. Near the hearth there were chairs for meetings and a doorway that led intae m'private chamber. When I had been young I had admired that door, thinking m'father could command his men from his public chamber then retire intae his bedchamber without havin' tae move through the halls. It had seemed powerful tae hae a private door. I had looked forward tae gaining that power, not realizing how solitary it would one day become — at one time these chambers had rung with the laughter of m'Mary and my young son, Eaun, lost two years ago tae the fever, but we dinna talk on him, he had been a year old at the time, a fine healthy boy until he was nae more.

Aenghus bowed his head. "I beg yer forgiveness, Yer Grace, I dinna mean tae be so glib about m'wife, twas insensitive."

I exhaled. "Tis unnecessary tae want forgiveness for yer good fortune, Aenghus. Our familial lands are meant tae be lived upon, the castle was built tae hae bairns wailin' in the nurseries and wives laughin' as they are carried down the halls tae make more bairns, this is the way of it... So it remains, we must come up with a task for ye."

My eyes drew tae the window as the room fell dark.

Aenghus said, "We hae had strange weather this week."

"Aye."

I strode to the window and looked out in the direction of the storm. It seemed tae be settled over the woods, just as it had been yesterday and the day afore. "Tis as if the sky has one mood but takes on another at the same time every day..."

I leaned out tae look left and right. "I hae never seen anythin' like it... yet here it is once more and always in the same place. Tis near Barran Moor...."

My brother joined me at the window.

"Daena it seem as if tis settled near the moor?"

Without waiting for an answer I asked, "Dost ye want tae go for a ride?"

"Aye, I never pass up a chance tae ride."

Moments later we had left the gates of Kilchurn and our horses were thundering up the causeway, followin' the familiar trail. We rode up intae the woods where we left the main trail for a side route tae Barran Moor.

By now the clouds above us, the whirling high bank of dark clouds, were seemin' tae collapse intae themselves. I rode toward the storm center as the winds buffeted us, slowin' our pace. Aenghus yelled over the wind, "Vigilance!" as a branch whipped dangerously across our path.

We emerged from the woods at the top of a small cliff and looked out over the moor.

I pointed at something that glinted at the base of the storm, something that looked as if the storm spiraled above it.

I yelled, "What is that gleamin' there, dost ye see it?" I turned m'horse tae race down the bank, my sight focused upon the spot where I had seen the glint, m'brother's horse galloping behind me.

The storm dwindled, the rain ceased, the clouds had diminished and rolled away.

I made it tae the spot, dismounted, and crouched beside the object. It looked as if twas crafted of rounded, burnished blade-steel.

Aenghus called out, "What is it?"

"I daena ken."

It seemed tae hum. My horse was agitated, I grabbed hold of his bridle tae calm him, then I reached out tae push the object, tae see what it was made of—

A loud clap from the trees on the other side of the moor, then another shot and another.

My horse reared. I held tighter tae his reins.

Two men were runnin' across the moor, wadin' through the burn, firing guns. Their guns fired faster than I had ever heard before, the shots, loud and dangerous.

I yelled for Aenghus tae "Run!" as the object grabbed m'hand, and seemed tae wrap around it. A pain shot up m'arm, and spread across m'shoulders. I tried tae detach m'self from its grip, watchin' m'brother ride away as the shots of gunfire sounded too near. I felt as if I were losin' the burden of m'body, becomin' separated from m'soul.

The roar of the storm rose.

I heard Aenghus's yell, risin' with m'own as all around me went dark and pain blinded me. I lost consciousness.

Chapter 2 - Livvy

2012
AMELIA ISLAND

My brother, Charlie, and I were crammed into the front seat of a truck as my grandfather, Lou, drove us careening down the mosquito-control road on Amelia Island.

He laughed. "Oooh, wheee, the wind is whipping. It's sand-blasting out here! This is peak storm-chasing, kids!"

Charlie said, "You say that every storm, Lou!"

I dug through the backpack between my feet looking for my safety goggles.

A branch whipped the front window. Lou said, "If I'm lucky it won't scratch the paint job." He turned left and careened us directly toward the center of the storm.

The back of the truck fishtailed in the sand. Our visibility went to zero. Lou craned forward over the steering wheel. "I want to thank you kids for coming to storm chase with yer old grandpa. Birdie told me this was too boring and you wouldn't have fun—"

Charlie laughed. "Birdie said *this* was boring? Fuck that, this is insane, sorry about the language Lou, you're my grandpa, you're supposed to be boring, but this is not boring. Besides it's Spring Break; the rest of my friends went to Fort Lauderdale. This is way more fucking fun."

Lou laughed. "I might get that quote notarized and put it on the wall of my office. 'Way more fucking fun than Fort Lauderdale'."

Charlie laughed. "I knew I was your favorite grandkid."

I pulled my safety goggles over my eyes. "Hey! I was invited too. Maybe I'm the favorite. I took a vacation from work to storm chase, I left my boyfriend back at home and—"

"And Chris might accidentally burn the house down."

"Yes, he's incompetent, but it's safe because he won't try to cook, he'll order out all week, but that's beside the point — the point is I came because Birdie's worried about Lou storm-chasing without chaperones."

Charlie said, "Let's be clear — you're missing work and a lame boyfriend, I'm missing Fort Lauderdale!"

"I win. I'm missing work *and* a grownup relationship. *Everyone* can see that."

As we sped over a dune, the truck lifted, and slammed down at the bottom. "You're squabbling over being my favorites — what about Dylan, off getting his degree? And Ryan, let's not forget Ryan, he's a soldier. How come he's not my favorite?"

Charlie and I groaned.

"Don't worry, you're *all* my favorites—" The back tires spun and then buried down into the sand. Lou turned off the engine. "Well, might as well go on foot, I couldn't see anyway."

I shoved my shoulder against the door to push it open, dropping into the midst of a howling, whirling, whipping tempest. Lou and Charlie were hunched against the wind, we were wearing goggles and windbreakers, but the wind was brutal, the sand blasting my skin.

I tightened my hood around my face.

The bank of clouds above us was dark, lightning struck near. Lou yelled, "Careful!" He dropped his equipment in the sand.

We crouched around and Lou began pushing buttons.

I yelled, "This is insane! This storm was *not* on the radar."

Lou said, "That's why we're here — this has been happening every day all week."

Charlie said, "Same time, too."

Another arc of lightning hit a nearby tree. Rain sprayed around on the wind. I crossed my arms and huddled against the brutal storm, scanning the landscape. The storm looked as if it came up from the ground instead of down from the sky.

I hadn't noticed at first. It was very odd.

I glanced down at Lou's weather meter and watched the numbers, the whole storm was behaving strangely. Then I noticed something gleaming right in the spot where the storm had been centered. "Weird! Do you see that!?" There was a small piece of something jutting out of the sand.

Lou looked up from his meter. "What is it?"

I crawled over a rock, hunched down, watched for a moment, then ran for the center of the waning storm.

As I grew closer I could see a small object, it looked live, energetic, powerful.

Charlie ran up behind me. "You're fucking crazy, Livvy!"

"Sure, we know that, but what the hell is it?" I dropped to my hands and knees and got close. It was the size of a Red Bull can, and was emitting energy. "Is it *causing* the storm?"

"I don't know. It seems like a gadget of some kind, but what kind?" Charlie looked down at his gauge.

I reached out and touched it — the metal of the gadget went liquid. It rushed around my fingers, adhering to my hand.

Terrified, I shrieked and glanced at my brother as behind him an arc of lightning zapped down and struck Lou who lifted up briefly, then was slammed down to the ground.

Charlie raced toward Lou, but I was frozen as a horrible searing ache ran up and through my arm, spread across my chest, and filled me with a pain that felt like being torn into a million tiny pieces, as if I were screaming out of my cells — my shrieking was deafening and torturous as I felt like I left my body and went unconscious at the same time.

Chapter 3 - Livvy

1560

NEAR LOCH AWE

I felt seared.

Scorched.

Coming up from under took a long time as the pain rose through me in waves. Inside my head was the sound of a deafening scream, erupting from inside.

I knew two things: I was injured, and I had probably been struck by lightning.

I truly hoped I was waking up in the hospital.

I also knew my grandfather had been struck.

I peeled open my eyes and stared up at a gray sky.

It was freezing cold.

I wasn't in the hospital — of course I wasn't. In a hospital I would be adrift on pain killers already. I surfaced up from under the pain and shifted my eyes left and right.

This looked like a forest. A dark dangerous forest.

There was a howling wind, shaking and rattling the top branches of the trees.

What the fuck?

I had been on the beach on Amelia Island.

I shifted my head to look around — *blurry.*

I realized I still had the goggles on. I pulled open my tight hood, *ow ow ow ow ow*, and yanked my goggles off my head. I wasn't in sand. The substrate under me was a mixture of mud and dirt, and thick with leaves.

I raised my left hand and dollops of thick rich soil fell on my mouth. I tried to wipe it off but had to spit to the side.

I heard an ominous groan.

My heart started to pound.

I shifted left and right, trying to look around, noticing a man-shaped lump nearby — *Lou? Charlie?*

"Who are...?" my voice was weak, barely a croak.

"Och nae!" He raised his head for a second. "What did ye do tae me, duine?"

I mumbled, "What did *you* do to *me*?"

He raised his head again, groaning from the effort. "Och, ye are a woman? Och nae!" He sat up and drew a knife. "Ye are a witch! What spirit is this — what darkness? What hae ye done tae me?"

It was crazy he was blaming me for darkness, when *everything* looked unlit, and there was no way I was taking responsibility for it.

The man seemed as if he was smudged all over with dirt, like a cloud of coal dust lay on him, but it was his whole self, and I suspected that it was an overlay that came from inside me, instead of on him. It was like looking at a photo with the color saturation decreased, the dark shadows going to deep black. And eerily, the volume of the world was faint. I could barely hear over the sound of my own breathing, my own heartbeat. A horse whinnied and sounded far away, but it was right next to me, saddled, carrying ancient-looking leather bags.

I glanced back at the man, he was historical looking, like a reenactor — this train of thought was interrupted when it dawned on me, *had he dragged me into the woods?*

That's when the pain subsided enough for me to get very very scared. "Who are you, what are you doing to me?"

"What hae ye done tae me?"

Why is it so freaking dark? I couldn't trust my eyes and wondered if I was possibly brain injured. *Would I know?*

The sound of my own breathing made his voice barely audible, "Are ye livin'? Answer me!"

"Yes."

"I asked ye, witch, what ye hae done?"

I groaned. "I'm not a witch, that is... why do you keep saying that? I am just a normal person. Until about a minute ago I was a normal person in Florida with a functioning brain, but clearly I have been struck by lightning or something. I was just with my grandfather and I reached out and touched the..." I jerked my head up and looked around.

I patted the leafy mulch on the ground, panicked.

I had touched something and now this had happened, *where was it?*

I found it under me and that was terrifying. I scrambled about twenty feet away and leaned against a boulder. This was good because now it gave me a far-enough-away view to keep my eye on the scary dude. *Was he planning to sex-traffic me?*

The scary dude who was sitting there, also keeping his eye on me.

His expression was furious, held on a, now that I looked, very handsome face. His hair was a warm golden color, tied back at his neck, a strand loose by his strong jaw, a perfect nose, glaring eyes.

He was hot, but also furious. His glare was not fun.

He rubbed his ears and shook his head.

I needed my phone to call Charlie, but I remembered with a dip to my stomach — it was connected by auxiliary cord to Lou's truck. I had demanded the cord, so I could choose the music. I now regretted that so much.

I should have let my brother play his terrible music. This is what I got for being a control freak, sex-trafficked by a hot dude in what looked like a primeval forest.

Hot dude was wearing a kind of dark wool coat, belted, with

what looked like a kilt, as if he had stepped out of a movie. *Was I on a movie set?*

Was this how brain injuries manifested?

My backpack was near the little gadget that caused this whole thing.

I timidly crawled toward it.

The man said, "Mind yerself, I warn ye, daena touch that device or I will run ye through."

"I would never. I just need my bag." I grasped the handle and slowly dragged the pack after me. I returned to the boulder and sat with the pack between my knees. "And by 'run ye through', you mean with your sword?"

"Aye. Ye are a witch, ye would deserve it."

"Look, I don't know what happened but I touched that thing." I gestured toward it. "Now I am here, possibly dead. That was it, all of it, I have never seen that thing in my life."

His eyes narrowed and he pointed a few feet away. "There are two of them, ye are in possession of two magical objects that ye hae unleashed in this moor. Tis yer dark magic that has—"

"I am not in possession of them, they're all the way over there, closer to you, actually. And I have never seen that thing, either of those things in my life. I am not a witch. I have never been a witch. I am a meteorologist."

"What dost this mean?"

"I study the weather."

"Tis nae possible—"

"What is 'nae' possible? Do you not understand meteorology?"

"I ken meteor, tis a root word tae mean atmosphere. I ken tis possible tae study it, as I hae heard tell of new inventions, a barometer I believe twas called, but tis impossible for *ye* tae be studying it as ye are a lass."

"Shit, dude, this patriarchal bullshit sucks, be better." I unzipped my pack, but the roar in my head was making it so I couldn't think. I zipped it again. "Have you kidnapped me — am I free to go?"

He didn't answer, instead he said, "I picked that apparatus up from the ground and dinna see ye anywhere close when it happened."

"I did the same thing, and you definitely weren't there." I looked around at the landscape, the shallow stream behind him, the boulders and rocks strewn around the field of woody plants and grass where we were faced-off against each other, then the rise of the hills behind us, walling us in with a tall deep forest. "I was in Florida, on the beach, with my grandfather and my brother."

"I was with m'brother as well, and... none of them are here now."

"What happened, *exactly?*"

"Was there a storm?"

I nodded.

"And I daena ken where Florida is, ye seem tae me tae be verra far from yer lands, but—"

"Florida? You know, the United States?"

He shrugged. "This is Scotland — ye see the ben there?"

I followed his eyes.

"That is Ben Cruachan, my castle lies at the east end of the loch..."

His voice trailed off when my mouth drew down into what my brothers called my 'comical frown'. It was my tactic to keep from crying, growing up with three brothers, I had learned not to cry in front of them. But I couldn't stop a big frown from settling on my face, a ridiculous expression that made everyone laugh at me, and now my mouth was bowed down, valiantly trying to keep the tears from welling up, not comically, at all. I wiped the tears away — hopefully before he could see them.

The stranger asked, "Are ye well?"

"No, I don't understand what is happening."

"I daena either. Ye arna a witch?"

"No, I am really not a witch. I am just lost. Or this is... this is a dream, I mean, *right?* This has to be a dream."

"I am here within yer dream? Ye hae conjured me? I think this is unlikely as I am a flesh and blood laird of these lands. Tis more likely that I have conjured you."

I chuckled through my fear. "So you admit that *you* are the witch."

He chuckled too, climbed to his feet, and sheathed his dirk. He walked over to the things laying in the dirt, crouched, and eyed them.

I stood, no small feat as I was very sore and disoriented, and joined him, though I remained a safe distance because I wasn't insane. "So *somehow*, I am expected to believe that I was transported by that whatchamacallit gizmo, from Florida to Scotland."

"Aye, or we are dead and are standing at the pearly gates." He looked around, shaking his head. "It daena seem true."

"Yeah, this doesn't seem like heaven or hell and I don't feel dead, though I kinda feel like what just happened might have killed me." I looked down at my clothes. "I hope when I'm at the pearly gates I will be better dressed."

"Aye, ye are wearin' verra odd clothes. Ye are dressed as a man."

I tugged the bottom of my pale green windbreaker down over the tops of my jeans and brushed dirt off my sleeve. The fabrics of the windbreaker and my brown backpack were shiny. My jeans were faded, the bottom hem was frayed over my hiking boots.

I muttered, "My coat is Patagonia, from the women's section."

He reached toward the gadgets.

I yelled, "No, don't!"

"I am nae goin' tae touch it, ye daena hae tae worry on it. I will never touch it again, but I need tae get it out of the open, tis too dangerous tae be layin' about."

"Is it hot?"

"Nae," he hovered his hand about a foot above it. "Tis cold as a stone, or a sword blade, yet... when ye touched it, did it feel alive tae ye?"

I nodded. "Like it hummed, as soon as I touched it it grabbed hold of me."

"Aye, it dragged me from the earth."

"And tore me to pieces."

He looked up at me, squinting, and nodding.

I suggested, "We could poke it with a stick?"

He said, "I daena trust it. What if it grabs the stick, and then m'arm?"

He picked up a handful of gravel, straightened up, and pointed. "I am goin' tae play chippy, I will roll it tae the hole there." He tossed a pebble against the gadget and it rolled a bit. He tossed another pebble and another.

I picked up a handful of gravel and began working on rolling the second gadget into another hole, tossing pebbles, knocking it so that it rolled or spun. The gadget would only go a half inch at a time, which was infuriating, but after a few tosses it became like a game.

He groaned when he missed. I gloated when I hit.

He watched me take a turn, then I watched him, until finally he knocked the object into the small hole. Two more hits and mine fell down in another hole.

I cheered.

He thought that was funny.

He scooped up some dirt and filled in the holes.

He looked up and down the gorge and up at the trees, and around at the mountain range and then he rolled bigger stones over the holes. He brushed his hands.

"You're marking the spot?"

"Aye, they are verra powerful and dangerous, but I daena think we ought tae lose them, we need to understand what they are."

"I agree."

Chapter 4 - Livvy

1560
NEAR LOCH AWE

I opened up my pack and rifled through it. I had my pink handgun holstered at the bottom, which was good, because I was not convinced this dude was safe. Some tampons, my house and car keys with the bright orange safety whistle and a tiny flashlight on the chain. I considered blowing the whistle, but... I glanced around, there was no one for miles. I had a tin of Altoids, too many hair bands, my copy of the Farmer's Almanac, which seemed really dumb in this instance, my phone charger was here, with the cord, but no phone. I had a Swiss army knife. I dropped it into my coat pocket. I had my weather meter, a bag of lint and a fire-starter kit, and a small first aid kit, basically just a few bandaids and an antibiotic cream, and a wad of CVS receipts, a pen. A protein bar. My wallet. A tube of mascara.

I unscrewed the lid on my water bottle and gulped some down.

He seemed to consider me for a moment. "Where did ye say ye were from?"

"Florida, I am a meteorologist.... It's..."

He looked blank and a little confused.

I decided to helpfully explain. "You know, where Disney World is?"

He shook his head.

"Actually, I don't really live in Florida, not anymore, now I live in North Carolina, long story — I went to university and got a job as a meteorologist and I live with a man named Chris, he's my, um... boyfriend." I didn't know why I mentioned Chris, it just seemed important that the dude know.

He looked up at the sky. "It looks as if we are goin' tae hae a winter storm soon, and I daena think we ought tae tarry for long. Dost ye hae any proper clothes in yer sack?"

I said, "No. I didn't... where are we going?"

"Tae m'castle."

"I don't know, *really?* Um..." My mind scrambled for what I was supposed to do in this instance — should I follow this strange man to a second location? To what he called 'm'castle'? If *ever* there was a red flag for a man who was going to be a creep, it would be one who called his house a 'castle'. I thought to ask if it had a torture room, but didn't want to put ideas in his head.

I had no phone and was completely lost. My mouth slowly drew down into my comical frown again.

His eyes narrowed. "Och nae, tis yer face pullin' down... ye canna stay here, where else are ye going tae go? Ye ought tae ken, I am the Duke. I am offerin' tae escort ye tae m'castle and offer ye lodgin' as ye seem tae be a maiden in distress and ye are a fine player of chippy for a lady, so I ought tae give ye a safe place tae sleep and a meal as ye are bound tae be hungry after our travails."

"Fine yes, all of this is true."

"But ye must change from yer clothes, ye canna walk around half-dressed as ye are."

I looked down at my body, completely covered.

He said, "Ye need a dress and tae cover yer hair."

"Oh." I put a hand up to my head, where my dark hair was long and loose. "What am I going to do?" Comical frown was on, tears were building up, but I swallowed them down. "This all sounds... I had no idea Scotland was like this... but then again I knew that Scotland and England had royalty, I just didn't know that I would ever *meet* one."

When I was growing up my mom always joked, 'What if the queen comes to dinner?' To make us mind our manners. It would work, but we were also smart-asses about it, there was no *way* the queen would ever visit our ranch in Florida. *What would mom think if she knew I met this hot yet strange man telling me I was not dressed well enough for his castle?*

She would probably say, "I told you so."

The man strode over to his horse — he was big, his shoulders wide. His whole vibe was like Channing Tatum. I hadn't expected to be in this close proximity to a man who looked like this year's Sexiest Man Alive, but here I was. In proximity.

I dropped my pack to the ground and pulled a mirrored compact from a side pocket and checked my face. I looked like someone who had been through an ordeal. I would have had a sickly pallor, but my cheeks had been sand-blasted in the wind. I had been told that I looked a little like Jennifer Lawrence, but they meant 'pretty'. Here I was looking like Katniss losing the Hunger Games. I brushed back my hair.

I was too self-conscious to put on makeup in front of him, so I put my mirror away.

He rubbed the horse's muzzle in greeting, then dug through a saddlebag. He pulled out a blanket, sniffed it, and grimaced. "It smells of horse and mud, but ye need somethin'."

He handed the folded wool cloth to me and then a smaller linen rag. He looked pleased with himself.

My frown deepened. "What is... what are you talking about?"

"Ye ought tae get presentable, as ye ken, *women* do."

I shook my head. A tear slid down my cheek, I dabbed at it with my sleeve.

"Och nae, ye are unable tae dress yerself?"

"In a blanket, yes — I don't know, what should I do with this?"

He took the small cloth, went behind me, draped it over my

head like a bandana, then tied it at the nape of my neck, pulling a bit of hair.

"Ow!"

"M'apologies, Madame."

I asked, "What is your name?"

"I am 'Yer Grace,' tae ye."

I teased, "So I'm to call you Your Grace? What is your *name* name, Your Grace?"

He stepped back and looked at my head. "This is an improvement, Madame, what is yer name and title?"

"I am Livvy, or rather Olivia, I am... no title."

"Ye arna married? What is yer husband's name, the man ye mentioned earlier?"

"I'm not married to... um.... His name is Chris."

"Your surname?"

"It's Larson, Olivia Larson, but everyone calls me Livvy."

"Ye sound English?"

"I'm not, I'm American."

He took the large blanket from me. "All right, Madame Livvy, ye should raise yer arms."

"Sure."

"...Yer Grace." He folded the blanket in half on the long end.

"Yes, Your Grace," I repeated, because I was not going to argue.

The blanket did smell like a combination of horse stable and body odor, but so did this fine gentleman in front of me.

Very close, his face near mine, he placed one end against my hip and then for a moment wrapped his arms around as he drew the other end to it. It wrapped once. He rolled down the top to hold the whole skirt in place.

"Remain still." He strode over to the horse and returned with a belt and wrapped it around my hips and secured it firmly. He looked me over.

He returned to his horse and brought me another piece of cloth. "Place this across yer..." He gestured for me to stretch it across my front. I held it across my chest while he cinched it in the back, tucked it, and shoved it all into the back of my skirt.

I felt and probably looked like a giant sausage since all of this was on *top* of my windbreaker.

I asked, "...and this is proper?"

"This is much better."

He drew his horse over and stood there, expectantly.

I crossed my arms. "Where are we going? I'm not just climbing on your horse when I don't know where we're headed."

He looked at me up under his brow. "Tis a long walk tae Kilchurn and I am hungry — are ye hungry, Madame Livvy?"

"Famished."

"Then ye will need tae get up on m'horse." He patted the saddle.

"Fine, but I don't know how I'm going to get up there when we've wrapped cloth around my legs." I did a few crouches and lunges to spread the 'skirt'.

He patted the stirrup, impatiently.

I put my foot in it and heaved while he helpfully nudged my ass up. I rocked for a moment, draped awkwardly over the horse.

He said, "Och, ye are as unskilled as a bairn, ye must swing yer leg around."

"I know, I know," I grumbled. "I've been riding since I was little, my family has a ranch. I just have a blanket wrapped around my legs."

He held onto my calf while I shimmied the blanket up while balancing on my stomach. Then I finally got my leg swung around so I was chest down on the horse's neck with my legs jutting out behind me.

I muttered, "Sorry boy. I know this is graceless, I am incredibly embarrassed."

The Duke said, "His name is Balach Mòr."

"Sorry, Balach Mòr."

The Duke levered my legs forward while I did a push-up.

I was sitting. On a strange man's horse.

My parents had never specifically warned me against this, but I guessed that was because it was so obvious. Don't get on a strange man's horse. Don't go with him to a second location.

He deftly put his foot into the stirrup, swung his leg around, and dropped into the saddle. The closeness of his voice startled me, right beside my ear. "Ye need tae move up just a bit..." He pushed my hips forward, then took the reins, made a clicking sound, and his horse followed his command. I used to ride like this when I was little, with my dad or my grandpa, except... this was a hot stranger

Somehow I had gone from the beach on Amelia Island to riding a horse with a strange man in Scotland, a Duke, and I truly thought I might have lost my mind.

Chapter 5 - the Duke

1560
NEAR LOCH AWE

The first things I noticed were differences in the path, the route was altered. I pulled Balach Mòr tae a stop.

I shifted in the saddle, looking up and down the land.

Madame Livvy asked, "Is something wrong?"

"There is something amiss, the stream has turned there, it is unfamiliar."

She said, "Oh."

I returned Balach Mòr tae the path and rode quietly. The lass rode well, after the blunder mounting earlier, she was relaxed against my front, and followed my movements. Her hair carried the scent of flowers, and she glowed with brightness as if she had a light within her. A spark tae her eye.

She was a beauty, twas almost enough tae lull me tae peacefulness, except the path wasna right, so I found my worries rising.

The forest was dark, beyond what seemed ordinary. Perhaps twas my eyes that were dimmed.

It was unfamiliar. And I worried on my brother, had he gotten away from the men?

. . .

Our path turned away from the woods and before us lay wide fields up tae the causeway that led tae Kilchurn castle... yet the castle appeared altered, it had only one tower roof and nae turrets. I turned Balach Mòr in a wide circle, while I looked in all directions. "Och nae, I daena understand... the castle is smaller, it is missing part of its construction."

Along the path and up and down the causeway traveled men on horses, some men on foot, some pushing or pulling small carts. In the loch were many boats, the wind gave the loch surface a chop, men were busy on the dock as the catch came in.

Madame Livvy was trembling. I tried tae explain my worries in a way that might bring her comfort. "Some of this is verra altered and I canna explain it, but there will be an explanation. I just hae tae see m'brother and m'chamberlain and..."

She said, "It's not that, it's that... this all looks very very old. I'm frightened."

"Ye must say 'Yer Grace', 'I am frightened, Yer Grace', tis the proper way."

"I am frightened, Your Grace."

"It does look dissimilar, but daena be frightened, Madame Livvy, I will come tae an understanding on it." Tae Balach Mòr I called, "Coisich!" We headed toward the castle gates.

The castle walls were familiar, Ben Cruachan beyond, the undulating hills, the wide loch, the colors of green and blue, sky and grass: all was familiar, but as we crossed the causeway I noticed that the people we passed were unfamiliar, not one face I recognized. As we neared, the unfamiliar began to stand out even more.

A large man who must hae been a guard, rode from the gate. I dinna ken him, and as he passed his eyes locked on mine and narrowed.

Might raiders hae infiltrated m'castle?

I grew more worried about m'brother and sister and all the

many cousins and yet... I couldna reconcile my worry with the state of the building, intact, and the people around us at ease. If there had been an overthrow m'castle would be in an uproar.

Madame Livvy was verra quiet.

As we came tae the gate, I said, "Daena speak. There is somethin' amiss, ye must watch me for signs what tae do."

"You won't leave me? Please don't leave me. I don't recognize anything and I'm really frightened and..."

"I winna leave ye, just follow me, be verra quiet and can ye please keep yer eyes down?"

"What do... what do you mean?"

"Ye are too direct, ye canna look the guards in the eyes or they will react."

"Ugh, I want to roll my eyes so hard I might get an eye cramp, but also... you are all that is keeping me alive, so... I will try."

"Ye need tae say 'I will try... *Yer Grace.'* Daena forget that I am a duke."

She repeated, "I will *try*, Your Grace."

She wiped her face on her arm and straightened her back.

I rode us in through the gates straight up tae the castle guard, not one man known tae me.

Chapter 6 - Livvy

1560
KILCHURN CASTLE

The only logical explanation was that I was inside a Truman Show situation. This had to be a movie set and a big budget film because no one was breaking character. Logically that was the only thing this could be. If this was logical then there was something really really wrong with the world, because that wasn't what was happening here — how could it be? What, I was storm chasing with my grandpa and brother and now I was on a movie set in Scotland?

Or maybe a big government psy-op. *But why would that involve me, a meteorologist with a desk job?*

Maybe I was insane, or dead.

But this felt real. This all felt real. Just very fucked up.

It smelled like old and shit and dirt and body odor and also fresh air and a cold brisk breeze that ruffled my headscarf. A headscarf! I was wearing a headscarf and riding a horse through Scotland with a Duke behind me, very close, so close it seemed as if he could breathe in the scent of me.

Had I forgotten deodorant?

Whatever, he would never notice because all of *all* of this reeked.

I was overcome by the sensory overload, cold, darkness, the

He pressed a finger to his lips. "We must get from this court-yard afore we speak on it, dost ye see the tall one, well dressed?"

I nodded.

"I am going tae give ye a coin, ye will approach her tae ask for a room." He dug through the bag at his waist. "Tell her I need tae speak tae the laird of the castle on the morrow." He pressed a coin into my hand.

"Okay, yes, I can do that." I was poorly dressed, out of my element, and felt incapable of doing *anything*. "You'll stay here, Your Grace?"

"Aye," he pulled me close and whispered, "but Madame Livvy, ye must not call me 'Yer Grace' now."

My eyes went wide. "What will I call you?"

"You will call me 'My Laird' it will call less attention tae us."

"Okay, this is confusing, but yes, Your *Laird*."

He groaned. "Nae, '*My* Laird'."

"What the... Okay, fine, *My* Laird."

He exhaled. "And keep yer eyes down when speakin' tae her — when ye raise yer chin tis apparent ye are from far away."

"Where will she think I am from?"

"Far *away*."

I straightened the cloth wrapped around my legs. "How do you know she's the one I need to talk to?"

"Anyone can see it, Madame Livvy. She is in charge of the castle and has been watchin' us since we arrived. Call her m'lady."

I gulped. "M'lady and m'laird." I walked slowly across the crowded courtyard to the door of the kitchen, where I could see a large fire in a hearth with stew pots, or more like cauldrons, hanging above it. On a long low table lay what looked like carcasses.

Flies buzzed around.

The tall woman narrowed her eyes as I approached.

I dropped my gaze. "M'lady we need a room for the night."

She asked, "From where do ye hail?"

"Um, I... far away."

She squinted. "Yer dress is verra odd."

"I need a proper one, um, m'lady, I am... I don't have anything else."

She put her hands on her hips. "Yer husband canna provide for ye? He seems verra capable. Ye ought tae hae a proper dress."

My eyes went wide, I thought for a moment that I might pass out. This was all too stressful. I supposed my face going pale was enough to convince her not to press, as the only explanation for everything about me was that I was clearly mental.

The woman huffed and put out her hand. I placed the coin into it.

"I will show ye tae a room in the back of the storerooms, ye can sleep there."

She gestured for me to follow and led me away. I said, "My um, my laird, needs to speak to the, um... the laird of the castle tomorrow, would that be possible?" I glanced over my shoulder — *was I leaving the Duke? What was I doing? Where was I going?* But I saw him — he was searching over all the heads in the court-yard for me. He finished with the stable man and pushed through the crowded courtyard toward me, catching up as I was led down a long stone tunnel to a small door.

The woman said, "I will arrange a meeting for ye with Sir Colin once he returns." She opened the door and the Duke had to duck to go in. There was a small bed with a thin straw mattress and beside it an end table with a pitcher and bowl on it. There was a filthy looking bowl in the corner.

The woman left.

The Duke, his head bowed because the room was too short, griped, "Nae hearth? This is the barest of rooms, fit for a servant. How dare they, I am the laird and master of this castle a hundred and ten years on."

I sat down and as my ass hit the planks the bed creaked ominously. I was clutching my backpack to my lap. My comical frown was back. *My face is going to freeze this way.*

I wailed, "I told her we were married, she thinks we're married!"

He looked concerned. "Madame Livvy, are ye well?"

"I don't know! I don't know what is going on!"

He rubbed his neck, "Och nae, I will break m'neck standin' here." He sat down on the end of the bed, a louder creaking sound, as if the bed were breaking.

There was a rap on the door.

I hastily smoothed back my hair and tried to not look freaked out while he opened it to a young woman holding a pile of clothes.

He passed the very heavy pile to me, then asked, "Dost ye want the young woman tae remain and dress ye?"

"No, I have a college degree, I can sort this out." He sent the young woman away while I looked through it, muttering, "How hard can it be?"

He said, "I ought tae stand guard outside."

I pulled up a piece of cloth. "Before you go, what is this, you think?"

"M'guess is the dress."

"And this would be the under dress?" I unfolded it. It was long and heavy.

He said, "I will call her tae return tae dress ye — this is a bit different from what I am used tae."

"No, I can figure it out."

He stepped out into the hall.

Chapter 7 - Livvy

1560

KILCHURN CASTLE

I got the long underdress on, backwards. Luckily it was voluminous so I could twist it around easily. Then I figured out that the 'dress' was a bit like a long thick overcoat, made of a saffron-yellow colored fabric, stiff like furniture upholstery.

When I stretched it and jammed both my arms in it, it would not pull across my back. My arms were stuck, the stupid dress would not fit. "Um, Your Grace, I mean, m'laird...?"

He put his head in through the door just as I figured out that there were ties at the sleeve.

"Never mind, I got this."

He left again.

I untied the sleeves and then easily pulled on the dress now that the top was like a vest with laces down the front. There was a piece of flat cloth to lay across the front with laces down the side. I hunched over to work on my front, but when I straightened up there was an awkward bunch at my waist. I had to redo the lacing and totally regretted I hadn't asked for help. Working on all of this gave me a horrible neck-ache, a tension headache, and a flop sweat.

Finally I got it all laced and rolled out my neck.

It had taken forever, I was famished. I remembered I had a

protein bar in my bag. I rummaged through, found it, unwrapped the end, and took a bite. *Yum, better.* I opened my water bottle and drank. *Much better.*

Though now I needed to pee and... was that bowl on the ground for peeing? Jesus Christ I hoped not. I would need to build up the nerve to ask the Duke.

I went to the door. "Um, Duke? Your Grace? Where do I um... relieve myself?"

His voice was low, when he said, "In the bowl, Madame Livvy."

I pulled up the voluminous skirts and crouched over the bowl and peed.

Then I shook dry and stood looking down at a bowl that was full of piss in my room. No flusher because this was a nightmare, apparently.

I pulled the sleeves up my arms thinking how smart it was to have detachable, adjustable sleeves, but then I thought, or more sizes and a store and fucking modern *civilization.*

I managed to get the top of the sleeves tied on my own, but I would need help with the rest.

I scrounged in the bottom of my backpack for a hair tie and twisted my hair back at my neck. I tried to look myself over with the compact mirror. I was only 80% sure I was right. Maybe less.

I called. "I'm finished!"

He opened the door and ducked to enter, his eyes drew up my dress. He ran a hand through his hair. "Och, Madame Livvy, ye are verra fine."

I smiled. "It seems right? I was guessing... I need help with the sleeves."

I held out an arm and he stood behind me and tied the laces, joking, "I hae untied laces, I am nae so good at the tyin' up."

Finished, I turned to face him. "Good enough?"

"Aye the saffron color is verra fine against yer..." He waved his hand.

I glanced down at my cleavage and laughed.

33

He ran his hand through his hair, straightened and smoothed the front of his coat. "Now we need tae find a meal."

"I need a meal so so so hard."

"What does that mean?"

"Oh, that's just something my brother and I say when we want something a lot, I want food, so so so hard... and I saw the kitchen, you'll want this to take the edge off." I passed him the quarter-eaten bar with the wrapper peeled back.

He looked at it quizzically.

I peeled off the wrapper and tossed it into my backpack. "This is peanut butter crunch with chocolate, try it, it's good."

He tossed the whole bar in his mouth, like a dude, and chewed, then he grimaced, and stuck his tongue out. "What is it?"

"You've never had peanut butter before, chocolate?"

"Nae." He licked his fingers. "Tis good tae ye?"

"Yes, they're each one of the great flavors of the world." I dusted my hands of the crumbs. "Your clothes aren't exactly right either."

"Aye, but I am too hungry tae think on anythin' but getting tae the Great Hall."

We left our basement room.

Chapter 8 - Livvy

1560

KILCHURN CASTLE

There were long board tables stretching down the room. Long benches for seating. A crowd of people sitting, eating, carrying on.

"None of this looks familiar?"

"Nae, this is my castle, but everything within is different."

We queued for food. "Since Sir Colin inna in residence I suppose we hae tae hold our plates out as if we are beggars."

"You never stood in line for a plate of food before?"

He whispered, "Nae, I am a duke, ye canna expect me tae *ask* someone tae serve me, they must serve me. Without question."

"That is very elitist of you."

He scowled. "Ye stand in line for food, Madame Livvy?"

"All the time, plus I feed myself from the pot sometimes, right off the stove."

"Ye cook for yerself, and then stand beside the hearth, eating straight from the cauldron? Ye daena hae a cook? Ye would eat in the heat and stench of the kitchen? I think ye are taunting me."

"I'm not, I'm telling the truth, but yeah, I get it, none of it sounds real to you, and none of this seems real to me, even though I'm right here looking at it."

"...m'laird."

I huffed. "M'laird."

The Duke stood straight and tall, his eyes continuously watching the room. I felt faint again, the smell of the food and the bodies was thick and musty, mixed with smoke from the hearth. It was difficult to see as the sun had gone down, and my sight was already dimmed. The faces around us leered in and out of the candlelight. Men were drunk in the corner. A musician played a fiddle near the hearth. The manager woman bustled in, her eyes caught mine, and she nodded, approvingly.

The Duke passed me a plate. I sniffed it, holding it close to my eyes.

He asked, "Ye are havin' trouble seein'?"

"Yes."

"It looks like cold mutton swimmin' in stewed turnip greens. There is bread."

I groaned as he grabbed a mug with some kind of drink in it. "What is that?"

He sniffed it. "Ale."

"Good, we need to start drinking."

We sat on a bench. I picked up the bread and tapped it against my plate, it was coarse, but soft on the inside. I dipped it in a bowl of what the Duke assured me was cabbage soup with barley. I picked at the mutton and had trouble stomaching the greens. The food was bland and poorly cooked and there wasn't enough spice, barely enough salt. I stared straight ahead at the wall across from me, hung with long flags with embroidered shields on them. I chewed a bite of food and then tried to swallow it and gagged.

He chuckled.

"Ye daena like the food, Madame Livvy?"

I tried a pickled pear and gagged again. "It's dreadful."

I watched the Duke through my side view, his jaw was set. His eyes never stopped moving, watching the entire room. He was tense. Through him I sensed how dangerous this was: both constant and acute.

The constant danger was everything about this place.

The acute was how the men behaved, as if they were begging to fight.

Just then a man walked down the row of benches behind us, his elbow jabbed threateningly toward the Duke, not connecting, but still.

The Duke glared.

The man laughed and continued walking.

I blinked back tears. I wondered if we would survive until morning.

I asked him, "What is your actual name?"

His jaw clenched and unclenched. "Dost ye mean, 'what is yer name, m'laird'...?"

"Yes, what is your name, m'laird?"

"M'name is Nor Campbell. I am the Duke of Awe, but here ye must call me simply 'm'laird'. Ye canna call me anything else as this is verra dangerous."

"Is it? I mean, I know it is, but *very* dangerous?"

"Aye, verra dangerous, but for now we hae a mug of ale, a bit of..." He prodded his food.

I grimaced. "We can call it gruel."

He laughed. "Aye, the gruel in this castle is a cruel trick upon us."

He slammed the rest of our ale and started to get up from his seat. "Would ye like a bit more ale, Madame Livvy? I want some so so so hard."

I chuckled.

He glanced around. "I will get it for us if ye promise nae tae speak tae anyone."

"Oh, right, like I'm going to go randomly around the room."

He looked at me oddly.

"Sorry, I meant, I don't know anyone, I promise I won't speak to anyone."

He waited.

I added, "...m'laird."

He left the table to fill our mug.

I stared straight ahead, until suddenly I was bumped by a big man, his hot breath in my ear, "What ye doin' on yer own?" And a bunch of stuff that sounded like it was in another language.

I shook my head.

One of the men he was with laughed.

"Where ye be from?"

I shook my head again and his expression clouded over.

"I am speakin' tae ye, where are ye from?"

"Far away," I mumbled.

He yanked me up by my arm. "A place where they daena teach ye respect?"

There were people everywhere, but not one came to help.

I panicked, "I'm from far away, the Duke and I are—"

"The Duke? The man ye are with is a duke?"

All the men started excitedly talking to each other.

His face got really close to mine, his grip on my arm was painful. "What is a duke doing, coming on Sir Colin's lands? He going tae cause trouble?"

"We ought tae put them in the dungeon until Sir Colin arrives." A crowd gathered, but still, they were not helping.

Suddenly the Duke's voice behind us. "Unhand her. *Now.*" He banged our mug of ale on the table

The man holding my arm shoved me away. "Yer lady said ye were a duke, what are ye doin' on Sir Colin's lands?"

The Duke drew his sword with the sound, shhhhheeeeeethhhh. He said, measuredly, "Mistress Livvy, go tae the group of women there at the end of the table and sit with them."

Five men surrounded him. I rushed down the table and perched on the bench beside the women.

One of the woman said, "Yer husband is askin' for trouble incitin' a fight with big Doloch."

I wrung my hands, but clamped my mouth closed. I would not cause more trouble.

A big man entered and commanded, "There will be no swords drawn in the Great Hall!"

One of the women said, "That's Bram, he'll bring an end tae it."

Another woman said, "He'll put him in the dungeon."

The Duke sheathed his sword, but voices remained raised — I understood snippets, "Ye are a duke?" A man bellowed, "Where are yer lands?" Doloch shoved the Duke and they glowered at each other, their chests bowed out. Every man had his hand on a sword hilt. It was very tense.

The Duke was outnumbered and I felt horrible, I couldn't believe I had outed him and caused so much trouble.

The Duke said, "Ye want us tae leave? We will leave."

Bram said, "Nae, ye are passin' through Sir Colin's lands, ye arna allowed tae leave until he grants yer passage."

The Duke shook his head. "I am not tae be held, tis a common thing tae pass through lands. I hae asked for the laird and hae been told he would return on the morrow. I was given permission tae remain in wait, but I will leave if ye daena want tae be hospitable."

"Ye haena given yerself a good reason for yer visit, nor an explanation where ye are from."

"I daena hae tae give ye an explanation, I am a duke. I can speak tae yer laird, and I demand this bawbag get out of m'face." He glared into Doloch's eyes.

Then Doloch laughed, mockingly, spit on the floor, said one last thing I didn't hear and sauntered away.

The house manager woman rushed up. "Master Bram will do his best tae keep the men from causin' more trouble with yer husband, but ye ought tae get him from the hall. Here is a bottle tae take tae yer room. Did ye hae enough food?"

I nodded.

She said, "I will hae Sir Colin see him as soon as he arrives in the morn."

I took the bottle under my arm and followed my 'husband', his stride brisk, as he crossed the Great Hall. He held the door for me, but glowered around at the hall behind us, threatening everyone not to follow.

Chapter 9 - Livvy

1560

KILCHURN CASTLE

I had no idea where I was but he led me down the halls, across the corner of the courtyard, and into the dark little underground storerooms, in the pitch black, and up to our room.

There was squeaking and scurrying as he opened the door.

"What the hell was that?" I clutched his sleeve.

"*Those* were rats."

For the hundredth time that day my chin trembled. "I need a light or... it's so dark." I squealed as I walked across the room, worried I might step on a rat, and ugh... my stomach hurt. I dug through my pack until I found the small flashlight connected to my keys. I flicked it on and swept it around the room. The contents of my backpack had been strewn across the bed and it was a mess. The rats had scurried, but then the light centered on the Duke's shocked face.

"Oh, this is uh... this is called a flashlight."

"How is it aflame?"

"I don't know how to explain it exactly. It's a little like a lantern." I held it toward him and flicked it on and off.

He winced, "The light blinds me and makes it impossible tae see."

41

I clutched the flashlight to my chest with the beam pointing down. "You can see without the light?"

"Ye canna?"

He ran his hand through his hair. "I must relieve m'self."

I turned my back while he went to the pot in the corner and urinated in a powerful stream. I busied myself scooping my things into my pack and zipping it closed, meanwhile wondering how we were going to sleep in this tiny bed. Then, for the hundredth time, the thousandth time, I wondered what the hell was going on.

"The household manager lady told me you can see Sir Colin when he arrives in the morning."

"Aye, after I meet with him we will try tae understand what has happened tae us." Finished urinating, he said, "Ye will sleep here, I will guard the door."

I blurted out, "I am so sorry I told them you were a duke, I am so so so sorry, I just... he scared me and it just seemed like a reasonable thing to tell him. I didn't know."

He said, "Daena worry on it, Madame Livvy, ye dinna understand. And how were ye tae ken that the biggest sack of pink reeking bawbags in the kingdom would want tae start trouble while we were eatin' our fine meal?"

I laughed.

He finished. "He meant tae start trouble. He would hae started it whatever ye said. "

"Oh, yeah, that makes sense... Your Grace."

A small smile tugged at the corner of his lips. "Ye are slowly growin' used tae m'title."

"You keep reminding me."

We both stood looking at each other. "So we time traveled?"

"Explain what ye mean."

"I was in the year 2012 and now I am in the year...?"

"We are in the year 1560, I was formerly in the year 1670."

"So you're back 110 years, I'm back..." I computed. "Oh no, I'm back about 452 years."

I comically frowned.

He drew his mouth down too. "And the food is terrible. I want more of the food ye had in yer sack."

"My guess is the rats got them." I really comically frowned even more, almost breaking my face.

He chuckled.

"If this is true, if we have truly time traveled, this is... I am so far back in time. Do you think we'll be able to get back?'

"I daena ken." He opened the door to go out. "I can only think on staying alive in this castle, Madame Livvy, I truly hope we will be able tae get back."

"You'll be right outside?"

"Aye."

The door closed behind him.

I peed in the full, disgusting piss pot.

I could hear the Duke right outside the door, adjusting himself as he sat on the ground.

I took off my hiking boots and I curled in the fetal position on the bed, without taking off my dress, because it would take too long in the dark with one hand and I was *not* going to put down the flashlight. Then I thought I heard something and my heart raced. I beamed the light toward the sound, then I thought I heard something from the other direction and I swung the light there. Then I swept the light all around and I was panicking, hard.

I tried to calm my breathing by counting: one two three. *It's fine, Livvy, this is just a dream anyway, this wasn't true, there was no way this was true, first, there is no science to—*

a sound.

I swept the light back and forth.

Nothing—

There is no science to time travel, it wasn't possible, and so it was likely a head trauma. Though it was weirdly specific and detailed and realistic...

I would have thought that if I was dreaming something it wouldn't smell quite so ripe.

Another sound, a sweep of the light, again nothing.

I pulled the scratchy thick wool blanket up to my shoulder. The mattress was a sack of straw over planks and it was very hard and small and stupid. I lay there with the flashlight clutched under my chin and knew without a doubt that I was going to die in the stone room with a dirt floor in the year...

I couldn't remember the year.

Tears rolled down my nose and cheeks and then I sobbed, hard.

Chapter 10 - Livvy

1560
KILCHURN CASTLE

I cried, trying to be quiet, but after a few moments I heard his voice through the door...

"Madame Livvy, are ye well?"

"No, I'm scared. I don't want to be by myself."

He pushed the door open, from where he was sitting on the ground with his strong wide back against the frame.

"Can I come sit with you?"

"Ye canna be outside yer room, tis unsafe, but ye can come sit beside me in the door."

I dragged the blanket with me, wrapping it around my shoulders. I sank down to the ground just inside the door. I leaned my shoulder against his back. "Is this okay?"

He said, "Aye."

We sat quietly, our backs leaned together, I was facing the bedroom, he was facing outside, he asked, "Why are ye weepin', Madame Livvy? I thought ye dinna cry."

"Why wouldn't I be?" I took a deep staggering breath. "I said I didn't cry in front of people, I was all alone. I'm lost, I know no one in the world—"

"Ye ken me."

"And you keep reminding me to say 'm'laird' and 'Your Grace.'"

"Aye, but I am also alone, Madame Livvy, lost as well. I am in another laird's castle while he is nae at home, and I am traveling without a guard. If ye dinna speak tae me with deference I would look weak... weaknesses are a sure way tae die."

"I never thought of it that way... m'laird."

"Ye ken, when ye say it, if ye want tae sound a proper Scottish lass, ye ought tae roll the sound a bit, laairrrd."

"M'laaiirrrrd."

"Aye, Madame Livvy, that is perfect. What else are ye weepin' on?"

I heard a bit of scurry from the corner just then, and swept the light around the room. "The rats."

"Ye daena hae rats in yer lands?"

"We have them, but not in our houses, or at least not in our beds. I've never had one go through my things before. Also it's dark here, much darker than where I come from. We have lights everywhere."

"It sounds dreadful. What dost ye need lights for in the night?"

"To beat back the rats, for one."

He chuckled, his voice low and deep and soothing. "Aye, I suppose tis a good reason. What else are ye worried on?"

I tucked my head against his shoulder, his shoulder length hair against my forehead. He smelled, but not unpleasantly, or maybe I had grown used to it. He had the scent of a man who had worked hard, mixed with spice and musk. I said, my voice very small, "During the storm, right as I was being ripped away, I think I saw my grandfather get struck by lightning."

"Och nae... ye must be verra concerned."

"I am, my brother was there, but... I wish I was there to help."

"One of my brothers was with me as well, someone was shooting at us, I told him tae run, but..."

"I hope he's okay."

"Aye, he is m'closest advisor. I daena want tae lose him."

I nodded, my head rustling up and down on the wool of his jacket. "I hope they're both okay, I hope we're okay... are you cold? Want to share the blanket?"

"Nae. I am warm enough."

I turned the flashlight on again, briefly, shined it around the room, then clicked it off. "You aren't married?"

"Nae, I lost m'wife and m'son a couple of years ago tae a fever."

"I am so sorry, m'laird."

"I am as well." He picked up the bottle beside him, pulled the cork out with his teeth and took a long swig. He passed it over his shoulder to me and I swigged and passed it back. I heard the clink as he put the bottle on the ground beside him.

"Who else do you have in your family? I have three brothers. My parents. Four uncles, six aunts, and all four of my grandparents."

"They are all living?"

I nodded, then added, "I hope so."

He said, "M'father died the year afore m'wife and son, m'mum is still living. I hae two brothers, both married. Aenghus, my youngest brother, has fathered his first son, and I hae a much younger sister for whom I am trying to find a suitable husband. I pray my brother escaped the danger, sometimes when I think on m'life and family I wonder if we are not cursed." He took a deep breath. "Perhaps I am most cursed of all. Three years ago I was granted the lands and the title of the castle we sit in now, and yet here I am in a rat-infested room off the stores. How far I hae fallen by touching that device."

He shifted a bit. "So ye believe by touchin' the device we traveled through time?"

"Yes, I believe so."

"Time traveled... this is a thing men can do? Och, I need another drink." He lifted the bottle and took a swig then passed it to me.

"I have never heard of any man time-traveling, *ever*." I took a big drink and wiped my mouth on the blanket.

"The church is quiet upon it, I hae never heard it spoken of before."

"I've heard of it, but only stories. I never realized just how frightening it would be. This isn't a charming tale of two people lost in time, this is terrifying." I clicked my light back on and swept it around the space again. I turned it off and we sat quietly for a bit until I said, "How are we going to get home?"

He didn't respond for a moment, then he said, "I daena ken, Madame Livvy..."

"I suppose it involves those devices again, we have to figure out how to work them. I don't like the idea of touching them again, but we might have to to get home."

"Aye I fear we must. We will hae tae touch them tae master them."

"I'll figure it out. It's just a gadget without the instruction booklet. Happens all the time. We just have to, as Lou would say, 'work the problem.'"

"Who is Lou?"

"My grandfather, he's a good combination of smart and reckless, he would just figure it out by poking the machine."

"Och nae, pokin' the machine is how we got in this mess."

"True... I'll figure it out. I just don't want to die here in the dark ages before we do."

"I promise ye, Madame Livvy, I will keep ye safe until we can get ye home tae yer family."

"Thank you, m'laird."

And then we grew quiet and I slowly fell asleep.

His voice in the night, my head jostling as he moved. "Madame Livvy, wake up."

I mumbled, "What?"

He whispered, "We must get up, I hae been warned we need tae leave. We must go tae the courtyard for our horse."

He closed the door.

I crawled, feeling for the flashlight, scrambled up, grabbed my pack, tossed my jeans and shirt inside, pulled on my windbreaker over the dress, and tried to open the heavy door. I yanked on it but it wouldn't open. I tugged. Nothing.

He had locked me in.

I pressed my ear to the door. Down the hall I could hear... *what was I hearing?* It sounded like a commotion. I threw the backpack to the ground, dug through it for my Swiss Army knife. Zipped up my coat. Slung the backpack on my back and stood facing the door with my knife aimed at it.

I pressed my ear to the door again. It sounded like a fight. A man's voice, was it *my* man? "Get back!"

A crowd viciously cheering.

Then a woman's whisper, "M'lady?"

The door handle jiggling.

I switched off my flashlight and tucked it in my pocket as the door creaked open. The manager woman was there, "Come, m'lady."

She disappeared into the darkness headed toward the courtyard. I slid through the door and followed her. I could hear a fight ahead of us and as I neared the courtyard I could see the Duke in the moonlight with his sword drawn, he was fighting the man from earlier.

He swung, Doloch swung. The Duke's sword was knocked from his hand and then men fell on him, beating him.

I clutched my mouth. "Oh no! Is he going to...? Oh my god, they're going to kill him."

The Duke was on the ground, a man stood over him, kicking him in the stomach.

The woman pulled me into a store room, and peeked out looking up and down the corridor. "The laird is nae arrivin' on the morrow, a messenger has informed the castle guardsmen, they hae been drinkin' and lookin' tae brawl."

"Where are you taking me?"

"Master Bram is seein' tae yer husband, he will meet ye at the gate." She grabbed my arm and pulled me down the tunnel toward the courtyard. We emerged in a darkened corner. I could see a group of about thirty men yelling and fighting.

She yanked my arm. "Follow me!" We rushed through a room and I did my best to stay right behind her though it was pitch black. Finally she shoved open a door and cold, chilly air hit me in the face.

She closed the door behind us and pulled me by the arm to the outside corner of the main tower house, down a small space created between the building and the wall, and then we came out at another door. A man waited there. He passed me the reins to the Duke's horse and they pushed me through the door to the outside of the castle walls.

Holy shit.

I was standing in the grass on a peninsula in a loch in the shadow of a stone castle in medieval Scotland.

I had just been escorted from a castle in the night, which seemed seriously unsafe.

Above me was a clear sky flung with stars and a deep chill that settled fear into my bones. I wasn't supposed to be separated from my guy. He was supposed to...

I looked up into Balach Mòr's eyes and I swear he looked down at me reproachfully.

"I know! I get it, I'm just as freaked out."

He whinnied.

I had a horse, I could ride, but where in the hell would I ride him to?

I heard yelling and it grew closer. I didn't know what I was supposed to do — go somewhere? Try to — the door behind me scraped open and two big men tossed the Duke out into the dirt.

Then they slammed the door.

Chapter 11 - Livvy

1560

NEAR LOCH AWE

He groaned, he was alive, but he looked...

I turned on my flashlight — his face was beaten up, he had a swollen lip, a blackened eye. "What did they do to you? Those assholes!"

He held his side. "Och, they tried tae beat the life from me." He looked down. "How big is the wound there?"

I shone the light on his side. "It looks like a scrape, does it hurt to the touch?" I lightly pressed and he winced.

"I kent we ought tae hae left as soon as they told me the laird wasna home."

I said, "Well, mistakes were made. I have a first-aid kit in my..."

"We daena hae time, we must ride." He groaned as he lumbered up, his right eye looking very swollen, his lip fat. He grunted and patted the horse's nose. "Och, Balach Mòr, ye tried tae warn me, but I thought a night in m'castle was nae too much tae ask."

He patted the saddle. "Climb up, Madame Livvy." He wrapped the reins around one hand, his other hand clutching his side, and leaned a shoulder against the horse. He put out a knee for me to step on. I scrambled up the side of the horse, almost effortlessly even with the thick skirts, but he barely noticed because his face was grimaced from the pain.

He said to the horse, "Och boy, now we are goin' tae get me up, are ye ready?" He heaved himself up with a grunt and paused at the top, making a phfshew noise. He inhaled, got his leg astride, and settled down in the saddle. He unwrapped the reins and clicked.

Balach Mòr carried us up the causeway.

The Duke kept his arm pressed against his side, sandwiched between us. His right arm held the reins and lay heavy across my thigh, his head butting against the base of my neck. The loch rippled in the wind and sparkled in the moonlight. He muttered, "Are they comin'?"

I glanced over my shoulder. "No, it doesn't look like it."

Balach Mòr walked us to shore, then through the fields, and then up a rise. The Duke was quiet. I tried to watch where we were going, but truly we were letting Balach Mòr decide where to go. The horse's pace was slow, a steady walk, as if he knew the Duke was injured.

The sky lightened. We kept moving until finally the Duke drew the reins to the right and the horse stepped from the path into the woods.

"We're stopping?"

He said, "Tis almost dawn and I need tae relieve m'self." He wrapped the reins around his arm again, groaned and sort-of-slid down, then he stumbled to a tree, his shoulder against the trunk, and pissed into a bush. He returned, but instead of climbing back on, he sat on a boulder then slid to the ground, his back against the stone. He asked, "Did I make it look graceful?"

"You made it look painful." I dismounted and dug through my pack for the first aid kit.

I crouched in front of him. "You're not as pretty as you were."

He groaned. "...now I am 'Yer Grace' once more."

I laughed. "You're not as pretty as you once were, *Your Grace.*"

"Ye think I am pretty on the regular?"

"I do, now let's see the damage."

He pulled his hand away and I caught a view of his abs ridging under his skin.

I was very close, investigating the bruise there, running my finger across his marred skin. "Take in a deep breath, does it hurt?"

He breathed in. I watched his chest rise and fall.

"It will be fine. It doesn't seem broken, I was worried you had a broken rib." I unscrewed the lid on my water bottle and pushed back his hair. "Tilt your head back, You have a cut on your cheek."

With my hand on his forehead I poured a bit of water on his wound. Then I recapped the bottle and used a bit of gauze to dab the wound dry. "Kind of regretting using the first aid kit already, when we just got here. Who knows how much I'll need it. Or *you'll* need it." I tore open a butterfly-style bandage.

"I am the culprit, brawling in the night."

"Getting almost kicked tae death, those guys were real assholes."

His head still tilted back, he asked, "What is it in yer hand?"

"This? It's a bandage, it's to hold the edges of the wound together so it will heal without scarring and ruining your handsome good looks."

I pressed the bandage to his cheek, then sat back on my heels and returned the first aid kit to the pack.

I got out my compact and showed him his reflection.

"Och nae, this is this visage of a monster, *this* is what ye think is handsome?" He turned the compact over to see the other side. "Ye are mistaken, Madame Livvy, I believed ye tae be wiser than this." He made a funny face into the mirror.

I said, "I was teasing. Your face is ridiculous."

He returned the mirror to me.

I asked, "When was the last time you slept?"

"I was sleepin' on the horse just now. Ye were in control."

"I was? I am very glad you didn't tell me because I have no idea where I am. We would be lost for sure. That would have totally freaked me out. But you need sleep."

"I daena need sleep, I need tae get us from this place in case we were followed."

"I don't think we were."

"Aye, but if it were my castle, I would hae asked my men tae follow, tae make sure the intruders removed themselves from my lands."

"I guess they would do the same..." I stood. "Excuse me, Your Grace, I have to pee." I wandered a little bit away, raised my skirts, crouched and relieved myself. Then I wandered back and said, "Probably."

He chuckled, "Were we still talkin' while ye were in the bushes?"

"Kind of, I really had to go, but didn't want to miss anything, probably they would follow us."

"Definitely they would, and the laird of the castle would be right tae be suspicious. My grandfather raised arms against his son, Duncan, and took that castle for our own."

My eyes went wide. "Your grandfather took their castle?"

"Aye, and all the lands. My great-grandfather was awarded the title, the First Duke of Awe, in the year 1600, but his castle was verra small, and there was another laird with more castles than he could hold — Sir Colin of Glenorchy, who, I would like tae mention, has barbarians for guardsmen and carries a shite title, a lowly 'sir', nae even an earl, whereas I come from a line of dukes, but I digress, my great-grandfather's son, my grandfather, was privy tae a secret."

I got comfortable in the dirt across from him. "A secret? What was it?"

"That the line of Sir Colin was weak. His son, Black Duncan, had a son, Colin, who dinna hae a son. They had many castles and tis verra verra difficult tae hold yer castle and lands when ye hae a weak line. Tis even more difficult when a neighboring laird has set his eyes upon it."

"So his barbarian guardsmen were right not to trust you?"

"Aye, my grandfather set his sights on Black Duncan's land and fought and won them. What if Sir Colin had been home and I had killed him or his son?"

"You might have saved your grandfather the trouble."

He said, "If I had killed Sir Colin or Black Duncan, who would m'grandfather hae gone tae war with?"

"And there is the issue with time travel, you might have changed time."

"Aye, tis all verra confusin', but it happened as it ought, and tis for the best that I was thrown from the castle afore I killed Sir Colin."

"Or if he had killed you...?"

He jokingly clutched his chest over his heart, "Och nae, Madame Livvy, ye think I would hae lost against a 'sir'? I am a duke! Dost ye ken what a duke does?"

"I have no idea what a duke does, as I have never met one before."

He grinned a big cocky grin. "I will tell ye what a duke does — a duke always wins."

"Oh, well, then I guess the good news is you didn't kill 'Sir Colin' because then another man might hae come along and taken the castle and *he* might have had sons. Your-grandfather might not have taken your castle."

"Tis a verra fine castle. I am glad tis mine. We hae added turrets, and enlarged the Great Hall, we also took their castle at Finlarig—"

"You took two of their castles?"

"I told ye, Madame Livvy, I am a duke, if I want yer castle I will hae yer castle. Finlarig is a rudimentary castle, but my

Kilchurn is verra grand, much nicer than this one. We hae ours verra comfortable."

I nodded. "I'm sure you do." I unscrewed the top of my bottle and found it empty. "Shit." My modern filtered water was gone, *that felt final.*

He gestured toward the stream. "The water there is good and cold."

I traipsed through the underbrush toward the stream bank and jumped from one flat stone to another in my saffron-yellow ren-faire-style dress, covered in a green Patagonia coat, in the medieval outdoors. It was like being on a nature hike, but insane. I balanced on a wide rock in the center of the water, wrapped my skirts around my legs, and knelt to hold the bottle under the rushing stream. It filled quickly and I drank from it: cold, cool, delicious. I scooped up more water and drank again.

Above me a falcon soared. Song birds twittered in the trees. The pines rustled as the breeze blew through them, a forest so thick it seemed like a person had never seen the interior of it. Wherever I looked there was not a bit of trash. I continued crouching, my eyes sweeping the landscape, then the horizon, and then the gorgeous wide sky, with the high cirrus clouds reflecting the sunrise. I drank again, then filled the bottle with more water, capped it, and stood. My eyes caught sight of the Duke, watching me — he looked away.

Chapter 12 - Livvy

1560

NEAR LOCH AWE

I handed him the bottle.

"Now it has water in it from your time, though, did you know that all the water in the world was here at the beginning and the exact same water is in my time in the um... future." I gulped. "Over four hundred years in the future."

He drank deeply and then wiped his mouth as he looked the bright pink bottle over. "The water tastes the same in every age." He screwed the cap on and off and then on again, watching the way it worked. Then he said, "So we need tae get ye home."

I nodded.

"I think it involves the devices, Madame Livvy, we must go back tae them. We must try tae get tae an understanding on how tae use them."

"I agree. But are you ready to move?"

"Aye."

"Where to?"

"We must go tae Barran Moor near the burn." He stood up with a groan, went to his horse, and put out his knee.

"Contrary to my earlier example, I do not need your help." I placed a foot in the stirrup and hefted myself up, with just a small nudge by his shoulder. "What does burn mean?"

He looked thoughtful, then said, "Burn is the stream that runs through the barren moor. All moors are barren, but this one wears the name."

"And while we're at it, what does Balach Mòr mean?"

"It means he is a verra big boy."

I said, "I have a horse named... I mean, I *had* a horse named Dewdrop. He died a few years ago. Now I have a horse named Dusty."

He stroked down Balach Mòr's nose and nuzzled against him. "I am sorry ye lost yer horse, Madame Livvy. Balach Mòr and I hae been ridin' taegether for a long time. Tis difficult tae think of going for a ride without him."

I patted Balach Mòr's mane. "It was not an easy loss. I love riding, I just don't do it very often anymore."

The Duke said, "Ye do it well."

"That is nice of you to say, considering, but these skirts are cramping my style." I tried to adjust the skirts under my ass, but lost balance and almost slid off, the Duke grabbed my knee to keep me from going over.

I clutched his arm.

"Och, ye almost went over, ye ought tae ken tae ride the horse means tae be on top of it."

I laughed, then watched him for a moment, he took a deep staggering breath.

"You cool?"

He narrowed his eyes, "Cool?"

"I meant, are you... um... well?"

"Aye, I needed tae get on top of the ache." He wrapped the reins around his thick strong wrist, and then held the saddle and heaved himself up behind me. He rocked his hips to get them settled, very close, and then he set Balach Mòr in motion.

We walked down the hill with a view of the valley below. "It's beautiful."

"Aye ye ken, Madame Livvy, my lands stretch from there," he pointed to the edge of the far valley, "and back..."

He attempted to turn to show me, but groaned and chuckled, gesturing behind us. "Verra far back that direction, ye will hae tae take my word on it."

I laughed.

I looked up, "Those are cirrus clouds."

"Are they? How dost ye come tae that?"

"I've just always known the names of clouds, The cirrus are made up mostly of ice crystals — and see the feathery bits there? That comes from the winds."

"Aye, we call them neul àrd, they mean a change in the weather is coming."

"I was going to say the same thing. Have you noticed that there hasn't been a storm?"

"Aye, until now they have been occurring at the same time every day."

"Lou said it was like that on Amelia Island too. I wonder if burying them stopped the storms?"

He pulled the reins to the left to direct Balach Mòr around a felled tree. "We will unbury them and see if the storm comes."

I looked up at the clouds, a falcon swooping in the air. "Yes, we'll test. The scientist in me says that if the storm doesn't come we'll figure out another test and another. We'll camp in the moor if we have to, waiting for the storm, but... the girl in me wonders, what if it doesn't happen? What if that was it with it?"

He was quiet as our horse picked a path through the woods leading down to the valley. "It stormed every day for a time, and then it threw us back here. We hae tae assume it will take us home."

"How come?"

"Because, Madame Livvy, the alternative is unbearable."

I nodded.

His heavy forearm rested on my hip. We settled into silence as we went and I thought about the weather, how the storm clouds would build out of the small device and how did it have so much power? And I wondered where the device came from — was it military? Or a terrible thought — *alien?* That would explain the amount of pain; it had to be aliens who came up with that, humans would have said, *fuck that.*

But if it was alien was it safe for human bodies? And how would I test, by using my body as a guinea pig for some kind of alien tech? And then I worried that someone from the government might be looking for it and would they think I stole it? And did our government know about time travel? Did I stumble on a secret? What if the CIA was after me now, or an even shadier group, something I didn't even know?

Or was I the only one in the whole modern world who knew about this gadget? And how could that possibly be the case? I was just a lowly meteorologist, living with my boyfriend Chris in a townhouse in North Carolina. I couldn't have stumbled on alien tech that no one else knew about.

And then I wondered about Chris. Did he miss me? Our relationship had been strained lately, by a... boredom? The best way to describe it was *indifference.*

But this might change that. In the movies this would be the turning point, the big life changing shock — Chris would probably remember how desperate he was for me, how much he loved me. And how from now on he would show me.

From now on.

When was now?

Now was 2012, I had to get back there.

When I was overwhelmed by it all I focused, once again, on My Grace's knee.

Chapter 13 - the Duke

1560
NEAR LOCH AWE

We arrived at the moor and dismounted near the stones I had placed over the devices and shoved them over with my boot and then Madame Livvy and I dug the dirt away until both devices were exposed. Madame Livvy said, "I can't believe you actually remembered where you buried them in medieval Scotland."

I scoffed. "Ye doubted me? This is m'home! There is the stream, here are the stones, there is the bird nest atop the pine, see the base? Tis fifteen paces tae here, with the peak of the ben right above it. Tis easy tae see, if ye look — the stones were out of place, all the other rocks are worn, these were jagged. Of course I remembered, besides twas only yesterday that we buried them."

She put her hands on her hips.

I crouched, peerin' down at one. "Dost ye think tis safe tae touch? It looks verra still."

"They're both very still, and we won't know if it's safe to touch without touching it, but hold on, let me make some notes first. If this is a test we should have lots of data."

She dug through her bag, pulled out a small book and began tae write upon a page.

"What are ye usin' tae write?"

"This?" She held it up. "This is a pen."

She drew a circle.

"Where is the ink well?"

"Inside." She drew the device and carefully marked the symbols upon it.

She straightened and crouched beside the other device and drew it as well. "The markings are a little different, I find that odd, but we know they went to different places, or *came* from different places, that might be why. This is the one that was nearest me, that one was nearest you... I mean, if they're a portal—"

"A portal?"

"Yes, like a door through time..."

I nodded though it dinna make much sense, but neither did the pen and I assumed she kent more of time travel than I.

She said, "So I assume this door goes to Florida, and that door goes to Scotland."

"I agree with yer assessment. We will hae tae wait for the next storm."

Chapter 14 - the Duke

1560
NEAR LOCH AWE

We left the devices in the middle of the wide moor and sought shade under an oak. She fiddled with a machine that she told me marked the weather, turning dials and writing in her book.

I held a fistful of gravel, shakin' them in m'palm, and then tossing them, plunk, plunk. "Women can read in yer time, Madame Livvy?"

"Yes, definitely."

I teased, "...Yer Grace. And what do ye call yer superiors if nae m'laird and Master and Yer Grace? Because ye canna remember tae do it."

"Well, Your *Grace*, we don't call them much of anything, 'Mister' before their surname, if it's formal, if not just, John, or Mary, you know... names."

"But what of men who carry titles?"

"I mean, there's the Queen of England, she is called 'your majesty,' I suppose, the Duke and Duchess are called, mostly, William and Kate. But maybe not to their face. I've never met them. I've never even been to England or Scotland."

I said, "Ye hae now, this is Alba, a land of beinn eireachdail, or as ye might say, magnificent mountains, and the men who rule them."

She passed me the water again. I drank, screwed the lid back on and said, "Tell me somethin' about yer world."

She considered for a moment, "Want to hear a strange weather fact?"

"Aye."

"So, sometimes, storms draw up water and then rain it down and every now and then, in the world, it ends up raining frogs."

I looked at her incredulously. "Are ye serious, Madame Livvy?"

"I am, you might be going about your day and suddenly a frog-storm happens."

"Och, I would be lookin' for shelter."

"Me too, I would be looking for a shelter so so so hard."

I laughed.

She pointed at the weather machine. "The atmospheric pressure is lowering... fast."

Dark storm clouds billowed above us, and then the wind began tae build and bluster. I drew Balach Mòr intae the woods.

Madame Livvy and I kept our sights on the devices in the middle of the moor.

"Now I wish we would have moved them farther apart, is this a double storm? Can you tell?" She crossed her arms, her hood flapped against her face.

The wind grew so blustering that we lost visibility, and there wasna any way tae approach the center of the storm. She placed her weather monitor and book intae her bag and slung it across her back. Then the winds grew tae a gale and we turned our back on it, and huddled taegether. I held m'horse firmly, tryin' tae keep him calm.

Finally, she said, "Wait, did you feel that? Is it ending?"

We turned to look out over the land. A swirl of dirt and gravel flung intae the air, then fell tae the ground.

"'Tis time." We rushed from the trees toward the devices,

Balach Mòr pullin' and tryin' tae keep me from reachin' the center.

She said, "I'm really scared! I don't know if I can touch it!"

"Ye can touch it Madame Livvy, ye are brave enough tae do it."

We reached the devices. I could see the one, mine, vibratin' and active.

Madame Livvy's wasna moving.

She plucked it up from the hole and held it in her hand, out on her palm. "Mine's not doing anything!"

"Nae!" The wind swooped and swirled around us. "Och nae!"

She looked down at it. "It's fine, it must... it needs a different time, it will do it later, you have to go."

"I canna leave ye, Madame Livvy, tis too dangerous for ye here."

"But it's okay, look! Yours is losing its power, you need to touch it and go."

"You need tae come with me, Madame Livvy, I will get ye home, but—"

The wind whipped around us.

I glanced over my shoulder at the device. "Ye must come! I canna leave ye here, twill be better, come with me and I will get ye home."

The last gust of wind seemed to die down. I glanced at the device again. "But ye must come fast, we will lose the time and we will hae tae live here in this godforsaken land for longer."

She put her hand through my elbow. I pulled Balloch Mòr and Madame Livvy tae the device and scooped it up... I felt the pain spread up my arms. I looked intae her terrified eyes and yelled, "Hold on, Madame Livvy, hold on!"

And the searing pain hit my full body and tore me away from the earth.

Chapter 15 - Livvy

NEAR LOCH AWE

I woke from a deep horrible aching unconsciousness and the first thing I noticed was the loud sound of shots being fired. I groaned and rolled to my side. I was lying on something lumpy, a pain in my rib — it was one of the gizmos.

I heard it again — loud claps, someone was shooting.

What the...?

To the right of me, the Duke. He was tense, listening, on his stomach in the dirt. He held the second gadget in his hand. The reins of his horse were wrapped around his wrist. "Madame Livvy, ye must be up, there is gunfire." He pushed up and jumped to his feet, crouching.

I mumbled. "What—?"

He grabbed my arm and dragged me up. "Ye must run!"

I yelled, "Ow ow ow," as I raced behind him. I had a splitting headache and was not ready to be in movement.

We made it to a safe spot behind a boulder. He peeked out.

I asked, "Where is it coming from?"

He pointed. "From over there, across the moor. I fear they were the men chasin' m'brother, could this be the same day?"

"I have a handgun." I dug through my backpack for my pink pistol. I had been carrying it ever since I had been scared shitless

CHAPTER 15 - LIVVY

walking home alone one night. My hands shaking, I racked the slide back, then aimed out over the rock in the direction of the shots, but I couldn't see anyone.

Then gunfire sounded. "Shit shit shit!" I aimed and fired, and burst into tears. "No no no no no." I had never shot toward a human before. Another shot sounded and I fired again. "I only have a few more bullets can we... shit... can we go?"

"Aye, Madame Livvy, come, follow me." He grabbed my pack, and crouch-ran deeper into the trees, leading Balach Mòr.

I waited, considered firing, but I didn't want to waste bullets, so I jumped up and crouch-ran after him.

Within the tree line, he put out a knee, "Mount!"

I stepped on his knee and scrambled into the saddle. He mounted the horse behind me, pushed my hips forward, and commanded Balach Mòr to fly.

This was the fastest I had ever ridden through the woods, I kept my head down, the Duke was pressed down on my back. I set the safety on my gun with shaking hands, just in case. It felt like we were flying, we left the woods and headed across the wide grassland that led to the causeway to the castle.

A man was riding at a fast clip from another path, headed the same direction.

I said, "Who's that?"

He said, "Och, tis m'brother!"

Our paths converged and his brother raced alongside us. "Nor! I hae been searchin' for ye since the storm!"

"I hae returned!"

We galloped on and then a line of more men fell in around our horse. The Duke said, "Daena be afraid, these are m'guards." We all thundered up the causeway, the guards yelling for the gate to open, and we stormed through and that was when I began to notice... everyone bowed or curtseyed as the Duke passed.

Men surrounded us to help with the horse, his brother asked, "What happened, Yer Grace?"

"I hae much tae tell ye, Aenghus, but we ought tae save it for my private chamber." While he spoke he put my pack in my lap and gestured for me to put my handgun in it. I slid it into the bottom and zipped the pack up. He continued, "We hae tae put men on the walls and we need a guard tae go tae Barran Moor tae search for the men who fired upon us."

He slid off the horse and put his hand up to help me down.

A man on the walls yelled, pointing in the direction we had come from.

The Duke said, "Madame Livvy, mind yerself, I will return, I must check on the walls." He rushed off across the courtyard, with people bowing as he passed. He and his brother took the stone steps in the corner up two at a time, then stood on the parapet, conferring with the guard.

I had no idea what to do with myself except talk to the horse. "Well, Balach Mòr, what do we do with ourselves? Just stand here and watch His Royal Hotness, the Duke of Awe, as he runs—" A stable boy took the reins of the horse and led him away, leaving me talking to myself in the center of the courtyard, wearing my hundred-year-old saffron-yellow dress, having been time-trafficked against my will by a strange gadget, shot at by assholes, and having been forced to use my self-defense pistol, which had been up-to-now just for show, and had woken up, yet again, in terrible, grimacing, horrible pain in front of a hot man who was also a Duke.

I did not like this one bit, except for the Duke of course, he was good.

I felt irritated with myself for this — I was in a relationship with Chris. Chris was hot, just in a different more modern way. Chris was handsome. Chris and I had avatars on World of Warcraft together, his was very bulked up and sexy, our toothbrushes were side by side on the bathroom counter — but I found myself watching the Duke... up on the walls, strong and straight, discussing with his men. I remembered his bare knee, and my eyes drifted up to see him again, and he met my eyes, checking on me.

I tried to look as if I was fine.

Though I kind of felt like crumbling to the dirt.

A lot of shitty things had happened to me that day, so many.

And somehow I hadn't made it home.

I kind of felt like I needed a cry, but I was in public and so I swallowed my tears, my mouth drawing down into my frown that did not seem comical at all.

The Duke glanced down. Then he jogged down the steps and crossed to me, as the people milling about the courtyard bowed when he passed. He came very close, his back to the courtyard, blocking me from view. "M'apologies for makin' ye wait, Madame Livvy. Yer face has drawn down once more."

"I'm just... I'm just really sad and this is... not what was supposed to happen... Your Grace."

"I ken, follow me." He led me into the main building and up a wide stone stair. "I hae asked m'brother tae meet me in m'chamber but we will hae a moment tae speak—"

"Were we followed to the castle?"

"I hae men on the walls and we sent a team tae scout for the villains." He pushed open a heavy door and we entered a grand room: a desk, a wide heavy rug covering the floor, a hearth warming the room. There were tapestries and even a shelf with a few books. "But a moment ago I saw what looked tae be a storm risin' behind the ben."

He drew me toward the window, set deep in the stone, and pointed in the direction. A few dark clouds cast a shadow over the north side of the mountain. He asked, "Might they hae been travelin' usin' one of the portals? Dost ye think they might hae left?"

"They might have, that would be a relief."

He turned from the window with a start. "Are the devices in yer sack, are ye touching them?"

My eyes went wide. "Oh shit, are they on me?"

I dropped my pack to the ground and zipped the top open. I didn't want to touch them so I tipped the bag and rolled them out, along with my pink pistol.

"Why dost ye carry a gun, Madame Livvy?"

"I got a little scared walking home at night from college. There was this guy, he was... kind of stalking me."

"Stalking?"

"Following me, scaring me... I've been shooting and hunting with my family for years, but..." I shoved the pistol into the bottom of the pack. "I mean, I never intended to fire it on a college campus or in a shootout with men in the seventeenth century, but I carry it because it makes me feel a little safer."

"Yer husband, yer laird, Chris dinna protect ye? Or what of yer father or brother, they could escort ye? They dinna mean tae keep ye safe?"

"I didn't live near them, the university was a couple states away."

His brow furrowed. "Ye went tae university far away from yer family?"

"And then I took a job there. I go home on vacation. It probably seems odd, right? Does your whole family live here?"

"Aye, most of them. Without the men of yer family tae ally themselves with ye, ye are nothing but a weak laird. If ye are surrounded by your uncles and brothers you will hae the guards ye need; with high castle walls ye will rule over lands; with bonny lasses, ye can grow a family. A man must have sons and nephews tae guard his family intae the future — none of what ye are sayin' makes sense. Why would yer father send a bonny lass such as yerself away?"

"He didn't send me away. He actually wanted me to stay, to help with the ranch, but I... I wanted a career in meteorology. So I left home to, you know, get educated."

"It sounds as if ye live in a verra strange world, I canna make sense of it."

"I think, even if you were standing in the middle of it, you wouldn't be able to make sense of it."

His brother rushed in. "Where were ye?! I was searchin' everywhere! And who has beaten ye and where did ye find this maiden?"

"Aenghus, that is a great many questions. This is Madame Livvy, Madame Livvy, this is Aenghus. She was in the woods near us when the men attacked."

"Who were the men and where did you go?"

The Duke asked, "How long were we gone?"

Aenghus said, "A full night! Twas evenin' when ye vanished. How dost ye not ken this? I looked for ye everywhere, I returned this morn with more men. I believed ye tae be dead."

"Nae, I was here, but ye couldna see me as I was in a different time — dost ye remember the object, there?" The Duke shifted the gadget with the toe of his boot. "Tis a device. I grasped ahold of it and burnin' pain afflicted me, I awoke outside the castle walls, but twas a different time. The castle was smaller, Sir Colin was the laird. I tell ye, brother, my mind is confounded with the occurrence."

"Ye sound mad, Nor." He tilted his head back. "What of this woman?"

"She found herself outside of the walls of the castle as well."

I helpfully added, "Except I was from a different place and time in the world, Florida, the year two thousand twelve."

"Florida?"

The Duke said, "She is speaking on the New World."

"Ye are both ravin' mad."

The Duke said, "Hae ye ever known me tae rave before? Do ye think that somethin' might hae happened in one night that would make me lose the tether on m'mind? Or dost ye think I might be telling ye the truth — that what has happened has been unknown in the world of heaven and earth, but it has happened all the same?"

Aenghus cut his eyes to me. "Ye trust that she inna a witch?"

"I considered it, but she inna, and ye ken, we daena believe in witches, brother, we are a family with beliefs based in the laws of God and man and we daena give credence tae the superstitions of black magic—"

"Except maybe dark fae."

"Aye, those are real, but we daena believe in auld crones wishing us ill. Besides..." He jokingly turned away. "She inna an old crone."

I joked, "I can hear you. I am still young."

The Duke chuckled.

Aenghus looked me up and down and shrugged

The Duke said, "She is a young woman from a different part of the world. She inna a witch, she has been in as much pain, as confused and lost as I hae been, we hae had tae band taegether tae survive it."

"Fine, she inna a witch, but tis a magic."

"Nae, Aenghus, twas verra real. I was confronted with the men of Kilchurn castle in the year 1560. I brawled with the guardsmen. I barely escaped with m'life."

"Ye might hae killed Auld Graybeard and saved our grandfather the trouble of havin' tae kill his son."

"It might hae created much more trouble —what man would hae gained the castle in his stead? Perhaps tae fight him before would hae strengthened him."

I said, "It's called the Butterfly Effect, changing the past will change the present. If we dislodged a brick, and it fell on the head of someone, maybe you would not be born — we could have changed everything." I gulped. I didn't like that idea one bit.

The Duke's brow drew down. "Are ye concerned that ye might hae changed yer *own* life?"

I nodded. "Yeah, my ancestors are from Scotland... who knows?"

The Duke said, "Then tis verra good that I dinna kill anyone." He turned to his brother. "Ye see, Aenghus, that her life has been complicated by this as well? Tis nae her fault. And I am sure she saved m'life, if I hadna been traveling with a lady I would hae been killed."

Aenghus said, "Well then I am glad tae hear it, Madame Livvy. Nor can be an arse, but he's my brother, I am glad he's returned."

The Duke said, "I need a meal."
Aenghus said, "Ye are always hungry."
"Aye, but where I hae been lodged the food was disgusting."
"Worse even than Auld Aymer's food?"
"Aye, if ye can believe it."

Chapter 16 - Livvy

1670

KILCHURN CASTLE

Aenghus left and the Duke said to me, "I am nae sure where yer room will be, I hae a few things tae organize — dost ye need tae ready for dinner?"

I said, "Are you saying that I am a mess and that I need to get ready for dinner?" I added, "Your Grace."

"It might hae sounded like that but I think ye look verra lovely. Ye ought tae ken though, ye are about tae meet my entire family, m'mum, my sister, my uncles, all of them."

"Then I for sure want to freshen up. This dress is okay?"

"I will send for m'sister tae help ye get dressed."

I stood in the middle of his chamber while he found his sister and then I was introduced to Lady Claray, a lovely girl who looked to be about eighteen, but possibly younger.

She was small, fair, had a wide grin, dimples, red hair and laughing blue eyes.

She seemed amazed that I was there. "Och, I am so pleased tae meet ye, Madame Livvy, but... Brother! Where did ye find the maiden? I daena understand!"

The Duke said, "I told ye, she was found under a tree brought upon a storm."

"Ye are jestin' with me, and I find it scurrilous. Daena ye think, Madame Livvy, that m'brother ought tae be truthful? Tis shocking tae think he would be makin' up stories."

The Duke said, "What dost ye ken, Claray? Ye were nae there!"

She put her hands on her hips and blew up the front of her face in a huff. "Tell me the truth."

He said, "I had an adventure, Claray. I was transported through a portal tae another time."

She groaned, over dramatically. "Madame Livvy, I apologize for my brother, he can be an arse."

The Duke said, "Claray!"

Then he said tae me, "M'apologies for Lady Claray, she is verra often a wagging mouth without any thought behind it."

Claray said, "Ye are the one telling me a fanciful story!"

I said, "I know I just met you, Lady Claray, but his story is true, there was a portal and we were taken through it."

Her face clouded over.

"Impossible. Inna it impossible, Madame Livvy?"

"I thought so, until I was in one place, touched a gadget," I pointed down at it, "and the next moment I was ripped through time to another place. There, in another time, I found your brother."

The Duke said, "Exactly. I touched the device and found myself wakin' in Barran Moor. Madame Livvy was there. I carried her on Balach Mòr tae the castle, this verra castle, but none of my family were there. Claray, ye were nae born yet."

"I daena believe one word of it, Yer Grace."

She knelt down and reached for one of the gadgets. The Duke and I both yelled, "No!" but she had it on her palm.

"It's some kind of vessel?"

I said, "Kind of, we've been calling it a portal, or a gizmo or a device or a gadget."

She rolled it in her hands.

The Duke ran his hand through his hair. "I wish ye would nae do it, Lady Claray."

"Why nae?"

"Because we hae learned one thing — daena touch the device. It might grab ye."

I added, "It's the number one rule."

Claray looked up at me, quizzically, "It inna grabbin' me, it inna doin' anything. There is nae movement at all, tis more like the candle than the flame."

I said, "It does seem to only grab us when it's activated or alive. I guess we can touch it when it's not. Thanks, Lady Claray, you've helped us learn something."

The Duke grinned. "We ought tae eat tae celebrate."

Claray rolled the gadget to the rug and stood. "Ye must excuse His Grace, Madame Livvy, he is always hungry and..." She looked me over shaking her head. "This dress is from...?"

"The past."

"Tis a lovely color, but tis falling off of yer form, we must set ye tae rights." She said to her brother, "Did ye hear that Madame Enid will be joining us tae dine?"

He sighed. "Och nae, I dinna hear it. Does Mam ken?"

"Mam *arranged* it, and ye ken why, she is verra set upon the match. Ye needs be ready." To me she said, "Follow me tae m'rooms."

Chapter 17 - Livvy

Claray fixed the ties on my shoulders holding on the sleeves, then helped me adjust the lace in front so that it was flat and not wrinkled. She spot-cleaned a dirty spot on my skirts, and then wrapped a shawl around my shoulders and tucked it in at the waist, saying, "Madame Livvy, none of this was right, who dressed ye?" as she cinched it all with a belt.

"I dressed without knowing how, and then your brother, the Duke, helped get the laces right."

Her eyes went very wide. "His Grace, the *Duke*? I daena believe it, he would never be so interesting."

There was a knock on the door and an older woman entered, looking flustered, talking as soon as she arrived. "I was coming tae tell ye that Madame Enid has arrived and..." She stopped still. "Who is this...? Is this the Madame Livvy, my son was speaking on? Och nae, His Grace dinna mention ye were so—"

Claray stood behind me, combing my hair. "What, Mam, what dinna he mention? Daena be rude — she is right here!"

"His Grace dinna mention she was so young and comely! Och nae, there is danger about, men attacking the castle, an unknown woman has arrived — I would nae be — I am *never* rude. I just believe I ought tae be *told* things."

Claray laughed. "Mam, ye sound as flustered as I was when I met her! But ye were told, almost as soon as we all knew, and ye ought nae be rude tae Madame Livvy, she has traveled a verra long way."

I winced as Claray tugged at a knot in my hair. "Lady Gail, this is Madame Livvy, Madame Livvy, our mother, Lady Gail."

Lady Gail looked me up and down then sighed. "I hae asked Madame Enid Holborne tae come all the way from Menstrie!"

I dug through my pack for a hairband and passed it to Claray. She looked at it oddly.

I said, "It's for holding my hair back." I twisted my hair and wrapped the band around it creating a low bun.

Lady Gail dropped the conversation and pressed close to see.

Claray said, "That is wonderful."

"I have more." I dug through my pack and pulled out five hairbands and separated them and gave two to Claray and held out three for Lady Gail.

She shook her head. "Nae, it seems verra... I canna."

"No, really, I have many of them, please."

She took them and deposited them in the bag at her waist. "Thank ye, Madame Livvy, tis a verra fine gift." She sighed. "What are we tae do with Madame Livvy?"

I said, "I don't exactly know what the issue is with me?"

Claray said, "My mother is conspiring tae marry His Grace tae Madame Enid, she has been doing it behind his back for *months*."

"And that involves me how...?"

"Because ye are lovely and she is concerned."

Lady Gail said, "Aye, I am concerned, Madame Livvy, do ye hae designs on His Grace, the Duke?"

"What? No, oh no, definitely not, I have a boyfriend, back home, it's serious." I added, "His name is Chris." Not at all sure why that was necessary.

Lady Gail narrowed her eyes and watched my face then said, "Well, that is a relief. And I will hae ye ken, Lady Claray, this is nae conspiring, this is planning. Sometimes His Grace daena ken what is good for him. He has been verra lonely and it is time for him tae remarry."

She added, "I must go and greet our guests," and left the room.

I dug through my pack for my makeup. Using the compact I put some mascara on my lashes, and then I unscrewed the lid on my natural pink lip shine, and brushed it on.

Claray clapped her hands, breathlessly watching. "Can I hae some? Ye look verra bonny!"

I held her chin and brushed a smidgen of mascara on her lashes and smeared the color on her lips. "That looks very pretty on you too." I pursed my lips and smacked them to spread the color.

She mimicked me.

I turned the compact for her to see.

She admired herself, but said, "I daena think I am much tae look upon, Madame Livvy, but ye are beautiful."

"You're so pretty!"

She scowled in the mirror then giggled wildly. "We must get you tae the Great Hall afore Madame Enid and Mam conspire tae hae the Duke married off afore we arrive."

"Will my being here cause trouble for him? Maybe I shouldn't go."

"Ye must eat, ye ought tae go, and aye, ye are goin' tae cause trouble, but His Grace haena had trouble in a long time, he needs it desperately."

"I don't really understand, but I am hungry."

"You and I will sit beside each other, I will keep ye from Madame Enid's malevolent looks, she can find fault in an heavenly angel, Och, she believes I am at fault for everything. Once she called me, in front of the Duke, ill-managed! Can ye imagine, Madame Livvy, tae think it of me?"

"I can't imagine it, Claray, you seem lovely, but maybe she

wasn't finding fault in *you*. Perhaps she was finding fault in your brother, and how he manages his family."

"Och nae! I never thought of it that way." She looked up at the ceiling considering, then said, "But she canna find fault in Nor! Only *I* can find fault in Nor!" She giggled again.

We left her room and began walking together down the corridor. "I will keep ye from Madame Enid's baleful looks and ye must protect me from the advances of Dunfermline. He is wanting tae marry me and I fear nae one will listen tae me on it."

"You don't like him?"

"Nae." Then she said, "I hae been *promised* that I will get tae give my opinion, but I kent these are the empty promises of a duke. If a man comes with land and status and negotiates for me, I daena see how Nor will take my side." Her face screwed up with worry. "How can I turn Dunfermline down? I can only keep tae the other end of the Great Hall so he winna corner me tae make his case."

"I will do everything I can to help."

She hooked her arm in mine. "Good, I think we will be great friends."

Chapter 18 - Livvy

1670

KILCHURN CASTLE

The Great Hall had appliquéd flags hung down the walls, shields displayed, a few large paintings for decoration. The ceiling of carved wood arched overhead. The windows had glass, and the hearth had a large fire, a nice crackling sound and radiating warmth, thick rugs before the hearth, and a smoky spice scent rising from it. Candles flickered on the tables. It was warm and convivial, and sort of reminded me of Hogwarts at Christmas. There was a long table, covered in a cloth, with chairs pulled up to it, and smaller side tables with chairs and benches. Places were set with plates and tableware. There were fine wine-glasses at the places nearest the head of the table.

The Duke wasn't there when we arrived, we milled about in the middle of the room, until he entered soon after, and everyone bowed their heads, even his sister and his mother, even me.

He walked through the room, addressing all who pressed forward, though there were those that remained behind, who didn't dare get close. I was close enough to hear him addressed "...Yer Grace..." and "...aye, Yer Grace..."

His back was straight, his wide shoulders set, his feet firm, he had changed into a clean coat and shirt. He looked rich and important, a sheathed sword at his hip. A kilt, his coat fitted. The whole effect of it, the Duke across the room moving through the crowd, having been, just hours ago, with me, now with all else... It was breathtaking.

He was dazzlingly hot.

An older man spoke to him next and beside him stood a lovely young woman with her eyes cast down.

Claray nudged me letting me know this was the woman picked for the Duke.

I watched her speak to him. She embodied all the classic 'young proper lady' kind of descriptions, like demure and chaste. I, on the other hand, even with the addition of the shawl around my shoulders, the makeup, the brushing of my hair, looked a little too unkempt and uncivilized. Not that we needed to compare us.

Why would we?

I was in a relationship.

With Chris.

He was hundreds of years away, but still, his name was on my internet bill.

None of this mattered. The Duke and I had just met. He was just a guy, like someone I had been trapped in an elevator with — I just had to get through it. I had to get back home. Chris and I were talking about getting a cat, so... and really, *honestly*, I needed to stay out of the way of the Duke's relationship. I wouldn't want to interfere. This was the past, Nor was supposed to marry this woman, probably. Who was I to change time?

The Duke asked the man how their travels were and then addressed the young woman. She answered, "I am well, Yer Grace," without looking up.

Lady Gail announced the serving of the meal and directed people to their seats. I was directed pretty far down the long table and tried not to let it bother me. Claray sat beside me. Her mother seemed shocked, "Ye ought tae be at His Grace's end of the table!"

Claray said, "Nae Mam, I hae tae keep Madame Livvy company, she is a guest!" So Claray and I were seated with some random people, while the Duke sat at the head of the table and the man with the young woman were beside him. Aenghus, Lady Gail, and another man who had a pointy nose and chin and long curly hair was at that end of the table too.

I whispered, "Lady Claray, tell me that isn't the man who wants to marry you?"

"It is! Och, can ye see m'troubles with it?"

"He is so old! How is that a thing?"

"He is a widower, he has children aulder than I."

"Oh no, that is... what are you going to do?"

"There inna anything I can do, Madame Livvy, if I must be married and I must. It must be tae the most advantage, and I... he is verra foul though. He has terrible breath."

I pouted in commiseration. "I am so so so sorry."

Her hands were clasped in front of her like a prayer. "If ye spoke tae His Grace, maybe he would—"

I shook my head. "I have *no* sway with his um... the Grace, the Duke, we only just met and—" I glanced down at his end of the table.

His eyes drew up and met mine. A bit of a smile spread on his mouth. The people around him were speaking, but his eyes were on me.

Then he withdrew them.

It had been very quick, and Claray hadn't noticed, as she picked at her dinner, disappointed that I couldn't help. "I ken, tis what I thought, I will keep tryin' tae talk tae him, maybe he will listen... I do wonder, Madame Livvy, how we women are tae hae our say? The men come and decide for us, and tis up tae us tae put up with it."

"Does no one marry for love?"

"Nor got tae marry for love, but she died. Malcolm married,

she is uninteresting, and lives in Edinburgh whenever she can, but he dinna *want* her tae be interesting. He married for her land. Malcolm is off traveling tae our other castles, that is why he inna here, ye would like him, he is verra fun — but most important, Aenghus got tae marry for love, but he is a man." She sighed.

A young woman dropped into the chair beside Claray. "We hae a full hall this eve, Lady Claray, did I miss any excitement?" Her eyes scanned the room. "I see Madame Enid is making herself comfortable and Dunfermline is making everyone uncomfortable. Lady Gail looks pleased about it all."

Claray said, "I am despairing, Ailsa, the whole dinner has been a misfortune — except I hae a new friend, Madame Livvy. Madame Livvy, this is Madame Ailsa, Aenghus's wife."

Ailsa said, "Aenghus told me tae expect Madame Livvy tae liven the room, but somehow ye hae both managed tae be at the unimportant end of the table! Did Lady Gail seat ye here?"

Claray said, "Aye, she did, but we are relieved, so I winna hae tae be near Dunfermline."

Ailsa sipped from her wine glass. "I see, but we are still downwind." She said to me, "My apologies, Madame Livvy, I daena usually speak so crudely."

Claray said, "Ye are all sweetness, ye are only rude tae help me survive."

Ailsa cocked her head at me. "What did Madame Enid say when she met ye? We daena usually have this much ado with the family meal."

Claray said, "She dinna say a word!"

I said, "I will be gone tomorrow, I do not mean to cause an ado or..."

Claray said, "Ye are causing a great amount of ado just by being here, there are one too many unmarried women in the Great Hall with a widowed duke for it tae nae be an ado."

"He was widowed two years ago?"

Claray said, "Aye, Mary and his son, Eaun, died two years ago, yesterday. We lost them both in the same day."

Ailsa said, "Twas a tragedy, he was once verra full of life, he is much withered and dour since."

"That is a tragedy." I glanced up the table again. His eyes met mine. He was thoughtful, spinning his mug.

The food was placed in serving dishes down the middle of the table, a carafe of wine between us. We had a first course of roasted salmon, and after many questions I figured out that there was an eel pie and a rabbit pie. For the second course we had turkey, pasties with a sweet glaze, some kind of root with bread crumbs and boiled spinach with cinnamon and ginger. There were breads and even some little cakes and I wondered if I could recreate the recipes. I might have been the only person from the twenty-first century to have actually tasted seventeenth century cooking *in* the seventeenth century.

Claray, Ailsa, and I drank wine and enjoyed the meal, and they launched into a story about a man they called Reeking Rhonag who would stink up the garderobe so much that no one could use the one on the north end of the castle. So the Duke decided to give him something to do every morning that would take him away from the castle so he would stink up the woods instead of their home.

We laughed so hard that Claray had to wipe her eyes.

Then she said, "Ye are so lucky Ailsa, that Aenghus loves ye so much, look over at him he canna take his eyes from ye."

We all looked up, and caught him watching Ailsa.

She blushed, "He does think I am verra fine. Tis nice tae hae such a wondrous husband."

I asked, "Do you have children?"

"We hae one bairn, he is sleepin'. Ye arna married, Madame Livvy? Ye seem auld enough tae be?"

I grinned. "Well, compared to you, yes, I am *past* old enough. I have a boyfriend, he's named Chris, and he's great, you know, and we're just not there yet and in my um... *lands*, we don't marry quite as young as you do here. We will wait sometimes and... I went to college. I have a career." I drank from my wine glass.

While I was speaking they both drew down their brows, as if nothing I said made any sense at all.

I finished as I put down my glass, "I'm really happy about the choices I've made." As if I was embarrassed. *Why was I embarrassed?* A week ago nothing about my life was embarrassing, it had seemed all great.

Mostly.

The young women here had no inkling what it was like to be in a relationship in the twenty-first century. It wasn't easy to forge a working partnership moving on from school, and into a thirty-year mortgage, while working two careers, and planning to have two children and a nanny. It was *complicated.*

I said, "We just haven't decided to get married yet. I'm sure we will, someday."

Ailsa said, "Yer father haena arranged it?"

"Where I come from we get to choose our husband, and then *when* to get married. It's all up to us."

Claray put her chin in her hand, her elbow on the table, looking wistful, "I would *love* that."

Ailsa shook her head. "I daena ken, that sounds verra difficult. How dost ye *choose* a husband?"

"You meet men, you date for a time, see if you like each other enough — *then* after a while if he *does* like you he asks you to marry him."

"The rest of yer family has nae say in it? If yer father and brothers canna advise ye on it, ye might not ken how he behaves among men —this is crucial, I believe. A man might be a lout or a churl and often tis yer brother's duty tae tell ye he is unworthy, and who would negotiate for yer dowry? And if yer mother canna advise ye on his manner? Och, it sounds difficult!"

Claray said, "*Every*thing sounds difficult tae ye, Madame Ailsa, because it has always been easy for ye, because ye are sweet and docile and yer husband loves ye..." She looked up and down the table. "Watch, Madame Livvy, Ailsa will bring him here."

Ailsa blushed red. "Ye want me tae show it?"

Claray said, "Aye, tis one of my favorite Great Hall pastimes. Ye want tae see it, Madame Livvy?"

"I would, show me."

"All I must do is this..." Ailsa tilted her chin up, and fanned her throat near her ear with long delicate fingers. Her husband, Aenghus, noticed after just a few seconds. He watched for a moment, then dropped his napkin and pushed back his chair. He strode tae our end of the table and up tae his wife's chair, he kissed her neck, right there. "Are ye well, Madame Ailsa?"

"Aye, I was just thinking of ye, m'laird."

He bowed and returned to his seat.

I laughed. "Well done!"

Claray said, "It works every time."

Ailsa smiled. "It really does, I am verra fortunate."

A woman entered the Great Hall and placed a baby into Ailsa's arms. Ailsa beamed and pulled a blanket from his face to show him. "This is my Ian, inna he a fine bairn?" Her eyes lit up with love as she looked down at the baby.

Claray grinned. "He is a verra fine bairn. He is the best nephew besides Eaun, may he rest in peace, the poor sweet boy."

Ailsa said, "Eaun was a fine boy, twas a tragedy when he and Lady Mary were taken from the family."

Our eyes raised to the Duke's end of the table. Madame Enid and Lady Gail were talking. The Duke looked bored.

Ailsa whispered, "Lady Gail is convinced she will match His Grace with Madame Enid, dost ye think he will go along with her plans?"

Claray cut her eyes at me. "I daena ken... he inna in the mood tae be married again. I daena think he will marry just because Mam tells him tae. He is a duke. He daena hae tae listen tae anyone."

Ailsa said, "We need tae convince His Grace tae look elsewhere. Madame Enid inna a good match for him, even with all the acreage she would bring with her."

She grinned. "Would ye like tae hold the bairn, Madame Livvy?"

The request shocked me. "I don't think I've ever held a baby before, I'm sure I'm not qualified, I don't think—" The baby was placed right into my arms.

Ailsa stood. "I must go tae the garderobe."

Claray whispered, "Watch, Madame Livvy, m'brother canna keep his eyes from her."

I glanced at Aenghus, his eyes followed Ailsa as she crossed the room then he jumped from his chair to accompany her out.

I spoke to the baby in my arms. "Hello, little one, how are you? I am a time traveler."

The baby looked up at me, waving his little hand around.

After Ailsa and Aenghus returned, the doors of the Great Hall banged open and a guardsman rushed up to the Duke and whispered into his ear.

The Duke stood, bowed to the guests at the table, and he and his brother left the room. Ailsa took her baby from my arms and everyone seemed nervous. "What is happening?"

Claray said, "I daena ken, but after the disturbance earlier, it must be dire."

We watched the door, everyone spoke in hushed tones.

Chapter 19 - Livvy

1670

KILCHURN CASTLE

A few minutes later the Duke and his brother stormed in and came right up to us. "Ye must go tae Claray's room. We will tell ye when the danger has passed."

Claray and Ailsa jumped up from their chairs and headed to a door in the back corner.

I asked the Duke, "What is it? Is it connected to us?"

"Aye, I believe so, a stranger has asked m'guardsmen if they had seen anythin' in Barran Moor earlier in the day — he is looking for the portals. He haena said it, but he is being deceptive."

"Should I come? I might have some insight — if he is a time traveler, maybe I will recognize something, his clothes, or how he behaves or..."

He nodded. "Aye, tis a good idea, follow me tae the balustrade."

He strode across the floor with me following close behind.

We took the stairs two at a time. I saw him wince a bit and hold his side as he climbed. He led me out onto a gallery. Guards stood there, holding bows, aiming arrows down at the courtyard.

He pulled me into the shadows. We were two stories above, the man was down in the courtyard on his horse.

He was rough looking, bearded, dirty, his clothes were all dark, and he had furs around his shoulders. He looked like he was from this century, or perhaps the one before, so I probably wasn't the expert. But then my eyes noticed his boots, they were rubber soled.

"He's a time traveler, definitely, it's his boots."

"I thought so, thank ye, Madame Livvy. Dost ye recognize the name, Johnne Cambell?"

I shook my head. "But it's a common name."

"Aye, could be." He stared down for a moment longer, then said, "Allow me tae show ye tae Lady Claray's room."

I followed him down the hall. "He won't be able to get the portals, right? You won't give them to him? Please don't, I desperately need the one."

He said, "I winna, Madame Livvy, I hae learned a lot from the men assaultin' us in the moor and the arrival of this man, Johnne Cambell. I am convinced the portals are verra powerful and they are dangerous in the wrong hands."

"Does that man have the wrong hands?"

His stride was long and purposeful. "Aye, he was being deceitful. He dinna directly ask for the portals, but was curious about the storm."

"If we were looking for the portals though, we would lie about it, and we aren't necessarily 'wrong' to have them. We need them."

"Tis true. But he arrived at night and he is traveling alone, but he dinna show me deference. He has nae asked my permission tae be on my lands. This is inconceivable, nae man would travel tae my castle, alone, with only the one sword and nae men — how can this be? Ye saw the trouble it caused when I entered a castle alone. I was even more suspicious because of what he said about the weather."

We came to Claray's door and he knocked and spoke through it. "I hae Madame Livvy tae sit with ye, Lady Claray."

I asked, as Claray unlocked the door, "What did he say about the weather?"

"He said the rain to the south of us had caused him tae seek shelter. But as ye ken, the storms were brutal and short. If he had been a witness tae the winds, he wouldna hae called it mere rain. He would hae described them differently. The storm was verra unusual. He ought tae hae noted it, but he dinna because he kens what they are."

"Very smart."

"I must go speak with him, I will be back when tis safe."

He left.

Chapter 20 - the Duke

1670

KILCHURN CASTLE

I stood in the courtyard, a stranger standing in front of me. I had ordered the stable lad tae take his horse, yet he had refused tae relinquish the reins. He instead appraised me with a malevolent cheek, his brow raised. Then he looked up and around at m'castle walls.

His clothes were worn and dirty, he wore fur around his shoulders, a wild scruffy beard. He had a sword at his hip. Madame Livvy was correct, his boots were from another time.

His horse carried heavy saddle bags. I considered that they might hold weapons, there werna any other point of so much gear.

I said, "Ye are unannounced and arrive without men, what is yer business?" The lack of men was worrisome, more so because he dinna seem concerned about it. My guards were agitated. He ought tae ken he was in a dangerous position, but he dinna seem interested in watching his back. This man, Johnne Cambell, had entered m'castle like a conqueror. He stood before me without seeming concerned for his life.

"Ye hae a fine castle here, Normond, Duke of Awe, a verra fine castle."

"Ye are addressin' me as if ye ken me, yet afore yer arrival, I hae had nae knowledge of ye."

"I am Johnne Cambell."

"Ye state it as if ye hae a point, as if it ought tae be familiar, but I daena ken of ye — are ye connected tae the Lowden Campbells?"

He scoffed. "The Lowden Campbells, nae, not the lowly Lowdens."

"Then ye are with the Argyll Campbells, yet m'cousin, James Glenn, haena mentioned ye. I feel he would hae as we talked a great deal about his men."

"I am nae anyone's 'man'. And the Argylls are beneath me as well."

I scoffed. "The Argyll Campbells are verra powerful. M'cousin, James, would find yer assessment of his importance verra amusin' just afore he runs ye through with his sword." I had m'hand restin' on my hilt and considered drawing the sword, just tae get tae the slayin' of this stranger, botherin' me with his insolence and audacity.

I pretended to be indifferent. "If ye arna a Lowden or an Argyll, but ye are a Campbell, I canna see how ye are important at all. Dost ye hae land? Nae, ye winna tell of it, tis nae known. Ye hae a strong castle? Nae, ye daena boast of it. I hae never heard of—"

"I will one day be a king."

I narrowed my eyes. "A king of *what lands*?"

"A king of a faraway land, a kingdom built by my brothers and I, after a good proper conquest, we are tae become the most feared and powerful Campbells in the history of the world."

"Yet I hae never once heard yer name."

"Och, but now ye hae, and ye winna forget it, as ye hae stolen something from me."

Och aye, as I suspected twas about the portals.

I slowly shook my head. "I daena ken what ye are speaking on, I haena stolen anything."

His brow raised and then he malevolently smiled and shrugged. "Ye hae something that belongs tae me, I dinna give it tae ye — if I wanted tae I could just demand its return—"

"Nae, ye winna demand anything of me. Ye hae nae army — ye are in nae position. Ye are an unknown, claiming tae be an heir tae a throne in a land that ye hae concocted. Ye hae made these claims as if it somehow gives ye a privilege ye haena earned — ye must be the most sore-brained bag of pig innards ever tae set foot upon my lands — a king? Ye are a common highwayman. Ye ought tae apologize for interruptin' my meal, and remove yerself from my lands."

"Och, I like ye, Normond the Wind-bluster, ye daena hae tae work so hard tae gain m'approval. "

I said, "I haena for one moment wanted tae gain yer approval. I hae wanted tae slay ye since ye entered my gates. I want ye off m'lands the day before yesterday."

Johnne Cambell exhaled and his voice was measured. "Ye hae stolen somethin' from me, Nor, tis a powerful instrument, a Tempus Omega—"

"A Tempus Omega? Tis a stupid name."

He glared. "It's too powerful, and ye are too weak tae control it. I could take it from ye, easily, but what is the fun of it? I prefer an alliance."

Holding the reins in one hand, he pulled a wee book from an inside pocket on his coat, pulled a strap from around it, and usin' a writing implement, much like the one Madame Livvy had used, noted something upon a page. He said, as he wrote, "...Lady Gail, Aenghus, the lovely Madame Ailsa and their son, Ian, a wee bairn..."

"What are ye writing?"

"The members of yer family who are in attendance this evening. When I return for the Tempus Omega, ye will provide it tae me, or I will make sure this evening is interrupted with more force."

He wrapped the strap around the book, and shoved it all back in his coat. "Ye daena hae any questions for me, Nor, for instance, how would I come back tae this time?"

My jaw tightened. "Nae."

"Thus proving what we already knew: ye hae one of my time travel instruments." He chuckled. "I suppose now ye see the dire and powerless situation ye are in. Ye will need tae keep that Tempus Omega safe."

"I haena agreed tae any alliance."

"Ye daena get tae decide, Nor. Ye hae what is mine, make sure ye keep it safe, keep it hidden, protect it, or yer family will pay the consequences." He mounted his horse. "I will return for it."

I asked, "In what time is yer kingdom?"

He spun it back around, the malevolent smile pulled at the edge of his mouth. "I *knew* ye had it, Nor the Wind-bluster."

I gripped the hilt of m'sword. "I demand ye tell me *what time.*"

"I am building a throne, a kingdom called Riaghalbane, in the year 2270." He looked around the walls. "Ye ought tae get some weapons, Nor, ye arna protected enough. There are dangerous time-traveling men about." He yelled, "Coisich!" smacked his reins against his horse and galloped through the gate and away.

My brother raced down the steps from his post at the walls. "What's our plan?"

"Hae men follow him. I want him off m'lands by the morn."

"Aye." He directed our men, and had a large group join him on the chase.

Chapter 21 - Livvy

1670
KILCHURN CASTLE

Lady Gail, Madame Enid, Lady Claray, and Madame Ailsa, holding her baby, were all in the sitting room in front of the hearth. Enid's behavior was altered, before she had kept her eyes cast down, now, without the Duke nearby, they were up, direct. Narrowed on me.

She looked like someone who had found her adversary and was drawing power from the challenge.

Her gaze was uncomfortable.

Ailsa said, "Madame Livvy, would ye hold the bairn again?" She placed him in my arms

"Yes, um..." I wasn't sure why I was expected to hold a baby, but it seemed like I ought to look half-capable since it was my second time. And Enid was watching, but I was a little worried the baby would squirm and slip out of my arms.

The baby looked up at me: a smile, a fart, its eyes rolled back and then closed.

Claray laughed.

"Is he okay?" A smell rose from the blanket.

Madame Ailsa said, "Of course! He has just had some milk, he will want tae be sleepin'."

She pulled the baby blanket open, unwrapped the dripping cloth off the baby's butt and replaced it with another. She tucked the blanket back around the baby and tossed the foul diaper over near the bowl. She did it so deftly that the baby didn't even wake.

"You want me to keep holding him?"

"Aye." She rose and poked the fire with a stick to bring up the flame.

Claray asked, "Where did you go with the Duke?"

"He needed to show me something." Enid's eyes were on me hard. *So so so hard.* I stifled a giggle by looking at a small painting of an older woman on the far wall. "I like that painting, is it of someone you know?"

Claray said, "Aye, my grandmother. She gave this tae m'grandfather when they were courting, and she gave it tae me because I admired it. Tis lovely daena ye think? She was a 'rare beauty' m'grandfather said, 'tae look upon her gave him edification.' Daena ye wish every man spoke tae ye like that, Madame Livvy? Tae hae such love, such poetic sensibilities!"

Madame Enid said, "I posit, Lady Claray, that tae always be preoccupied with love is proving ye hae a unserious mind. Ye best be careful or ye winna hae a man find ye worth marrying."

Claray's eyes went wide.

Her mother pursed her lips and shook her head.

Claray huffed.

Ailsa said, "I think Lady Claray has kept a proper balance of a serious mind with a preoccupation with love, she will be alright as long as she keeps them in turns."

Enid folded her hands primly. "I will agree that tae hae them in turns, tae keep yer yearning for poetry tae a minimum, tae stamp down yer desires, tae nae paint yer face as if ye were tae be on a stage — *these* mixed with a mind that yearns for truth and serious service tae her laird, are the way of womanhood. Lady Claray would do well tae allow the parts of her better nature tae take a turn for once."

Claray clamped her lips closed.

Lady Gail changed the subject, "How is yer dear mother, Madame Enid? Why did she remain at the estate?"

Enid said, "Mum remained at Menstrie tae—"

Lady Gail said, "I do hope she is not unwell!"

"She does suffer from unease. I am sure she will recover soon enough, but she understood the necessity of *my* coming as soon as I was sent for. It was a long trip, as ye ken, and verra tiring, too tiring for her. I hae been strained by it. I do wish my mother had been able tae make the journey with me."

She smoothed back her hair and continued, "But as ye may hae heard, just as Father and I set out, Laird Galloway and his new wife were expected tae visit Menstrie. Laird Galloway is verra important, but we could not delay our trip here, as ye had asked for my attendance as soon as possible — if one is requested by the Duke, one *goes* tae the Duke."

Lady Gail said, "I am certain yer mother has much tae do tae prepare Menstrie for Laird Galloway's visit."

Enid daintily inspected her fingernails. "*Everything* must be perfect, and Mum felt she could barely accomplish entertaining the Laird without me, but father decided that as the Duke seemed so sincerely *earnest* tae call me tae Kilchurn that I was allowed tae attend tae His Grace's needs."

I glanced over at Claray who did a very small, barely perceptible eye roll.

Lady Gail said, "We knew that with the anniversary of Lady Mary's passing that His Grace would be in need of company. He does keep tae himself a great deal. We are grateful ye were able tae come as a diversion from his troubles."

Enid cut her eyes toward me. "His Grace needed me, of course I came."

The baby began to squirm, Ailsa took him from my arms and cooed to comfort him, then said, "His Grace haena been alone much since the anniversary. He has had many distractions."

Claray counted on her fingers. "He has been caught out in a

storm. There are men battling him. A new acquaintance from far away. An auld family acquaintance visiting from the lands tae the east. And now a stranger at the door has interrupted our nightly meal. We hae had so many distractions we dinna hae a chance tae dance."

Lady Gail said, "Lady Claray! This is a verra dire situation, ye must not make light of it — what if something happens tae yer brothers?"

"Och nae, nothing could happen tae m'brothers, they were born tae fight. They hae been brawlin' with each other my whole life, I would like tae see someone try tae battle them!"

Enid said, "Lady Claray, tis unladylike tae speak of battling and brawling."

Claray raised her chin. "I am glad I am not a lady then. I am the younger sister of a duke and I hae watched him spar. I think tis fun tae watch. I am glad he is the kind of brother who allows it."

Enid pursed her lips, as if to say 'that is the *first* thing I will put a stop to' and I kind of wanted to kick that expression off her face. I was new here and already didn't like her.

There was a knock on the door and the Duke and Aenghus entered. "Lady Gail, ladies," he bowed. "We nae longer need tae hide. We hae sent the stranger from the castle. Our guardsmen are stationed upon the walls. We hae men camped in the woods. We believe tis safe tae go tae yer own rooms."

The women stood. Ailsa asked, "Aenghus, m'laird, ye will be on the walls tae night?"

"Aye, I must be on guard."

"Then I will invite Madame Enid tae sleep in my chamber, as I am sure she will prefer the company. Madame Livvy can stay here with Claray."

Claray clapped her hands.

Aenghus asked, "Mam, would ye like an escort tae yer chambers?"

Lady Gail said, "I ought tae hae Nor escort me, tis verra late and he canna linger here in the middle of the night." She glanced at me, as if I were the one keeping her son here in the middle of the night.

Chapter 22 - Livvy

1670

KILCHURN CASTLE

Aenghus, Ailsa, and Enid left after their goodbyes and Claray waited until the door closed behind them before she turned on her mother. "Mam, dost ye hear how she speaks tae me?"

Lady Gail said, "I did, Claray, I heard it — Madame Enid has strong opinions about how ye should behave."

The Duke crossed to the hearth, crouched there, poked at the fire, and added a log. "What dost ye mean?" He gestured for me to sit on the chair nearest the fire.

Claray crossed her arms and huffed. She started to speak and then didn't. She scowled.

The Duke stood and brushed off his palms. "Out with it, Claray, ye must tell me everything as I am yer laird and master."

"This is the difficulty, Your Grace, ye are my 'laird and master,' as ye say, and ye are tae decide everything for myself and I am just yer mere sister without a say in *anything*."

"I told ye ye would hae a say in things...? Did I nae?"

"Ye said, Yer Grace, that I *might* hae a say in one thing, and tis the most important thing. I am afeared that if I hae a say in this other thing, I will use up my one chance."

The Duke chuckled. "Sister, are ye sayin' ye want tae save yer time tae hae an opinion for a different thing? Ye think I might give ye only one chance for it?"

"Aye. I do truly believe it. This is about marriage. Ye might give me only one chance for it... and I do desperately want tae keep my opinion for m'own self, but I canna bear it..."

She balled up her fists and looked at the ceiling as if in silent prayer. "I hae tae say it, I canna be quiet and let it happen..."

"What must ye say? My heavens, ye are carrying on, Claray." He teased, "If ye hae something tae say that would interfere with an opinion on yer own marriage it must be verra important, as without yer say I am liable tae marry ye off tae the first auld man who comes askin' for ye."

Her eyes wide she said, "Ye wouldna! Would ye? Oh, please tell me ye wouldna!"

A smile spread across his face. "Och nae, sister, ye ought tae sit down, ye are becomin' overwrought."

Lady Gail said, "This child is working herself up intae a tither."

The Duke took his sister's hand. "Sister, I am teasin'. I will take yer opinion intae my decision on yer marriage. I will do m'best tae make the match advantageous for ye, and winna hold any of yer myriad other opinions against ye. Out with it. What is it ye want tae say?"

"Brother, ye canna marry Enid Holborne."

He looked shocked. "This is on the table? Ye think I am plannin' tae marry Madame Enid?"

Lady Gail said, "I daena understand why *everyone* is so set against it. Tis nae a terrible idea. She is of a good bloodline. Twould be an auspicious alliance of our families."

The Duke said, "This is why she has come tae visit? Did ye tell her father that we were goin' tae host her visit, as I am lookin' for a wife? This is an underhanded dealing without speaking tae me on it first."

"How could ye not know, Nor? I invited a young woman tae visit and ye feign misunderstanding the purpose? I invited her tae spend time with ye, so ye could see she was pleasing. Ye had tae see this was my purpose — I am a verra good mother but I am nae supernatural."

The Duke turned to me. "First, Madame Livvy, m'apologies that ye are havin' tae be a part of this family discussion. I hae a great deal tae tell ye on our visitor this eve, yet here we are havin' tae discuss Lady Gail's designs." He said, "Second, Mam, I kent ye were leaning this way, pushin' Madame Enid forward for my consideration, but I hae chosen tae ignore yer machinations, but there is a large gulf between leanin' and plannin'. Please daena plan. And tae m'sister, Claray, ye hae tae ken, ye daena ken everything. I am nae planning on marrying Madame Enid."

Claray said, "But see this is the problem, Nor. Ye say ye daena plan, but then ye daena plan and daena plan until one day ye are in the middle of the plan and then tis too late tae say 'daena plan.' Then ye would say, "Tis too late tae stop now, the plans are set!' When would ye want me tae tell ye: she is ill-suited for ye, she will make ye unhappy, she is full of a sour disposition and a controlling air—?"

Lady Gail said, "She would run a very smart household."

Claray said, "But at what cost! We are never tae laugh again? Tae speak our mind? She wanted me tae not watch the boys when they spar! She wants me not tae rush in the corridors, she orders me tae keep m'tongue." Her hand on her forehead she said, "Och nae, Yer Grace, I canna bear it, how am I tae survive?"

The side of the Duke's smile went up, a crinkle of smile lines. "It sounds as if most of yer complaints about Madame Enid involve yer happiness nae mine."

"If I am unhappy, ye ken ye will be unhappy as well."

He chuckled. "I ken it, ye will never let me smile again."

"That is not what I meant, I meant she is not suited for *either* of us. We are much alike, ye ken. Ye understand me. Ye ken I am not tae be stifled. Tis the way our father wanted me tae be."

Lady Gail said, "Yer father did spoil ye terribly. Perhaps a civilizing influence, with a firm hand, and a model of control would not be such a bad thing?"

Claray said, "Mam! What of love?" So wonderfully over-dramatically that I had to bite my lip to stifle my laugh.

The Duke said, "I see, Mam, that ye are verra set on finding a match for me that is prudent and alliance-building. I appreciate yer effort, but I must reiterate my decision: I am nae planning tae marry. Madame Enid is a fine woman but she is not tae become the Duchess of Awe. I winna hae a duchess, not again — my decision is final. Ye must end yer conniving on the issue. And, sister, ye hae given me yer opinion, but it haena weighed in my decision. I came tae it on m'own. I ken ye are looking after me, but ye are not my protector. Ye must settle down intae yer own place, daena step out of line."

"Are ye saying I must be more of a lady?"

"I am saying ye must not believe yerself above me, tis not on ye tae decide my affairs."

"Aye, Yer Grace." She bowed her head.

"And Madame Enid's particular attributes are nae excuse tae be rude tae her, she is our guest. I want ye tae make yerself available tae her first thing in the morn. Ye will sit with her and be at her beck and call for the day."

"This is my punishment?"

"Nae, this is yer duty. Did ye just now advise me against marriage? If ye are stepping forward as an adviser, ye are also stepping forward as the sister who will keep our guests comfortable."

"Aye, Your Grace, I will."

"Good, and again, I am verra sorry, Madame Livvy, that ye had tae be a part of the discussion."

Without thinking I said, "No problem, M'laird."

Lady Gail cut her eyes at me. "He is *Your Grace.*"

The Duke said, "I asked Madame Livvy tae call me m'laird."

Her eyes widened. "Tis beneath ye unless tis an endearment, and she is not *endeared*. Is she endeared?"

"Nae."

"My apologies, Lady Gail, I misspoke." I bowed my head as I had seen the women do.

She nodded, her worries assuaged, apparently.

The Duke said, "Madame Livvy, much was revealed with the visitor, but the hour grows late. I will tell ye about it in the morn, then we will make sure tae get ye home."

"Good, thank you, Your Grace," I made sure to add it because his mother was watching. The Duke put out his arm for his mother and they went to the door.

Chapter 23 - Livvy

1670

KILCHURN CASTLE

As soon as they left the room, Claray, scowling at the floor, said, "I had tae say it, daena ye think, Madame Livvy? I couldna let it pass, she is verra dreadful and someone needed tae say it tae His Grace."

"Yes, probably, and when I intervene with a friend I often feel worried after, as if I've overstepped even though I know I said exactly what I needed to say — is your mother upset that I didn't address him correctly?"

"Aye, but ye canna let it bother ye, she was verra broken when m'father passed and Nor is young tae be a duke, she worries on him, and she is concerned because of the way he looks at ye."

"How does he look at me?"

"As if he thinks ye are beautiful, as if he thinks the sun rises when ye enter the room."

"Oh."

She breathed out. "Och, I hope I dinna overstep. Nor has too much on his mind tae hae me worrying him, but yet I *do*. If I left it alone though he would hae more tae worry on. And, ye ken, m'mother was going tae hae him married tae Madame Enid without delay."

Claray's lady's maid and a couple of other servants entered the room and began helping us undress.

She said, "Now I hae tae spend the whole day with her when I would rather spend it with you."

"I think I am leaving tomorrow."

"But you just got here! I like ye and daena want ye tae leave!"

"I like you too. I hope your brother will listen to you about your marriage."

She said, "I pray he will, father would hae wanted him tae, on his deathbed he advised Nor tae care for me. Tis a kind and generous thing tae hae a father who thinks on his daughter that way. He dinna hae tae, he could marry me tae anyone he wants. I am verra blessed."

"And you haven't met the man you want to marry yet?"

A young woman began working on Claray's laces, and another worked on mine, we stood face to face while they worked on undressing us.

Claray said, "Nae, but I think whoever he is, he ought tae hurry, as I winna be able tae hold them off forever. Tis my duty tae marry, and soon. I do hope there will be a man of a fine stature and a clever wit, who is verra fond of me and wants me tae be just as I am — does he exist?"

"I truly hope so, Claray, he is what we *all* need."

Down to our chemises, we took turns peeing in the bowl which had a horrible stench, and was embarrassing to do in front of someone else, but it gave me a chance to see how she did it: a crouch, a wiggle, she made it look easy. Not like me, I looked like I might fall into the bowl, the strain on my thighs was incredible. I was fit, I should be able to crouch, but a crouch for a poop was a whole 'nother thing.

Her bed was a four-poster, but was small by modern day standards, and was uncomfortable. There were warm blankets stacked on it, and we were to share, laying side by side she asked, "Do you have older brothers, Madame Livvy?"

"I have two older, one younger."

"Och nae," she laughed. "They must be full of ideas on how ye are tae be."

I thought for a moment. "They kind of are. They don't boss me around, they don't get to pick who I marry, those ideas are long past, but they do have opinions, *many* opinions. I always wanted a sister."

"Me too. I was verra glad when Ailsa came intae m'family, though she is so in love with Aenghus that she will only ever take his side in everything. I would like, just once, for her tae take *my* side in an argument with him."

The night was dark, our room smelled like smoke and fire, dirt and must, but also warmth and conviviality. The lady's maid was nearby, sleeping by the hearth. Our voices were hushed. "Do you argue with Aenghus a lot?"

"We argue a great deal. Where Nor wants tae be fair, Aenghus wants tae be right."

I chuckled in the darkness.

Then we were quiet. I looked over at the small sliver of a window at the dark night sky, but it hit me that outside these strong thick walls was a medieval night — cold fear gripped my heart.

There wasn't a phone for centuries.

My face screwed up into my frown.

Claray looked at my face. "Och nae, sweet Livvy, did something frighten ye?"

"Yes, I'm just... so afraid. This world is very different from my own and I'm homesick, I think, and... I don't know exactly why, but are we safe, are we going to be okay?"

She was almost nose to nose with me and stroked down my hair. "Of course we are goin' tae be safe, Madame Livvy, hae ye seen m'brothers? They are the guardians of us. They hae been takin' care of our family for*ever*, ye ought nae be scared. There is a full guard out on the walls and if ye listen — listen..."

We lay there quietly listening and then there was a sound, like a faint 'Caw!' as if a far away bird was calling through the night.

"That would be the guards signaling tae each other. They hae a whole language tae keep us safe."

"That does make me feel better."

"And Nor is the Duke, he is even better at it than m'father, though daena tell m'mother I said as much. M'father was kindly and sometimes lost wagers. Nor never fails. He is strong and everyone kens it. Another family would hae tae be desperate tae want tae battle against the Duke of Awe. He is afeared for miles around, so ye daena hae tae be worried, Madame Livvy. He will protect ye."

It took a while but finally Claray fell asleep.

Then I lay there listening to the sounds of the guard on the wall, their signals carried through the clear, cool night air. The fire in the hearth burnt down, its rumble quieting, the sounds of Claray grew, she breathed deeply, a little noisily. I could not sleep.

The night had been quieter than any night of my life, even on hunting trips with my dad and brothers. It was as if in the modern world there was always something in our gear or equipment that hummed with energy. This was stone cold quiet. Here there was nothing that hummed but humans and animals for *centuries*, this was an ancient silence and I was in the middle of it.

There was a snap and pop from the fire and it made my heart race.

I tried to center my breathing, but I had the blanket up to my nose, my eyes traveling back and forth looking at nothing, because it was so damn dark.

I heard a call, it sounded like a bird of prey, and another, a call from man to man. When Claray had explained the call sounds it had made me feel better, now the hair pricked up on the back of my neck.

I sat up and stared out the sliver of a window at the night sky.

I glanced down at Claray. Her eyes open, she said, "Is somethin' amiss?"

I nodded, my eyes wide, a full-blown dread settled in my soul.

She listened, then said, "They are just callin' tae pass the time, ye ought tae sleep Madame Livvy, ye will become agitated."

"I think I already am."

"We can hold hands."

We held hands and a few moments later she was fast asleep again and I was staring at the pitch black medieval castle-gloom.

Chapter 24 - Livvy

1670

KILCHURN CASTLE

I must have fallen asleep eventually because a knock woke me with a start.

The Duke whispered, "Madame Livvy, will ye rise? We ought tae make haste."

I sat up and looked around, dazed.

Claray said, "Where are ye goin'?"

I muttered, "I don't know."

Claray called, "Brother, where are ye takin' her?"

His voice through the door. "Tae send her home, it may take a full day, we ought tae leave afore first light."

I climbed from the bed. "I'm going? What time is it?"

She sat up. "But, Yer Grace, I daena want her tae go."

The Duke said, "Ye daena get a say in it, Lady Claray, ye needs tae do as I command, or ye will see the inside of the dungeon."

"Ye would put me in the dungeon, for what offense?"

"For arguin' incessantly, I hae made a law, tis not allowed."

"Fine, Madame Livvy is a'readyin'."

She rose and passed me a skirt. "Pull it up over the shift." Her lady's maid rushed in and took over, and wrapped a belt around my middle, cinching the skirt at my waist.

Claray said, "Lower yer arms." And wrapped a blanket

around my shoulders, criss-crossed in front and tucked in tightly at my waist.

"What is this called?"

"A plaid."

"Interesting, it's not plaid though, I thought plaid meant the pattern. This is solid blue."

"The pattern is a tartan, this wrap is the plaid." She stepped back and looked me up and down. "Good enough, ye ought tae hae a finer dress, and proper stays, but ye are leaving, I ken tis selfish, but I daena want ye tae take my dresses away."

"Oh I absolutely agree, you don't want this plaid?"

"Nae, that is verra common, tis yers and if ye hae taken this one, I will be able tae get another."

There was another knock, "Are ye coming, Madame Livvy?"

Claray called out. "Brother, it takes a moment tae dress a lady, dost ye want Madame Livvy tae be clothed when she opens the door?"

The Duke's voice, "Aye."

I sat on the edge of the bed and pulled on my reeking socks, and shoved my feet into my boots and tied the laces.

I scooped up my pack, hooked it on my shoulder, unable to put it fully on because my shoulders were bound by the tight plaid, and hustled toward the door, yanking it open and almost running into the Duke.

"Oh! I'm ready."

He smiled. "I see that, ye look a verra fine Scottish lass, good morn, Madame Livvy."

"Good morn, Your Grace."

He turned and started walking down the corridor, his lantern shining a dim light around his legs. He turned back and said, "Ye ought tae follow."

"I don't want to follow, it's pitch black and I... I don't want to rush headlong into a frightening thing, I am not to be just called for and whisked away, this is freaking me out. Why are we leaving in the middle of the night?"

He stopped walking and returned to standing in front of me. The corridor was briskly cold. "Madame Livvy..." He looked up and down the corridor. "I hae much tae tell ye but we daena want tae be overheard."

I nodded.

"I want tae get ye home. And I hae been thinkin' tae do that we need tae return tae the moor. We need tae be there with the portals when the storms begin—"

"If the storms begin..."

"Aye, if the storms begin, and tis likely that there will be men awaitin' us. We ought tae go now, under cover of darkness. I ken a place where we might hide while we wait for the storms."

"Okay, that makes sense."

He said, "Dost ye hae all yer things?"

"Yes, do you have the portals?"

He patted two small sacks that hung from the side of his belt. "Aye."

"Can I say goodbye to Claray? I forgot."

He rapped on her door. Claray peeked out. "Madame Livvy, ye forgot tae say goodbye."

The Duke said, "That is why she has returned."

She exclaimed, "I hae a present for ye!" She rushed away and returned with a dried flower. "This is a stalk of heather from outside our castle walls."

I put it up to my nose and breathed in the scent. "It smells like the air here, thank you."

I dropped my pack to the ground and dug through it. "Here is um..." I found my mascara and lipstick and gave them to her.

She said, "Thank ye, Madame Livvy, I had a hope ye might," and clutched them to her chest.

The Duke said, "We must go."

I hugged her again. "I loved meeting you."

Claray hugged me goodbye, "I am sorry ye were so fearful, Madame Livvy, I am glad ye will get tae go home," and I was led away by the Duke. To keep up with his stride I had to take a step and a half to each of his steps. He was quiet as if he were thinking.

At the stair he shook his head and said, "Were ye truly frightened?"

"Yes, it was one of the worst nights I've ever had."

"Och nae, the worst nights? In my magnificent castle?"

"It's not your fault, I just... I'm not used to the sounds, or lack of sounds, and maybe I'm afraid of the dark. That is something I didn't know about myself. I feel panicked, my heart is racing, I can't really see."

He took my hand, "Come with me."

He led me up the spiral stair at the end of the hall, a cold draft rushing down it, causing me to shiver. He drew me up, kindly, slowly. He left me at the door and strode out onto the walls. The guardsmen there, bowed.

He sent them away and then he drew me to the railing.

There was no moon, but a star-flung sky.

"There inna a moon taenight, I ken tis verra dark, but instead we hae the jewels of the Duke of Awe, the stars that shimmer in the sky over Kilchurn.

I gaped up at the sky. "It's beautiful."

"Aye, tis a clear night, sound travels verra well. The men along the parapet are guardin'. Within my walls ye are safe."

"Claray told me I was, I just had a hard time remembering to breathe."

He breathed in and gestured for me to breathe in too. We both stood on the walls side by side and breathed in and out looking out at the stars.

"Better?"

"Better."

"Then I ought tae tell ye about the visit from Johnne Cambell."

"Did he know about the portals, about time travel, was I right?"

"Aye, he was a time traveler, he threatened me, he said he would harm m'family, he kent a great deal of us."

"That's a lot you've been dealing with."

He shrugged. "I am used tae dealing with dangerous things, there is always a..." The side of his mouth went up in a smile. "I winna finish the thought as I daena want tae frighten ye again."

"Thank you... so he threatened you because he wanted the portals?"

"He told me he was goin' tae leave the portal with me, he called it the Tempus Omega, and that I was tae keep it safe until he returned as if we hae an alliance. He is under the impression that he rules my actions through threat."

"He doesn't?"

"Nae, he daena ken who he is dealin' with. I hae an advantage."

"What? You do?"

"Aye, Johnne Cambell dinna ken we hae two of the portals. He thinks I only hae one. That must be an advantage."

"Yes, yes it is, that's a great advantage. I'm not sure how, but it has to be. Until now I thought our only advantage was the gun that's out of ammo."

"We hae also learned the first rule: Daena touch a movin' portal."

I sort of laughed. "Whoohoo, look at us, winning!"

He said, "We are winnin' so so so hard."

I laughed, but it wasn't really funny, not freezing cold on a castle wall in the seventeenth century, not sure I would ever get to go home. I didn't know if this could be called winning.

"The portals are verra powerful, I see it now, so I will travel with ye, see ye safely back home, then on the next storm I will return here. I will keep the two portals."

"You will come to Florida?"

"Aye, I will come tae this magical place called Florida, where the women wear pants and learn tae read."

"It will be your turn to be frightened."

He chuckled.

"Why are we up so early?"

"I had trouble sleepin' as well, we might as well go."

We left the walls and descended to the courtyard.

His horse was waiting for us. I climbed on, and the Duke got into the saddle behind me.

His brother rode up.

"Aenghus is coming with us?"

"Aye, for a guard and he will bring Balach Mòr back to the castle."

Aenghus waved a hand. "Good morn, Madame Livvy, fine weather for a ride." He added, "Ye certain ye daena want me tae remain with ye, Nor? I can bring more men."

The duke said, "Nae, we are goin' tae be secretive, remain hidden, I canna do it with the horses nearby and an army is out of the question."

"Fine, I will leave with the horses, but ye hae tae promise nae adventure without me."

"Ye hae had too many adventures already, I promised yer Ailsa ye would be home for the midday meal. Ye will return with the horses, I will continue on as quiet as possible, without m'brother lumberin' through the underbrush beside me."

"Are ye sayin' I am too noisy? Careful or I will return with yer horse and ye will hae tae walk tae the moor."

We left through the gates and rode up the causeway toward the mountains. I said, "Is this morning? It feels like the middle of the night."

The Duke said, "Nae, Madame Livvy, tis morn, we are just before the dawn."

I shivered. "How much before the dawn?"

"Ye are cold?"

"Yeah, my coat is in... where is my coat?"

"Tis in one of the sacks, I can get it for ye once we are within the tree line." His left arm wrapped around me, I leaned back a bit, huddled within his arm. His breath beside my ear as we galloped towards the woods.

Aenghus's horse galloped along behind us.

Then, once in the woods the Duke slowed the horse. "Hold the reins." He leaned back to dig through the saddle bag.

I pet Balach Mòr's mane and brushed my hand down his withers and shivered.

The Duke found my coat and draped it around my shoulders. He pressed forward, holding the coat to my back. "This is better?" His voice rumbled deeply near my ear. He took the reins.

"Yes." I buttoned the hood and the top button under my chin, wearing the coat like a cape.

Our horses walked through the woods. I tried to think of what I was feeling with his arm around me on his horse in the early morn of a long ago Scotland. Some kind of Stockholm Syndrome, probably. I was dependent on him for my safety, health, wellness, like the whole thing — *everything*.

Beyond an empty gun I had almost nothing.

And I really liked the feel of him, that was nice.

For a split second his cheek pressed against my head — was that me, or did he do that?

He said, "Dost ye see the tree there, Madame Livvy? Tis an ancient tree..."

I said, "Mmmhmmm," because the horse was lulling me to sleep, and I was wrapped in the Duke's arms.

Chapter 25 - Livvy

1670

NEAR LOCH AWE

"Madame Livvy?"

His voice reached my mind, bringing me to consciousness. "What? Are we there?"

"Aye, we are near the banks of the Barran burn, we are goin' tae give our horse tae Aenghus and finish the journey on foot." He pulled the horse to a stop.

I stretched.

He shook out his arm.

"I'm so sorry, was I heavy?"

"Ye were verra asleep, but nae too heavy."

"The sun is coming up."

"Aye. Twill be a beautiful sunrise."

"I really really wish I had a cup of coffee, this morning begs for it."

He dismounted and put his hands up for me to slide into, I kind of slid into his arms and down his chest, and there was a pause for a moment, chest to chest — sexy, except my hood had slid forward awkwardly hiding my face. He dropped my feet to the ground and adjusted the shoulders of my coat so that it fell in a normal way.

Aenghus took the reins of the horse. "You're sure about this

118

Nor?"

"Aye, watch this direction for storms, if ye daena see one return for us before nightfall. If ye do see one, then I am likely gone tae a place Madame Livvy calls 'Florida'."

"Whether I see one or not I am likely tae come check for ye afore nightfall."

I dug through my pack. "A gift for you, Aenghus." I handed him the bag of lint and the fire starter kit.

He looked at it quizzically.

"The lint will catch fire in a second. This is the flint, this is the strike." I struck the rod against the flint and sparks flew.

Aenghus said, "Och aye, tis verra simple!" He put the kit inside his sporran. "Twas a pleasure meeting ye, Madame Livvy, and Nor, be cautious."

The Duke said, "Dost ye think if ye are nae there that danger will befall me?"

"I ken without a doubt that if I am nae there ye will be like a bairn, mewling in the bushes, askin' all the wolves tae care for it."

"Tis nae true! I saved ye from the..." The Duke gestured around. "Everything, I am always rescuin' ye!"

Aenghus shrugged. "I hae tae pretend tae let ye rescue me or ye mewl louder."

"Says the younger brother who I used tae hae tae carry home from the fields because yer feet were sore."

Aenghus laughed, turned the horses and left us alone in the woods.

I asked the Duke, "How much farther?"

"Near an hour of walkin', Madame Livvy."

We made it, finally, and because we weren't sure if someone might be lying in wait, we tried to remain cautious and hidden. We crouched down behind the underbrush, then crept down a small graveled bluff.

We came to a shallow cave under a ledge overhung with a veil of roots and vegetation that would hide us from view. In front of us was the wide riverbank, at least a football field length across to the thin stream, and farther still to woods on the other side.

As we climbed in behind the ledge he said, "Och nae, this is tight, I hae hidden here before but I was much smaller."

"You hid here, why?"

"Tae jump out at m'brothers, we were in battle, the boisterous kind."

I sat down on the inclined ground, my feet sliding in the gravel. I had to hike up my knees and plant my feet to keep from sliding out.

He said, "Hold ontae the root there. The tree is strong enough tae hold us." He folded his body in beside mine with his head hunched down. "We winna be seen but we will be verra uncomfortable."

He pointed. "There is the place where we found the portals. Dost ye see it, beside the rocks?" He peered up and down the moor. "I canna see anyone."

"But we have to assume they are there."

"Aye, we ought tae, but we might be wrong. Johnne Cambell told me he was leavin' and for me tae keep the portal safe. He demanded an alliance. I dinna agree tae it, but perhaps he has called off the battles. Twould be good if we are left alone."

He adjusted his ass in the dirt to try and get more comfortable.

It began to rain. It was not one of the storms we were waiting for, this was drizzle and drip, an enveloping grayness, and we were surrounded by a sound-dampening thrum.

A rivulet of mud went by my skirts. "We're in a dirt cave, rain is just what we needed."

He said, "Twill help us tae hide. I hope it inna a frog rain though."

"A frog rain would suck so so so bad. You know what? I don't like the portals being connected to your belt — what if they start up and whisk us away? I feel like I want to be ready, I want more control."

He untied the two sacks.

I looked in one and noted the marks. "This one took us to the past in Scotland." I returned it to its sack and passed it to the Duke who placed it to his left.

I said, "If it starts moving, kick it away."

I checked the second sack, just to make sure. "Yep, this one has the markings for going to Florida." I spoke to the portal, "Please take me back to Florida. Please. And to do that you must activate, please, yesterday you didn't and that is... that sucks, please activate."

I returned it to its small sack and the Duke shoved it about four feet in front of us in the rain.

He said, "When it turns on we will jump on it."

I gulped. "I'm scared."

"Ye are more frightened if the portal daena turn on."

I nodded.

He continued, "We ken the storms occur at the same time, it happened regularly for days afore I found them. There is nae reason why they ought tae stop now."

I worried, "What if they need to be out in the middle of the moor...? What if they need something... something we don't know?"

"If the time draws near and they arna turning on, we will kick them out intae the moor, so that they will."

"That's a far kick."

He chuckled. "I am verra determined."

I teased, "Or if they don't turn on we can try to figure out why — maybe not kicking, maybe some examining. We need to figure out how it works."

"Yer plan sounds suspiciously as if we would hae tae touch them."

"Yes, that does sound like it, I do not like that idea. Let's wait and do that *after* we see if the storm comes."

"We winna ken for a time."

"So we just wait? Hoo boy, I am going to get really nervous."

He nodded, picked up a bit of gravel, and loosely shook it in his hand.

Shoulder to shoulder we sat there as the sky turned orange and the sun came up in the east.

"This is so beautiful."

"Aye."

I rested my chin on my arms wrapped around my knees. "This sky looks like God painted it."

"Aye, it does."

I put my cheek on my knee and watched the side of his face. "My grandpa studied meteorology because, as his father said, 'Blue skies are fleeting, we must be ready for the change of weather that's a'coming.' That's why my family has a ranch, why we learn to use firearms, and why we study the weather, it's all because we know that the sky will change... we ought to be prepared."

The Duke nodded. "When I wake I go up tae the walls first thing and decipher the sky, the direction of the wind, the amount of clouds. It helps me decide on the tasks of the day."

"How cool is it that four hundred years from now people are still waking up and needing to know the weather of the day? It connects us all through time." I yawned.

He said, "Ye can use m'shoulder if ye need tae."

I put my cheek on his shoulder. "It's just that I usually wake up to a warm cup of coffee, now it's been days without."

"I hae heard of coffee, and travelers hae mentioned a coffee shop in London. I am interested in going tae taste it. What is it like?"

"It's dark brown, aromatic — it's a type of bean, roasted and ground, with hot water poured over it. Just about everyone in the world loves it. We have whole shops for buying cups of it. We drink it full of milk and sugar, yum. When you come to Florida you can have some."

"It does sound verra good." He pulled a bit of bread from a bag laying beside him in the dirt, tore it in half, and passed me a bit.

I said, "I can't wait to show you Florida, but it is going to be really overwhelming. And I'm worried that... what if you come with me and then you can't get back here? It feels mean to take you away from your family. Every time we touch these portals it's a huge risk."

"I am willing tae take the risk tae make sure ye are all right." He bit into the hard bread and chewed.

Tears welled in my eyes, the familiar pull of my mouth pulling down. I blinked them back. "You're not frightened of the trip, Your Grace?"

"Nae, tis something that must be done, and soon ye will be home, I promised ye, and so I need tae do it. Are ye frightened, Madame Livvy?"

I nodded, my head rubbing up and down on his shoulder. "But this is helping, having your shoulder is nice. I don't know what I would have done without you. I was hundreds of years in the past, didn't know how to feed or clothe myself. Who knows what would have happened to me."

"I daena ken how much help I was, I almost got us killed by brawlin'."

"That was terrifying, but at least we didn't have to finish eating that dinner."

He chuckled.

"It feels good to laugh, this has been what my grandmother would call an ordeal."

"Aye, but the ordeal inna over, Johnne Cambell has threatened me."

"So he just time travels around, threatening people — is he going to screw up the history of the world?"

"I daena think he cares. He seemed careless about the usual

way of history and years passin' by. He wants power above all else. I ken many men like this, he will need tae be reduced."

I nestled my cheek against his shoulder. "He sounds dangerous. More so that he can jump in and out of time."

"He kent a great deal of me, but he dinna ken all... It gives me an upper hand." He looked down at me. "Daena worry, Madame Livvy, I am a Duke, these are my lands, he canna win against the Duke of Awe."

He peered back and forth, up and down the gorge again then continued, "I am the most powerful laird in the region, he has made a mistake challenging me."

I nodded. "He doesn't know we have two portals—"

"He daena even ken about ye."

"*Thankfully*. That makes me feel a lot better... So you have more information than Johnne Cambell, that's a good thing. And if one of these portals is powerful, two is much more so."

A smile lifted the edge of his mouth. "Aye, and ye strategize, ye are nae like most women."

"I don't know about that, if you think women don't strategize, you are not listening."

He chuckled.

I said, "I don't know how this is going to go down, but thank you for taking care of me here. I don't understand how we met, but I really liked meeting you, you've been... really helpful." It wasn't exactly right, I wanted to say he had been comfortable, but also hotly unsettling, and like a close friend and also a mysterious stranger — he was all those things.

He had been my protector for days.

He pressed his cheek to the top of my head. "I dinna mind, Madame Livvy, it has been a pleasure meeting ye... ye are the only brightness in this dark time."

"You've been that for me, too, I will miss you after this is said and done."

His head nodded against my own.

Chapter 26 - Livvy

1670

NEAR LOCH AWE

We had these powerful portals, but we didn't know how to use them. It was a little like having a nuclear warhead buried on your property, not very helpful and likely very dangerous.

Men wanted these portals, they were hunting for them, tracking them, willing to kill for them. And I might be drawing them toward my family, which sucked.

This was possibly very risky, but I wanted, needed, to go home.

Whenever I closed my eyes I saw Lou lying in the sand, clutching his chest and the fear in my brother's eyes when he saw me disappearing, or whatever it was that happened.

How many days had I been gone?

I woke up a while later, confused by my surroundings, my face pressed into wool. It took me a moment... I had my head in the Duke's lap.

I pulled myself up, sending a cascade of gravel out of the cave. The Duke pressed a finger to his lips. *Wheesht.*

My stomach plunged, my hair stood on end.

He pointed behind us.

I listened. Men were on the path above us, mere feet away.

Then there was a short vibrating buzz from the portal ahead of us, the one that was a portal to Florida. The man above us got quiet.

Another buzz.

The man above us yelled, "There!"

The Duke slid forward, stood, and kicked the portal in the sack ahead of us about thirty yards. The sack billowed as it went, and then the portal flew from it end over end, beginning to really vibrate now. It landed near the stream and energy erupted from it, like an explosion.

I threw my arms up over my eyes and my head as the blast of wind blew us against the cliff. Above us a column of cumulonimbus clouds boiled into the air.

Holy shit.

The Duke drew his sword and turned to fight the men who were racing down the embankment.

"Ye must get tae the portal, I will hold them back!"

I had the horrible choice to make, go forward into a vicious storm, against a powerful wind, to ride a horrible pain-searing journey, or stay here and...

I glanced over my shoulder, three men, struggling against the winds to attack the Duke.

I was unarmed, there was no way to help.

He yelled, "Go!"

I plowed through the wind. My skirt and hair pulling straight behind me, the winds at a gale force.

Lightning struck a log about ten feet to my left, it sizzled and then caught on fire and the fire blew across the bank.

I should not fucking be out here in this.

A funnel spun around, I couldn't go any further. I got down on my knees and tried to crawl, the wind was brutal, a torrential downpour started, like a bucket of water thrown on my face.

I lay down with my hands over my head, because there was

nothing else I could do, but there was one saving grace, no one else would be able to get closer.

I tried to be an unattractive object to lighting.

Then the wind switched.

My skirts shoved up.

I scrambled up and crawled forward, glancing behind me — the Duke was wrestling one of the men gaining on me, beating the hell out of each other.

I needed to gain ground. I scrambled to my feet and ran.

But then about ten feet away the wind switched, buffeting me from the right side. I stumbled and fell hard on my shoulder. The Duke had hold around the waist of a man who was plowing toward the portal.

The Duke yelled, "Get tae it!"

"Without you?"

He didn't answer. I pushed shoulder first through the wind, an arm up to block the gale, five steps and I would be on it — I was breaking the rules of storm chasing, unprotected, fighting my way into the eye of the storm.

I was there!

The energy at the center was insane.

I reached for the portal but then there was a blow to my back, knocking me hard to the ground, another sharp pain up my shoulder, blinding wind above me, lightning lit up the sky, as if it was arcing all around me. The Duke grabbed a man off me and they were fighting, the Duke under him, they rolled toward the portal.

Then the Duke was on him, raining blows on his face, but the man was reaching for the portal, his fingers almost on it.

I scrambled up, dove across his legs and onto the portal as if it was a fumbled football on the field. I clutched it to my chest, the man's hand twisted in my hair jerking my head back, *letgolet-goletgo!*

As the portal grabbed hold of my arms a searing pain spread

across my chest, my mind panicked, was I going to have a heart attack holding it to my chest?

It felt like my hair was ripping off my scalp, there was a heavy feeling, someone landed on my hips, the full weight of a body on me, but that was okay, I was suffocating, dying, screaming, anyway... might as well get on with it.

Chapter 27 - Livvy

I came to, in the sand on a beach, I was damp.

I glanced around. I was lying in the tide, a bit of a wave lapping around my feet. It did look like that spot Lou and Charlie and I had been storm-chasing in a few days ago, but I couldn't be sure. There were low trees, scrub oaks, I think they were called, and... a muffled grunt beside me. I twisted.

The Duke was groaning, an arm thrown over his face. So whose leg was this across my arm?

The other dude.

He shifted.

I said, "Duke, Your Grace, *Duke*, are you awake?"

He startled. "Och nae," his head up he looked around. "Och, Madame Livvy, watch out!"

He lumbered up as I looked over my shoulder, and the man punched me hard in the face.

I shrieked and held it, too much pain on top of too much pain. It was hard to focus as I heard the sound of pummeling, and looked up to see the Duke holding the man's head under the water until he stopped struggling and drowned.

A bigger wave came up and the Duke dove back to keep from getting doused.

The wave hit me, rolled me, and tried pulling me into the ocean.

The Duke grabbed my wrist and dragged me from the water

He scooped up the portal laying in the surf, and the sack with the second portal and dragged me through the sand and up to a dry dune. He dropped my hand and collapsed down on his ass and then lay back with a groan. "Och nae, tis verra painful, distressin', and horribly bright."

Just then the overcast sky broke open and rain poured down.

"Welcome to Florida."

~

It took a while to gain focus. I had been staring out at the ocean, the waves lapping on the dead man in the surf.

Then I grew more conscious. I was staring out at a dead man in the surf. I needed to get the fuck off this beach. *What did I have?* Nothing. Not even my backpack, now in a cave in a distant century.

I mumbled, "Stay here. Watch for people," and rushed toward the dead man. I waited for the wave to pull back then I dug through his pockets, keeping my eyes averted because his eyes were open. He looked like something out of a horror movie.

He wore modern fatigues, and had a coin in his pocket from a long ago time, but other than that, nothing.

I ran back to the dune where the Duke stood, the sack with the portals tied to his belt, watching up and down the beach.

"In lieu of burying him, we need to get out of here. But first..."

I looked around for the weather station that Lou would have set up... I found it strapped to one of the legs of the boardwalk. "Follow me." I strode over to it and pushed the power button — powering it off and then waited for a few minutes and turned it back on. I didn't know if that would be a good enough signal. I just hoped that Charlie was monitoring it.

I scanned up and down the beach; there were lots of McMansions, but the closest house was a small beach cottage that looked lifeless and empty. And might have less security. We began to walk as rain continued streaming down.

Chapter 28 - Livvy

2012

AMELIA ISLAND

The Duke was quiet, head down, he moaned.

"Too bright? Even in the rain?"

"Aye."

"Keep your eyes shut, I'll try and keep you from falling." I took his arm and led him. "One foot in front of the other, keep going, exactly like this." We bypassed the house's deck and went to the bottom-floor garage. I peeked through the window. There were no cars, the place had a vacation rental sign and no signs of life.

The side door had a deadbolt and no window.

"Come with me, let's see if I can jimmy a window." He followed me as I slogged up the steps, my soggy, sand-covered skirts dragging behind me. At the top deck I looked right and left, still no one to be seen, and there was a sliding glass door, old-school style. "I got this, I break into the one at home all the time. You got your knife?"

He pulled out his dirk and I showed him where to pry. While he pried, I lifted the handle and a second later the door slid open.

I stuck my head through and looked all around to make sure there weren't any alarms and then I waved him in and closed the door behind us.

He stood still, looking dumbfounded.

I led him by the arm to the sectional couch and sort of pushed him down into it. He was too wet and covered in sand, it was incredibly irresponsible of me, but there was too much to do and I needed to think.

We had needs to meet: shelter, water, food, safety, get home.

"Lay your head back and close your eyes. Let me look around for a moment."

He put his head back, groaned, and mumbled, "...Yer Grace."

I chuckled. "Yes... Your Grace." I went through the cabinets, found glasses and filled two with ice water from the refrigerator dispenser and drank heartily from one and carried the other to him. I stood dripping wet in front of him. "The fridge is empty, I'm famished but we'll have to wait for food."

He drank from the glass. "Tis ice cold!"

"Yes. Yes it is... there's so much to explain, but I have a lot to figure out, we've broken about fifty laws."

I drank down the rest of my water. Then I went to the bathroom, located a stack of towels, and began drying off my hair. I brought a small stack for him to dry off with. I placed them beside him on the couch. He opened up an eye and then closed it again, quickly.

I perched on the couch beside him and picked up the yellow phone on the end table. I only had one of my family's numbers memorized: Mom, so I dialed it and she picked up on the first ring.

"It's me."

"Livvy! Livvy, we've been so worried!! What are you... where are you?"

"Mom, I have had a shit time, how long have I been...?"

I listened to her explain that I had been gone for almost twenty-four hours, a whole night, and they had been frantic about me and were so worried and—

Yet I had watched the sun set and rise three times.

"Is Lou okay?"

"He's good honey, he had an indirect hit by lightning, he said he was 'shaken, not stirred.' Charlie got him to the hospital, Junior and Birdie drove up there last night, Birdie sat in the hospital while Charlie and your uncles searched for you all over that beach. They've been up all night looking for you. This morning Lou was transferred to our local hospital, they said he gets to come home tomorrow."

Tears streamed down my cheeks. "Mom I need help, I can't really explain what happened, not over the phone, but... I need someone to come get me."

"Of course. Charlie was about to head back up to look for you, what's your address?"

There was a magazine on the coffee table, I read the address out to her. She hung up to call Charlie.

The duke had one eye open, watching me. "Who were ye speaking tae, Madame Livvy?"

I looked down at the handset.

"This is a telephone, see the wire? It's connected to my parents' house, really far away. My voice went through the wire and my mother's voice came through it to me." I replaced the handset on the phone and sat quietly for a moment. I pulled a tissue from a box, blew my nose, and wiped my eyes.

The Duke asked, "Madame Livvy, is yer grandfather well?"

"Yes. He's in the hospital but he will be out tomorrow. I'm just so relieved." My chin trembled. I tore the tissue into pieces and then pulled another one. "I know it's weird but I think I'm in shock. I am even more frightened by coming home, as if I expected to wake up and learn it was all a dream, but it wasn't — we really were time traveling. That was my mother's voice on the phone and she didn't know where I was all night, she's really upset."

He was sunk back in the couch, I was perched on the edge.

"And I am traveling with a duke. It was touch and go there for a moment, I didn't think you were going to make it."

"Of course I was goin' tae make it." He sheepishly grinned.

"Bringing him was a mishap, I will admit, but killin' him was always the plan."

"Well, here you are, wet on the couch in the future. What do you think so far?"

"From inside m'eyelids tis verra alike the past. There is a great deal of rain."

For lack of something better to do, I turned in my seat and used the end of a towel to push his hair back and wipe water and sand off his forehead. It was close and intimate, to brush his hair back, to clean his skin. My face close to his — he had sand on his brow. I exposed a dry end of the towel and gently brushed, wiping it away.

His arm rose and his hand went around my wrist and he gently pulled me, directing me across his lap. It was fluid how it went, as if this was just the next step. I was concentrating on his skin, his full lips, his chiseled jaw, his lashes resting on his lower lids — so close that I could make out the grains of sand and next moment, I was crawling onto his lap, my legs astride, without embarrassment, without a thought, as if it were the most natural thing in the world.

I changed the edge of the towel to a drier, cleaner edge and leaned forward on his chest and brushed the sand from his temple. While I concentrated, his hands lay on my thighs, the scent of him, musk and effort, a bit of spice and sweat, the sound of the waves crashing on shore, the thrum of the rain, the dark grayness of the world outside.

I brushed some sand off his earlobe and whispered, because I was close, *better?*

Aye Madame Livvy, ye are making it all better.

My temple pressed to his cheek. We were breathing in unison, breaths that were becoming shorter, faster, like panting, my skin against his stubble. I drew my lips along the edge of his jaw until the corners of our mouths were a centimeter away — and then we kissed.

My lips were a softness against his pressing, my lips parted to his pressure, our tongues met in sweet tastes, his warm breaths, his solid form between my legs, his hands sliding up my thighs. I lost sight of everything for a long moment kissing him warm and hot, the taste of him... *oh*...

I withdrew my tongue, bit my lips, pulled my mouth from his, very close I said, "I don't know what that was, it was..."

My heart raced. I took a deep ragged breath.

His hand rose and cupped my jaw, "I ken what it was, Madame Livvy..." He brushed my hair from my face and put it behind my ear. He pulled the towel from my grip on his chest and used the edge to wipe at my face, a very gentle brush of sand from my cheek.

"I mean, that was really lovely," I said, "but we should stop. I have... Chris, you know? This is very confusing, I just met you. And we live in different times."

He nodded, and left the towel on his chest between us and dropped his hands to his sides. We met eyes and stared deeply into them. It was as if we were consoling each other, silently. The phone rang.

"Och nae!" He clamped his hands over his ears.

I dove off his lap for the phone. "Hello?"

It was my mom. "Your brother was already on his way, he saw the weather station turn off and on, he was going to check it out, so he'll be there in about an hour and forty-five minutes."

I said goodbye and placed the handset back on the phone. "Now we just have to wait for over an hour."

I went to the sliding glass door and looked out at the beach. The lapping waves were rolling the dark form of the dead man in the shallows.

I tried to think of how the body would be traced back to us — *could it? Would it?*

I closed the drapes, throwing the room into darkness and curled up beside the Duke on the couch, my arm wrapped around his, our hands clasped.

I fell asleep.

. . .

I woke up a while later and peeked out the door at the beach. The rain was really beating down, the tide was high. I couldn't see the body anymore.

I looked at the Duke. "I am famished are you hungry?"

He said, "M'whole middle aches from hunger."

Chapter 29 - Livvy

2012

AMELIA ISLAND

Charlie's big truck splashed through puddles and pulled to a quick stop in front of a mailbox. His windshield wipers working overtime, swish swish swish, his lights on in the rainy gloom. The Duke and I rushed out into the downpour, me telling him over my shoulder, "We're going to get in that thing, a truck, it's going to be crazy, you'll just have to deal."

Charlie jumped out of the truck, ran around, and bear-hugged me in the rain. "Jesus Christ, I thought you were dead. Where the hell did you go? What happened, Livvy, that was insane!"

"I know, I have so much to tell you but right now I need to help the Duke with all of this." I gestured my arms, wildly.

"Who, this guy, the *Duke?*" Charlie looked the Duke up and down. "You'll explain it all in the truck though, right? Who the hell punched you, did this dude punch you?"

"No, he rescued me, come on, let's get in — faster than this."

I was drenched, Charlie was wearing a raincoat, I was not. The Duke and I looked like drowned rats. Charlie jogged back around the truck and climbed in.

I opened up the back passenger door and gestured the Duke in. He shook his head. "Och nae, I will walk..."

Charlie was peering out at us, "What the hell, Livvy, y'all need to climb in the truck."

"I'm trying." I said to the Duke, "You can't walk, it's too far."

Rain poured down. "I need a horse, ye said ye hae horses."

"We have to drive to the horses, you have to climb in, it's like a carriage, like a horse. It will take us on the road, just going on a little ride. It's going to seem crazy, but you just have to do it."

He put a hand on the door and another hand on the seat. "Ye are sure on it? We could call yer men tae bring the horses tae us?"

I said, "That's not how it works, and the faster you do it, the faster you get in, the faster we get food. Are you hungry, Your Grace? Want me to shove my shoulder against your ass and push you in, like you did to get me up on the horse?"

"Nae ye daena need tae." He heaved himself up and awkwardly dropped into the seat, keeping a foot on the step outside.

"You have to pull your foot in, I have to close the door."

He pulled his foot in. I slammed the door shut. I opened the front passenger seat, climbed in, and sat down. "Thank God you have seat covers, I have a century of dirt and grime on me, mixed with the mud of a thousand storms. How's Lou? Oh, and before you answer, we need food, we need so much food."

"Lou survived, Lou about scared the shit out of me, and you fucking disappeared. What was up with that, and now you're back at the same place? How the hell did you do that—?"

I pulled the visor down and directed the mirror so I could see the Duke's face. "How you doing?"

He was looking all around at the inside of the truck and bouncing a little on the seat. "Tis a verra fine carriage."

I grinned, unbuckled my seat belt, and not answering my brother, climbed over the seat into the back.

"Livvy, you're getting mud all over the seats!"

"I know, but I can't help it... he's in a truck for the first time ever, I don't want to miss any of it." I pulled my leg over and dragged the soggy skirts behind me into the back seat. I exhaled,

139

AMELIA ISLAND

because that had been a lot of effort. I remembered to strap the Duke's seatbelt across his lap and then I put mine on too.

I took his hand between us.

Charlie looked at me through the rearview. "Maybe you need to tell me what the hell is going on?"

"I time traveled."

He kept his eyes on mine in the rearview. "Bullshit. I've been out searching for you all night, I'm exhausted. I deserve better than this."

"I'm not making up a story. I time traveled to the year 1560. This man, the Duke of—"

Nor said, "I am the Duke of Awe, Nor, of the Campbells of Awe."

Charlie said, "Cool name, but um, that story is still bullshit." He turned a corner at about twenty miles per hour and the Duke clutched the seat and the door like he was going to fly from the truck, but he had a big grin on his face.

"You like going fast?"

"I do like it, verra much. Tis verra bright though, I hae tae keep my eyes shut."

"Just wait, we are going to go even faster."

Charlie passed back a pair of sunglasses. I put them on the Duke as Charlie got us up on the main road and sped up. The Duke gripped the handle.

I asked, "I wonder if you've ever gone this fast before?"

"Never."

Charlie's eyes flashed into the rearview, his brow drew down. "This is all bullshit, what the hell is going on?"

"It's not bullshit. I time traveled. I have been in the year 1560 for a couple of days, and then I was in the year 1670 for a couple of days, it's been an ordeal."

"Bull—"

"Stop saying bullshit."

"I will stop saying bullshit when you start telling me where you were."

140

The Duke said, "Madame Livvy is tellin' ye where she was, I was with her. We were at Kilchurn castle in the year 1560. Can this carriage go even faster?"

"Are you from Scotland? I one-hundred-percent know they have trucks in Scotland."

I said, "This is what we're trying to tell you, he lives in Scotland, I met him there, because I was in Scotland! But it was the year 1560 and then the year 1670. That's why he has never been in a truck."

Charlie turned a corner and said, "Bullshit."

"What do *you* think happened to me?"

"You died."

I gestured to myself. "Clearly *that's* bullshit — what's the other explanation, now that I'm in your backseat?"

"I don't know, I thought maybe you got picked up by a tornado. The police wouldn't help me look, they told me I had to wait before making the report, so Tim, Dan, Junior, and I were looking for you in the woods in the center of the island."

He pulled up in the drive-through of the Dairy Queen. "What do you want?" and ordered for himself while I studied the menu.

I rolled down the back window and leaned out to direct my voice into the speaker. "Two cheese burgers, four large orders of fries, two extra large sodas, two blizzards."

Charlie said, "You got your wallet?"

"No, dude, I don't have my wallet. My phone was in Lou's truck, not that any of it would have helped anyway. I was in another century, no cell service. Besides that, when these evil assholes were chasing us I lost my backpack. I got nothing."

"You better pay me back, the Duke here sounds like he should be able to afford our food."

"He's from another century. Any money he has is not going to work here anyway."

Charlie exhaled irritatedly as he paid.

· · ·

He passed the bags over the seat. I put the drinks all around us in cupholders. And then, as Charlie pulled us from the parking lot onto the highway off the island, I dug the Duke's burger from the bag and peeled the paper back. "This is a burger, it's going to be delicious, but go slow, or you'll get sick. This is a lot of... probably too much food."

Charlie watched me through the rearview mirror as I explained the burger to the Duke. "The only other explanation is that you were taken up by aliens. Were you taken up by aliens?"

"Nope, but it was a little sci-fi, and who knows where the time-travel tech comes from, it looks pretty alien to me." I drank some Coke. "Oh man, this is delicious. I need to go slow too, there hasn't been sugar in days."

The Duke watched me take a bite of burger and mimicked me, taking a bite of burger and chewing. He nodded.

I pulled the lid off his Blizzard. "Here is a spoon for this."

While he ate some of the cold ice cream I passed him a couple of French fries dipped in ketchup.

His face drew down in a grimace.

"You don't like it?"

He smacked his lips and pointed at the Blizzard and the fries. "Tis too sweet and verra salty."

I sipped Coke through a straw.

He mimicked me, slurping, then grimaced.

I giggled. "You don't like the Coke?"

"Horrid!"

He finished his burger in two bites.

Charlie said, "How the fuck has he never had Coke?"

"Because he's a time traveler! That's what I'm trying to tell you. I've been riding on horses for days, look at my clothes. Where do you think I got this outfit from? I'm wearing long skirts!"

"I don't know, some weird cult kidnapped you?"

I huffed. "I know this is illogical, but try to *be* logical — did you see anyone there? Were there kidnappers there?"

"No, just that strange little object."

I put down my Coke, "Yes! Exactly!" I pulled one of the gadgets from the small sack on the seat beside the Duke. "This thing!" I leaned over the front seat and held it in front of him as he drove. "You saw *this* right? Under the storm? Well, it *causes* the storm, and if you touch it when it's alive—"

The Duke muttered, "Daena ever touch it when it is movin' unless ye are ready for a horrible experience."

"Yep, it drags you through time. It hurts like shit, by the way, it's truly awful."

Charlie darted his eyes back and forth from the road to the gadget, then he touched it, timidly, and then he returned his hand to the steering wheel. "You expect me to believe that this thing jumped you through time?"

I returned the portal into the sack. "Yes, I know it's a stretch, but it's..."

My eyes drew to the Duke who took some fries, dipped them in the Blizzard, like me, grimaced, took a sip of Coke and spluttered. "Och nae, tis more horrid as it goes."

I stifled a laugh. "I am sorry it is so unpleasant. You want the... what do you like of it?"

"The meat was fine, the rest of it," he sneered, "Tis awful."

Charlie sped up, the Duke held his stomach.

He put some French fries in his mouth and retched then took a small sip of Coke and gagged.

Charlie said, "Jesus Christ, has he never had fast food before?"

"No, he hasn't had any of this at all, and this is his first time in a truck, on a highway, and he's getting carsick. *That's* what I'm saying."

Charlie mumbled, "Bullshit," then said, "But tell me what happened, we're spinning around the beginning of your story, let's get to details."

I launched into the story of the last few days: I ended up beside the Duke in the year 1560, we had to ask for lodging in a castle, we had to leave the castle, we jumped with the next storm, but not here, we ended up in the Duke's castle. I explained it was

143

the same castle just different times. Then we waited until the following day, another storm, we jumped here, the Duke coming along to make sure I was okay.

All the while Charlie repeatedly said, "Bullshit," or "No way," but I could tell he was believing me more and more.

Then, from the corner of my eye, the Duke took a small bite, grimaced, put it on his knee, took a sip of Coke, retched, and his drink dropped to the floorboards, the top popping off and Coke splashing everywhere.

Charlie yelled, "Hey!"

The Duke clutched his stomach and turned absolutely green.

Charlie fishtailed the truck to a stop in the shoulder of the highway as the Duke clutched a hand over his mouth and heaved.

I reached across him, shoved the door open, and unlatched his belt. The Duke fell from the truck to his hands and knees and vomited in the grass. It was sprinkling rain down on us.

I scrambled out of the truck and perched in the door with my hand on his shoulder, averting my eyes so I didn't vomit too.

After he finished, he groaned, wiped his arm across his handsome mouth, and sat back on his heels. "Och nae, that was a foul meal, Madame Livvy, ye were able tae finish it?"

I chuckled. "Yes, it was delicious."

He groaned. Cars whipped by us, a semi-trailer honked, loudly. He closed his eyes.

"In hindsight though, you didn't need any of the other stuff. I should have gotten you four burgers. That is not the right food for you at all when you're traveling faster than you've ever gone."

He lumbered up to his feet. "I was enjoyin' m'self on the ride and then it turned."

"You feel okay now? We still have an hour, at least, to go."

Cars whipped by, buffeting us with wind from their wake. "Will we get tae go fast again?"

"Yes indeed." Charlie held out his burger wrapper. "Here, have mine, fixed it for you, get back in the truck."

. . .

I climbed in then the Duke climbed in. I reached across and pulled the door closed. I strapped on his seatbelt.

"Thank ye, Madame Livvy."

Charlie pulled the truck back onto the highway. We rolled the windows down, for some air.

"Is that good?"

"Aye." He leaned his head toward the window so the wind blew through his hair as Charlie got the truck up to seventy miles per hour.

I said, "Charlie's burger is two patties and he took off all the parts, here's a couple of burger patties. Ketchup scraped off. One has cheese. Two slices of bacon. And then, no more Coke." I moved his drink to the other drink holder. "What do you want?"

"This ride requires a whisky."

Charlie said, "I don't know if I... you know what, check under the seat — there's a toolbox? It might have a flask in there, from a job."

I pulled the toolbox out and unlatched it. There were a few light mechanic's tools and a flask. I opened it, sniffed. "Yep. Here ya go."

He had the burger wrapper on his knees. He swigged from the flask. "This is verra good." He ate the burger without anything extra.

I tried to hand him a French fry and he shook his head. "Nae, if yer flyin' down the road ye canna eat anything distasteful. Ye must stick tae the basics."

I laughed, "Those are meat and whisky?"

"Aye."

Charlie said, "Whisky and Coke is very good too."

"Nae, I am not that courageous."

I looked out the window. "You're seeing so much new."

He chuckled. "I'm not seein' anything, m'eyes are shut tight behind these... what dost ye call them?"

I said, "The sunglasses?"

Charlie said, "Okay, fine, I am starting to believe you."

"Not to digress from my story, but did you tell Chris what happened?"

"Yes, Mom called him, and she's probably calling him right now to tell him you're found."

"He didn't come though? Was he worried about me?"

"No, he didn't come, we didn't know what to tell him really, we were in search mode, and you know, he said he had to work." Charlie met my eyes in the rearview.

I said, "But he was worried?"

"Mom said he sounded worried."

Chapter 30 - Livvy

2012
LOU-MOO RANCH

We pulled up under the sign that stretched over the drive, Long Moss Ranch, a distinguished name for a cattle ranch, but everyone called it Lou-Moo ranch, after the men — a line of Lou Mullers of which my grandpa was the fourth, my uncle Junior was the fifth.

Charlie put our security code into the keypad, the gate swung open, and he drove us up the long drive to the main house. We passed the massive live oak that was hung with Spanish moss, and pulled up in front of the mansion, or as dad liked to call it, the big-ass house.

My dad had married into the family, and was, as he said, "Just happy to be here." He had moved in and helped run the ranch with my uncles. Lou was the patriarch. He ran everything from his big ass house, while his sons had smaller houses scattered around.

Ryan, Dylan, Charlie, and I, had grown up in a house farther up the road, but we pulled up in front of the main house and Mom and Dad and my uncles, Junior, Tim, and Dan, were all waiting for us on the porch.

I opened the truck door. "Climb out, pretend to be cool. No judgment, but most of my family is judging you."

The Duke groaned and climbed out. He kind of awkwardly bowed.

I clambered down the side of the truck into the arms of my family.

My dad asking, "What the hell happened to you?"

My Uncle Tim asking, "Who the hell is this guy?"

Held in Mom's endless hug, I asked, "Can we sit? I have a great deal to tell you and we need to sit, and we might need some food for the Duke."

The front door opened and my grandmother, Birdie, rushed out. She was plump and short with steel gray hair, always wearing denim blue. "Livvy! Oh my God, Livvy! I thought you were dead!" She threw her arms around me. "I didn't believe them, then I had to go to the bathroom. I said, 'Lord, please don't let my Livvy drive up while I'm taking a dump,' and guess what happened? You drove up!"

I laughed as she rocked me back and forth in her arms.

My mom said, her eyes wide, "Birdie, our Livvy has just informed us that this is a duke — Livvy, have you been kidnapped, are you in some kind of cult?"

Birdie let go of me and looked the Duke up and down.

"Mom, dukes aren't cult leaders, they're a *title*. He's *nobility*. This is the Duke of Awe." I introduced, "Duke Nor, this is my grandmother, Birdie, my father, Dave Larson, and my mom, Joni Larson, my Uncle Junior, my Uncle Tim, and my Uncle Dan."

The Duke bowed again. "At yer service, Madame Birdie, Master Dave and Madame Joni, Masters Junior, Tim, and Dan, tis a pleasure tae meet ye all."

Birdie fanned herself. "Well, Jiminy Cricket, if this is a cult where do I sign up? He sounds like he stepped out of the pages of the Highlander story."

Uncle Tim said, "Good show, we watched every episode."

Mom said, "Come up and get something to drink, are you hungry Duke, um, Awe?"

"I am usually called, Your Grace—"

Her eyes went wide.

"But the family of Madame Livvy in the new World may call me Nor, daena tell my mother." He chuckled. "And aye, I am verra hungry."

I said, "But he will definitely want something meaty. Like seriously, just meat on a plate."

Birdie said, "Perfect! We have sausage in from the market. And I have a wonderful dry cheese. Do you like a dry cheese, Nor the Duke? Paired with Dijon mustard it's lovely."

Mom and Birdie climbed the front steps into the house, with all of us following. Mom said, "I have to call your brothers, Livvy, first thing, I promised I would call as soon as I saw the whites of your eyes."

My mom asked, "You want to go clean up and change? You're damp and sandy."

I glanced at the Duke and shook my head, I didn't want to leave his side after just arriving. "Nah, I'm damp and sandy, but it's okay, kinda want to sit and talk for a moment."

Birdie said, "Well, you need to wash up in the kitchen sink then, before you get to eat."

I led the Duke to the sink and ran the water, squirted soap on his hands and wordlessly guided him through the scrubbing, rinsing, and drying so he wouldn't be perplexed in front of my family.

The kitchen was large and open to the dining area where we sat at the table. There were meats and cheeses spread out on trays in the middle of the table with some crackers on the side.

The Duke had a glass of ice water beside him and a bottle of beer. He gave the beer a taste, smacked his lips, and gazed at the label, then he looked all around at the room.

The kitchen and dining area were decorated in farmhouse country, the predominant color was sage green, there were open cabinets with Birdie's collection of ceramic pitchers. The counters were marble, the seats wicker, it was tasteful but busy, with little knickknacks, family photos, and pieces of collected art on most surfaces. I wondered if the Duke was able to focus on every tchotchke, every picture on the wall, every piece of equipment. Or anything at all, he was seeing so much for the first time.

After that gaze around, he kept his eyes down at the table in front of him. He would raise his eyes if he was speaking, then look back down.

I supposed that was self-protection.

Gathered with my family around, Birdie held my hands, misty-eyed, because as she said, "I thought Lou's blasted storm-chasing had been the end of all the people I loved, we were broken, totally broken!"

I clasped her hand. "I am so sorry you were worried about me, Birdie, it was awful, all I wanted to do was get back."

Junior said, "So your story is you time traveled? Seriously, you expect us to believe it? We are more skeptical than that, the family of Lou Muller doesn't believe in magical fairytales. We are reality-based, there is no science to support it."

I shrugged and sort of jerked my head at the Duke. "I can't explain it, I don't know the science, but I know I am sitting beside a duke who is here from hundreds of years ago—"

Charlie chimed in. "I saw the dude take his first drink of Coke, it's got to be true. There isn't a person on earth who has not tasted Coke or at least heard of it."

My dad asked, "When were you born, Nor the Duke?"

I teased, "Dad, it's *Nor*, or the Duke, or Your Grace."

"It's hard to keep straight."

I nodded. "Exactly! That's what I kept telling him!"

The Duke chuckled. "I am beginnin' tae understand why Madame Livvy had such a difficult time usin' m'titles." Then he answered my dad, "I was born at Kilchurn, on the edge of Loch Awe, in the year 1645, the eldest son of the Duke of Awe, the grandson of the former Duke of Awe. M'grandfather gained our title after he fought and won the battle at Doune, takin' the castle from Black Duncan, the son of Auld Gray-beard, Colin Campbell. Kilchurn has been our home since." He met our eyes then quickly looked down and continued, "My father passed three years ago, twas then that I became the current duke."

My mom asked, a glint of a plan in her eye, "Are you married, Nor?"

I rolled my eyes, "Mom, don't start, he's not..."

Mom said, "Not *what*? He's a duke, he's traveling, time traveling, with our daughter, and he might be an eligible bachelor."

I said, "Mom, I'm not... I'm in a relationship."

She said, "I know, I know, with *Chris*." She sounded, not for the first time, sarcastic.

The Duke said, "I am a widower. M'wife and m'young son died of a fever two years ago."

Birdie said, "I am so deeply sorry for your loss."

My mom said, "Yes, I am so sorry, Duke Nor." Then she gestured as if to say, *I told you so,* to me.

I huffed. "He has been promised to an eligible lady, Madame Enid, from the neighboring..." I gulped when the recent kiss flashed through my mind. "He and I are just friends." I glanced at the Duke whose eyes were on my face as I spoke.

I flushed. I opened the sack and rolled the two portals out on the table with a small cascade of sand around them. "This is what we are calling the portals."

Charlie tentatively pushed one causing it to do a half roll before righting itself as if it contained a weight inside.

Junior said, "This caused the storms?"

I said, "Yep, when it's live, or moving, a storm rises, if you touch it—"

The Duke said, looking down at his hands, "Daena ever touch it when tis alive."

"We know this to be true. If you touch it you will jump through time. We both learned it the hard way."

We all looked at the portals.

Uncle Dan said, "What the hell is happening? Are we all buying into this hoggimapoggy?"

Birdie said, "It's Occam's Razor, Danny, the simplest explanation is probably true."

Uncle Tim said, "Mom, you're saying that *time travel* is the simplest explanation? What about 'my niece has a head injury'? How about 'Livvy has taken up with a wild band of Ren Faire cosplayers and she's teasing us,' what if she's become a Shakespearean actor and she's method training? All of those are simpler reasons!"

Birdie said, "They are not simpler reasons! If it's a head injury, how does she have a duke beside her? We all see him, right? He's not the ravings of a hallucination! And the other two would involve her behaving in a way that is contrary to her nature. If she wanted to join a wild band of Ren Faire cosplayers she could just tell us. What would you say, Joni, if your daughter told you she was traveling with the Ren Faire?"

"I would say, 'Have you made sure to pack your toothbrush? And do you need gas money?' When I was following the Grateful Dead, finding gas money was half the trouble."

Birdie said, "Exactly." Then she said, "And Livvy would never be a method actor, she doesn't have the talent."

I laughed. "Yep, this is true."

Uncle Tim said, "She was so bad in the fifth grade school play, I tried to sneak out."

I said, "I feel like with practice I could get better, but why bother?"

Birdie laughing patted the back of my hand. "Sweet sweet dear, no you couldn't. Believe me, you said your lines with all the passion of a telephone pole and then you repeated them a second time because you weren't listening to yourself!"

We all laughed, even the Duke.

Grandma wiped her eyes. "The simplest explanation is that my granddaughter is telling the truth. She has time traveled."

I grinned at the Duke. "That only took a few long hours to convince them. Want a tour of the ranch?"

He said, "I first need tae visit a garderobe."

Everyone looked blankly.

"The bathroom! Of course, it's been hours."

I led him into the downstairs half-bath, and flipped on the blaring light. Then I quickly turned it off when he winced.

There was a candle on the toilet tank. I opened a drawer, found a lighter, lit the candle, and said, "This is the toilet, go there. This is the flusher, when you're done." I turned the handle on the water faucet. "This is for water to wash up after." I turned the handle off. "Hot and cold. And this is the paper to wipe yourself. If you, you know... need to wipe. Then you throw the paper in the toilet and flush it down."

His brow drew down.

I said, "I know it's a lot, just think, it's *exactly* the same as at your castle except this is the bowl, this is the pitcher, and instead of someone cleaning up after you, you flush to whisk it away. Got me?"

He said, "Aye," then he laughed. "Are ye goin' tae stay in the room, Madame Livvy? We hae relieved ourselves in front of each other, but this room is verra small. I daena think ye want tae be in such tight quarters while I am achievin' it."

"So true."

I left him, closing the door behind me and seeing my grandmother and mom standing there with their arms crossed.

I whispered, "What?"

Mom said, "Don't 'what' me, Livvy, you are smitten with him."

"I am not. Not at all."

The toilet flushed.

"Besides, I have Chris."

Mom said, "Whatever on Chris, you know how I feel about him."

I crossed my arms. "Yeah, I know... if anything I have a crush, just a little crush, but mostly the Duke and I are friends, because we had to save each other.

Birdie said with a hushed voice,"Ah yes, the mutual rescue of young love. I haven't let myself look, but I bet he has hot knees. Have you taken a good long look at his knees?"

I grinned. "I have *so* taken a long look at his knees, they are very very hot."

The toilet flushed again.

Mom whispered, "...And the shoulders, whoa Nelly. I think I was having a hot flash the whole time he was at the table."

I said, "Mom! Dad is going to hear you."

She laughed. "Your dad said the Duke was hot, even Dave Larson can see it, it's not like I'm saying *anything* that we don't already know. He's hot as hell and you're smitten with him."

The Duke cleared his throat, reminding us that he was a few feet away. The toilet flushed again.

We hustled from the hall.

Chapter 31 - Livvy

2012

LOU-MOO RANCH

I called Chris.

He picked up the phone. "Hey babe! You're back!"

"Yeah, um, that was—"

"I was so worried, when your mom called I didn't even know what to do."

"Yeah, they had no idea, I'm back now, it was—"

"She said Charlie and your uncles were out searching for you, but everyone thought you were dead." It almost sounded like an accusation.

"I'm not dead, I was storm-chasing with Lou and—"

"He's going to get himself killed one day, along with all of you."

"He's in the hospital still."

"I'm sorry, that was asinine of me, is he okay?"

"Yeah, he's okay, he's coming home tomorrow." I had been about to explain time traveling but realized I didn't want to go through that again, it would take too long and here he was accepting the story as it was: *Livvy was lost, now Livvy was back.*

I was standing in the formal living room facing a bookcase with my great-grandmother's collection of knickknacks, including a small pewter castle. I peered at it, suddenly wondering why I had never noticed it before.

I asked, "What are you doing this week? Want to come down and—"

"Livvy, I wish I could — I got that project at work and no more vacation days, we're saving for a house you know, gotta work. When will you be coming home?"

I pulled open the glass door and picked up the pewter piece and turned it over. On the bottom it was printed: Edinburgh Castle.

Who in my life had traveled to Scotland? I couldn't remember ever seeing this before, but there were a lot of little figurines and paperweights — maybe I hadn't noticed it because it wasn't relevant?

"Livvy? When are you coming home?"

"Oh um..." I closed the door and turned from the cabinet. "Let's see... I took off the whole week, so I might as well stick with the plan, I'll be back Sunday."

"Okay great, I'll be here all day waiting for you."

"Good." I awkwardly added, "I guess I'll be going to work first thing Monday morning."

"Yeah, Cynthia filled in for you, but she is not doing well. Everyone will be thrilled you're back."

"It's not rocket science. Do I need to call and tell them I'm alive, let them know I'm okay?"

"I didn't tell anyone... you were only gone for one night, I wasn't sure what happened and your mom was not sure, so yeah, it's all good."

"I need a vacation after this trip."

"We're saving for a down payment, gotta put in the hours. We'll build our vacation up and take one in the fall."

"That's a plan."

I heard the Duke's voice in the kitchen and wondered what he was talking about. "I gotta go, we've got... I'll see you on Sunday afternoon. Love you."

"Sure, see you then, love you too."

We hung up.

On my way to the kitchen I passed Birdie. "Who went to Scotland?"

"What do you mean, Livvy? *You*, just yesterday?"

"Who else? There is a figurine from Scotland in the cabinet in the living room, I never noticed it before."

"What do you mean?"

We returned to the room and stood in front of the cabinet. "Have you seen that before?"

"No, but it doesn't mean anything, I don't know half of what's in this old house. Too many ghosts, too many ancestors, passing down all their stuff. Who knows..."

"But you don't remember someone going to Scotland?"

"Not that I can remember, but what do I know? Ask your dad, maybe his family did. He might have put it there. But in the meantime, sweetie, you need to go take a shower."

"I am damp and sandy—"

"Among other reasons."

I laughed. "Birdie, are you telling me I stink?"

"To high heaven."

I sniffed my pits. "Yes, I desperately want one, but..." I looked down the hall, "Will you make sure the Duke is okay? I'll just be gone for a moment."

"You'll be gone for longer than a moment, but we will make sure the Duke is taken care of, I think we ought to send him to the showers too."

"Uh oh. Maybe I need to...?"

"Let's let Charlie handle it, don't you worry about it, dear, you go attend to the cloud around you."

Chapter 32 - the Duke

2012
LOU-MOO RANCH

Livvy's father stood at the edge of the tub pointing at the faucet. "...and you've never seen one of these before?"

I shook my head. "Nae."

"See this lever? You'll push it up," water sprayed from the showerhead, "and then you twist the handle a little to the left, right here, see? This is hot water." He put his hand in the spray. "Hold on, it has to warm up. That's why you need to know this position, because if you don't have the position it'll never get the right temperature." He kept his hand under the spray and I memorized the position of the lever.

Finally, he said, "Perfect." Then he looked around the bathroom. "You're going to climb in and wash centuries of grime off you." He picked up a bottle. "This is shampoo for your hair. These are soaps."

He looked around. "These are the towels for drying off."

"Thank ye for showin' me, Master Dave."

He smiled. "It had to be me, Charlie was laughing too hard to take it seriously."

Charlie called from the other room, "Glad I didn't have to show you how to use the toilet."

I chuckled. "Twas Livvy who shewed me that, but I had tae tell her tae use the bowl in our room in the sixteenth century. We both had tae learn somethin' new."

Charlie stuck his head in the door, his eyes wide. "Livvy literally had to go in a bowl in the room while you watched?"

"There was a garderobe, but aye, there is a bowl in the chamber for convenience. I averted m'eyes."

"What the hell is a garderobe?"

Junior called from the outer room, "Don't let Charlie bother you, Nor, it was one of your fellow Scottish guys who invented the flushing toilet."

"This wondrous invention? Och, he must hae smelt the garderobe on a balmy summer day and become inspired."

Master Dave waved Charlie away from the door. "Let's let Nor enjoy his first shower with indoor plumbing." He looked around the now steamy room. "Sorry about Charlie."

"My brother Aenghus is much like him, I am used tae the wit and sparrin'."

"Anything else?"

"Nae, I think I understand the basics. One question, how long ought it tae take? I am tryin' tae decide if I must go verra fast, or if I ought tae draw it out, and I canna make sense of it."

"You ought to take about a five to ten minute shower. Maybe twenty, since it's been a long time."

I joked, "It has been centuries."

Charlie in the other room said, "Stay in there until the water runs clear!" and laughed some more.

Dressed, after the shower, I met Madame Livvy in the hall. She grinned, "Well done, except, a bit of lather still..." She wiped the side of my hair. "You smell really good."

"Ye smell verra fine as well, Madame Livvy."

She leaned on the wall, facin' me. "You're taking a lot of the modern world in stride. I'm impressed."

"Ye find it impressive, Madame Livvy? I am a duke in a strange land, standin' in front of a bonny maiden whose father has had tae explain how tae wash m'self, while the bonny maiden's brother found the whole thing verra amusing. I daena fault him for it, twas amusin', but it inna *impressive* for His Grace, the Duke of Awe, tae be in this position."

She grinned. "You think I'm bonny?"

"Och aye."

"Thank you, and I do think it's impressive, think how much you've seen for the first time!"

I shook my head and joked, "I haena seen anything, I hae kept my eyes closed tight, especially if I canna understand it."

"So you're not looking at anything? Really?" She laughed. "Your eyes haven't been shut the *entire* time."

"Aye, but even when ye *sometimes* see me with m'eyes open and looking straight at it, I canna truly see it, because I daena ken what it is."

She led me tae the stairs.

I continued, "Or I am makin' up stories for it. I say tae m'self, 'Yer Grace,' I hae tae call m'self 'Yer Grace' as nae one else will and I feel verra diminished for it, 'Yer Grace, this is simply a verra fine carriage,' and 'Yer Grace, this is a manor house, though altogether altered from the usual style,' and 'Yer Grace, this is a kitchen, though it daena hae Auld Aymer sweatin' over the fire, yellin' and carryin' on in the middle of it.'"

"Still, I think it's very impressive, Your Grace, even with the making up of stories to get through it. You were in a truck today, you went eighty miles per hour."

I grinned. "I did like goin' fast, and thank ye for the 'Yer Grace', Madame Livvy."

"You're welcome."

She led me out ontae the porch, a warm afternoon, a steam tae the earth after the rain earlier. We looked out over the grass.

She said, "I had no idea I was going to travel to Scotland, meet a duke, and then bring him home, so I didn't pack well — here I am wearing jeans in front of you. You're seeing that, right?"

I glanced down at her legs and joked, "Nae, I canna see those, m'eyes are verra closed on yer lack of proper dress."

Chapter 33 - Livvy

2012
LOU-MOO RANCH

Charlie and I took the Duke on a tour of the ranch. We kept it to the outdoors, to things that were familiar enough, mostly — he stared up at the sky. "Madame Livvy, what are the stripes?"

"Those are condensation trails from an airplane."

He blinked. "What is an ayrplen?"

"It's an, um... a vehicle, like a truck, that flies through the sky."

He watched the sky for a moment, then said, "Och nae." And then shook his head from it, and said, "What curiosities are ye goin' tae shew me next?"

He only glanced at Lou's massive barn and I decided to not to freak him out by showing him the big tractors parked inside, too much at once — instead we showed him the fields, the grazing pastures, the sty and the coops, and the orange trees. He had an orange tree in his greenhouse, but it was small, and the few oranges it produced were precious. When I showed him how many trees we had he was astonished. "How many oranges for each tree, Madame Livvy? How many trees?"

"We have about one hundred acres for trees, about a hundred trees per acre, so that's ten thousand trees, and they each yield about four hundred oranges, so about four hundred thousand."

The Duke blinked. "Four *hundred* thousand? This is a great many oranges. Master Lou must hae immense wealth."

Charlie said, "It's not immense wealth, but he does well. This is a good ranch, though it is a lot of work." We walked him to the pasture to see the cattle. When he saw the split-rail fence he investigated the way it connected and kicked the wood to check its sturdiness.

We all leaned on the top rail and Charlie explained all about the breed of cows we stocked, and how many. The Duke asked questions and they conversed for a long time.

Then Charlie was called away and the Duke and I remained there, quietly watching the cattle ruminate.

"Whatcha thinking about?"

He had his forearms leaning on the top rail of the fence, a foot up on the bottom rail, raising his knee so that it showed from under his kilt, his light- gray shirt, loaned to him by Uncle Tim, matched his eyes. His hair was shoulder length, but tied back, a bit loose at his jaw. He looked incredibly sexy, at ease, his shoulders stretching his shirt. He grinned. "I am thinkin' on yer immeasurable wealth, Madame Livvy, and how yer brother, Charlie, dismisses it as inconsequential."

"I know it seems that way, in comparison. We *are* wealthy for the time, but truly this is just a normal amount of wealth. There are some people who are wealthy beyond my imaginings. Billions."

He frowned. "That is a made up number."

"Yes, yes it is."

He said, "Yer family is callin' me Nor, ye could if ye wanted."

I laughed. "I finally got comfortable with 'Your Grace'."

He teased, "Took ye long enough."

The sun was going down, a lovely pink sky glowing over the pines to the west. I said, "It's almost dinner time... I'm hungry again."

"Och, there is so much food here, ye eat whenever ye want."

"We are peak food production."

We both looked out at the horizon.

"Your eyes are better, you can see?"

He raised the sunglasses and wiped his eyes with his arm. "They still water, and although I jested earlier about not seeing it, I want tae see it. This is a world I hae never seen before, a land that daena exist in my time. I never believed I would see the New World, and here I am..."

He pushed away from the rail. "I must return home though, Madame Livvy."

"I understand, you have a big family and they need you. You have to protect them and... you'll get married and there will be babies born. It's your life, we have to get you back to it."

"Aye, and yer life is here."

"Yes, this is my home." My eyes swept the pastures. My apartment in North Carolina entered my mind, but I pushed it away. That was my apartment. This was home. I promised myself I would visit more.

I exhaled long. "I'm going to miss you."

He met my eyes. "Dost ye think, Madame Livvy, that in the history of the world there hae been people who hae met through time like this? Are we the first of them?"

"I don't know... I can't believe we're the first, but how come I have never heard any real accounts of it before? It's all fictionalized stories."

"Dost ye think that the stories could be made up from real events?"

"Maybe but it would be hard to keep it secret. We... we have only done it a few times and so many people know about it, and we already left a dead body on the beach." I gulped.

"It bothers ye?"

"Yes, it's hard to get the image of his body rolling in the surf out of my head."

"It might help ye tae remember that he wanted tae kill ye, sometimes life is choosin' tae kill or be killed, ye canna regret stayin' alive."

I nodded.

He said, "If people ken about time travel they would hae tae keep it secret, the portals would be verra dangerous in the wrong hands. I am growin' tae realize that if the wrong person has control of them they could do a great deal of damage in the world. We ought tae be more secretive."

"Yes, you're right, and I was thinking, you need a gun. I will give you one, for protection. I'll tell Junior to choose one from our gun safe."

He nodded, reached out and pushed the hair back from my face, and tucked it behind my ear. "Twill be verra difficult tae leave ye."

I frowned. "It will be hard to watch you go, Your Grace, I mean, Nor." I kicked the dirt. "Will you get married to Enid? I mean, I know it's not my place, but I just want you to know, I think that... Nor, she is cruel to your sister. She doesn't like Claray much and... it doesn't bode well for household harmony."

"Och, ye are also suggesting I will marry Enid? How come a widower is seen as someone tae be married off tae the first unmarried woman who comes along?"

I said, "I think I heard that it had been two years since you lost your wife; your family, and I, we just want what's best for you..."

"Aye, it has been a long two years."

"Nor, it might be time to marry, to treat yourself to some happiness, just, you know, some advice — aim for harmony."

He cocked his head to the side. "And what of ye, Madame Livvy, will ye marry soon?"

From the house Mom called, "Livvy! Dinner!!"

I smiled. "Perfect timing to interrupt a question for which there is no answer."

We began walking to the house. "He haena asked ye?"

"No, and it used to make me crazy, I couldn't understand why he wouldn't but now... not sure I would want him to. But that has nothing to do with you. Not really."

Chapter 34 - the Duke

2012

LOU-MOO RANCH

I sat at the table again with a plate in front of me that held sausages. I watched the people around me eat and imitated them. There were fine silver implements for stabbing the meat, a knife at every place setting.

Beside the sausage were some greens and some boiled root vegetables. They passed around a bottle that, when squeezed, poured a blood-red sauce upon their plates that they sopped all their food intae.

They ate and talked boisterously about stories and plans, and laughed a great deal, teasing each other, a similar thing tae m'family back home. I supposed that this meant that all families through time were much alike, laughing and yellin' and carryin' on.

Their voices were loud and caused my ears tae ache. The sausage tasted of salt and needed tae be washed down. The beer was too cold and shocked m'throat. Madame Livvy sensed I was uncomfortable, so she lowered the lights and put a candle in the middle of the table.

The flame helped, but it had a sweet scent that filled the room and caused m'head tae swim. When I drew my eyes tae the walls there was color and pattern and shapes and so many words, and the likenesses of her family, done in a way that was verra lifelike, and then, the music — it came from the walls around us, everywhere, a voice singing filled in behind our voices as we spoke. This all created a cacophony in my mind that was difficult tae think through.

Master Dan said, "So Livvy mentioned we need to give you a gun, how about we go to the shooting range tomorrow morning, teach you some basic skills with a modern gun. We'll send you back with a rifle and some ammunition, sound good?"

"Aye, Master Dan, I thank ye for the attention tae protectin' m'family." I rubbed my hand up and down on my face.

Madame Livvy asked, "How are you, Your Grace?"

Charlie said, "Livvy, you still callin' Nor 'Your Grace'?"

"No, it just slipped, habit... it's what everyone calls him, he's a *duke*."

I glanced from Madame Livvy tae her brother.

Charlie said, "So a duke is a big deal?"

Madame Livvy said, "A big deal? Yes. A duke is just below a king."

Madame Birdie said, "Dear me, we should have gotten out the fancy china."

Madame Livvy said, "I had to learn to call him 'Your Grace' and then 'm'laird,' and his mother 'lady,' and it was a *lot*."

I chuckled. "Madame Livvy took a verra long time tae learn it, twas so so so hard."

Charlie laughed. "Did you teach the Duke that?"

Livvy said, "I am very proud. He taught me to say 'Your Grace' like a lady, I taught him to say so so so hard, like a frat boy. But I had to use his title, to keep us from being killed in a medieval castle."

Charlie asked, "How?"

I said, "I had nae men as guard, traveling alone with a woman, she had tae show me deference or else nae one would believe m'worth. None of ye hae a title?"

Livvy's father said, "This is not the usual way, no, my wife is likely to call me 'butthead.'"

Livvy's mother laughed. "That is not true, you will confuse him. I only ever call you a butthead if you are being a butthead."

I said, "Now I understand why it was so difficult tae convince Madame Livvy tae use the phrase."

Livvy said, "It was, so difficult, but he calls me Madame Livvy, so eventually I got used to it."

Her father chuckled, "So if I call my wife Madame Joni, she won't call me butthead anymore?"

Livvy's mother said, "That might work, although if angered, I might call you 'Master Butthead." He kissed her cheek.

I looked down at my hands, the headache spreading across my brow.

Madame Livvy spoke, "Do you want to lie down? I can show you to the guest room."

I nodded. "Aye Madame Livvy."

She said, "We had a big day, we time traveled and everything hurts. I think it's time for bed. I'm going to show him the guest room, is it okay if we leave our plates?"

Madame Birdie said, "Yes."

Madame Livvy led me up the stairs.

In the bedroom Madame Livvy turned down the blankets on a large bed.

There was a bright light overhead that caused me tae wince. I had tae clamp my eyes closed once more.

She asked, "You're wincing, it's painful?"

"Aye. It feels as if I hae a horse standin' upon my head."

"That sounds awful. You want the blinds up or down?" She raised a window coverin'.

The landscape was blissfully dark, the sky a deep velvety blue, with stars flung across it. "I would like tae see out."

"I think there's enough ambient light, let me turn this off."

The light was snuffed out and I was able tae open m'eyes once more.

She pointed toward a door. "There's the place to relieve yourself."

"Thank ye." I looked out the window, rapped upon the glass, clear and flat, easy tae see through. "Will I need tae take a guard duty?"

"No we don't have to guard at night. We have alarms, sensors in case something happens, no worries."

"What is a sensor?"

"We have a system, devices that can tell if there is someone moving nearby, the alarm will be loud to wake us up, it's good, it will warn us."

He nodded. "I will try nae tae worry though that seems ill-considered. Who is sleepin' here in the house?"

"Uncle Tim, Birdie, Charlie... Junior has his own house, his girlfriend lives with him; Uncle Dan has a mobile home; my parents, Dave and Joni, have their own. I'll um... sleep down the hall."

I picked up a framed image of a man and woman from the table beside the bed.

Madame Livvy said, "Those are my great-grandparents, Lou's parents. The photo was taken when they were just married."

"This is a photo?" I turned it over. "What is a photo?"

"It's a... hold on, I'll be right back." She rushed from the room.

I sat quietly on the edge of the bed, and placed the frame back upon the table.

She returned a moment later and sat down beside me. She held up an object that looked as if it were a mirror. "Smile, Nor."

I smiled.

Then she showed me our likeness, frozen on the object. "This is a photo. The camera is different than the one that took that photo, but it's the same concept. I could put this in the frame, it would be me and you, just like this couple on their wedding day."

She looked down at the image of us. "I took three, but let's try again — we look boring."

She held the object up again and we both looked up. She leaned against my chest and my arm went around her. "Better."

I said, "I believe I look like a ghost, as do the couple in this photo, as if I hae been dead for many centuries. I am auld, as they are. And yet they are young, from last century? I am from long years afore that. I am verra weary from thinking on it, Madame Livvy, I am verra out of time."

Her face grew solemn. "You are out of time, but you are not a ghost, you are a man, like an explorer, like Columbus who discovered the New World. You have crossed time on a vessel and when you arrive at the distant shores you are still a man there, still a real man, you still exist. When you go home you will be returned, a man, His Grace, the Duke, the head of your family. You will still be important, but you will be wiser for having seen this new land, you know, Nor?"

I nodded. "Aye. And I like it when ye call me Nor."

She smiled. "Good, I like it too, Nor — and that was a lovely smile, but it must be so much better than that. I am taking photos of a man from the seventeenth century. This is historic, can you make a funny face?"

"I think m'current pained expression is a verra funny visage."

"Ha, but, Nor, there is nothing funny about seeing you in pain. You'll need to override it to make this photo important." She held up the object again. "Stick out your tongue and... perfect."

She showed me our image. I was laughin', lookin' upon her face, she had her tongue out, humorously, leaned against me.

She said, "We look really really happy. This will be good to remember you by." She looked at it a moment more, then stood up. "I must go to bed, I'm sleepy, good night, Your Grace."

"Good night, Madame Livvy."

She left the room.

Chapter 35 - Livvy

2012
LOU-MOO RANCH

I got up, dressed, then went down the hall to knock on the Duke's door. He was sitting on the bed, waiting, with the door cracked. He smiled when I stuck my head in. "You look like you feel better!"

"Aye, the sleep did wonders, though I am famished, will there be a meal in the Great Hall?"

"Yes, kind of, breakfast at the kitchen table. Follow me."

I led him downstairs.

Mom and Birdie and Charlie had gone and left us a note that they were picking up Lou at the hospital.

Dad and the uncles were already at work.

I got out a dozen eggs to scramble.

"Ye are goin' tae cook?"

"I love cooking. It's my favorite way to unwind. But I also love to have someone help, so here's how we're going to go. You're going to crack all these eggs into this bowl." I passed him a carton of eggs.

I put bacon and some sausage in a pan and began frying it

while he whisked eggs according to my directions. I poured us each a mug of coffee, leaned on the counter and passed him a mug. "Blow in it first."

He blew. "Blow more, you want it to be cool enough, no pain, not after the headache last night."

He blew some more.

"Now sip."

We both sipped.

I moaned with pleasure. "What do you think? Is it as good as I promised?"

He chuckled. "I dinna taste anythin', m'tongue is scalded."

I took another sip. "Try again, it's cooler now, but also, maybe you will like it with cream. We have to test all the ways for you to find the perfect taste."

He took another sip.

I poured cream in mine. "Taste this one now."

He tasted my coffee.

"Whatcha think?"

"I prefer the black."

"Good, and now you know."

He took another sip of his. "Tis a tragedy tae find out how I like m'coffee right afore I leave tae a world without."

I said, "Yes, yes it is. Oh and that reminds me." I poured him a small glass of orange juice. "Drink up. It's got vitamin C."

I made a couple of pieces of French toast with sourdough bread, because I wanted the taste of syrup. I used the rest of the eggs to make a massive mound of scrambled eggs.

He sipped the orange juice and we ate our breakfast standing in the kitchen while I found a bottle of vitamins to send with him. "These are for your family, make sure Claray gets some, and Ailsa, they're child-bearing age, they need one a day." He nodded along though I knew he had no idea what I was talking about.

. . .

The door opened and my family bustled in, with Lou in their midst. I threw my arms around him and hugged him and buried my face against the shoulder of his jacket.

"Well now, aren't you a sight for sore eyes," he said, "I heard you had an adventure."

"I had such an adventure." I introduced them, "Nor, Duke of Awe, this is my grandfather, Lou Muller."

They shook hands.

Lou said, "You can call me Lou, no Mister Muller, or whatever your manners call for, apparently you kept my granddaughter alive in a seventeenth century castle, and you predate me by centuries, I think it will add to my stature to have someone as old as you call me Lou."

The Duke smiled. "Alright, Master Lou, I will abide by yer wishes."

Grandpa laughed. "Well shit, that is just dandy, how did I never realize storm-chasing was going to get me a glimpse into another dimension?"

Birdie said, "You knew it was going to kill you someday, I tell you all the time."

He waved her words away. "Pshaw, woman, you told me it would kill me forty years ago, you have been wrong on it every time since, someday I will die of old age, and you will be left crowing, 'I told you it would kill you!' And I have instructed all the kids to roll their eyes."

We all laughed.

Dad said, "I married into the family, but I don't remember those instructions."

"I'm telling you now, if Birdie is saying 'I told him so' after I die on the toilet brushing my teeth, please, son-in-law, roll your eyes for me."

Lou hugged Birdie and kissed her cheek. "I am very sorry you were worried about me, my sweet Birdie." Then he hugged me. "I am very sorry I was so worried about you, my Livvy-bear."

Then he looked at the Duke. "So let's talk about the Duke amongst us — what's the name of your castle?"

The Duke said, "Kilchurn, on the edge of Loch Awe."

Charlie began working on his phone. "Uh oh." He turned it around to show me. I looked and then showed it to the Duke. "Do you see?"

"This is a photo of my castle?"

"Yes, it's a photo of your castle — it's a ruin." I zoomed in on the details and showed him the broken down wall.

His brow drew down and he blinked looking at it. Then he shook his head and looked away.

"That's unsettling to look at?"

"The castle holds my family. The walls were built tae shelter them, fortified tae protect, there ought tae be guards upon the wall — aye, tis unsettling tae see the walls torn down."

Charlie smacked his hands together and rubbed them briskly, "We need to get you that rifle. I'm thinking a Winchester."

Mom said, "You don't want to set off an arms race and start a war."

I said, "It wasn't a war that made the castle a ruin, it says here that it's a ruin because of lightning."

Lou said, "We still need to get the man a proper gun, it's only fair if people are attacking him."

Mom said, "Good point."

Lou said, "And the whole history of the world is one big arms race."

We all went out to the fields to practice shooting and give the Duke a rifle.

Chapter 36 - Livvy

2012
AMELIA ISLAND

By lunchtime he was armed with a rifle and ammunition.

He had a cooler full of treats for his sister, his brother and his wife, and his mother.

And Charlie had given him a parka for really cold days and Uncle Tim gave him a pair of waterproof boots.

The Duke and I loaded up in Charlie's truck and began the drive to Amelia Island.

We didn't know if he needed to time travel from there, but we didn't want to risk doing anything differently. As Charlie put it, "If you change the location do you end up in a different place?"

We all agreed it was a very good point and not something we should risk.

I sat in the back with the Duke, the middle seat between us. Charlie and I sang along to some music and taught the Duke the words to one of the songs. We rolled down the windows when he felt green. We talked quietly, and at last were silent. This was a long drawn out forever goodbye after all.

Close to Amelia Island I said, "I have a present for you, I don't know why I didn't give it to you already... I think I was nervous you wouldn't want it, I mean, why would you? This is goodbye and nothing good comes of not saying a proper goodbye and knowing that we aren't going to see—"

Charlie turned on his blinker and pulled around a truck carrying timber. "You're rambling."

"Oh yeah, but... don't listen, I'm talking to the Duke."

"I'm going to shut up but seriously the Duke doesn't want to hear you babble."

He turned the music up in the front seat.

I said, "Anywho, this is for you." I pulled my bag to my lap, dug out an envelope, and passed it to him.

He pulled the flap open and peered in.

I said, "It's the drawing I made of the portals, with the markings and there's something else, our—"

"Och, tis our photo?"

I nodded. "I picked my favorite, I hope it's yours, I..."

He held the photo, the smiling one: I was leaning on him, his arm around me. "I like it verra much." He continued looking down at it.

Then he flipped it over, but clutched it in his hand and watched out the window as the world went by. "Tis verra interesting how the world has changed, yet it remains the same. I once loved a woman named Mary, and she gave me gifts that caused m'heart tae beat with fondness, and now tis hundreds of years in the future, I am in something called a 'truck' and I am driving through Florida in the New World, and ye hae given me a present, Madame Livvy, and it has caused m'heart tae beat fondly once more, something that haena happened for me in a long time. I dinna believe it ever would again — the world stays the same." He looked down at the photo once more.

My face drew down into my frown and I blinked back tears.

Finally we pulled up at the beach and parked at the public access.

Farther down there was crime-scene tape wrapped around a stand of trees.

The Duke and I hadn't mentioned the body to Charlie. The less people knew of our involvement, the better. It hadn't been our fault that we were chased through time. There were no guards or police cars. We assumed the body had been found, but it didn't involve us, we were just tourists visiting the beach. We carried our boxes and bags down to the sand and arranged them to look like we were enjoying a beach day while we waited.

Charlie asked, "What do you think the police tape is? Because of Lou's heart attack and when you went missing?"

"Maybe," I said with a shrug.

He walked over to the pole where Lou's weather station was strapped. I watched him as he checked the mounts to make sure it was secure.

The Duke placed the two portals in the sand in front of us. We knew which one went from Florida to Kilchurn in the year 1560, and which one went from Kilchurn 1560 to Kilchurn 1670. The Florida one had carried us from Kilchurn 1670 to Florida, current time, but would it return him there? We thought Nor would end up in the 1500s and would have to *then* travel to the 1600s but we weren't sure. I jokingly offered to go with him to help, but this might become a never-ending cycle.

He put them out so he would know which was which, we didn't know much but we wanted no surprises.

When they went live he would grab it and do what needed to happen to get back to his castle.

We sat and waited.

I dragged my fingers through the sand and sifted shells through my fingers. "The shells are pretty here."

The Duke put the bag with his rifle over his shoulder. He sat on the cooler of food.

Charlie asked, "Do we know if the cooler will go with him?"

I said, "My backpack went with me. I was wearing it though."

The Duke said, "My horse went with me. I held his reins in my hand."

Charlie said, "Sounds like it might work then."

I said, "You and I just need to stand well away."

"Oh I will, I'm going to run so far that way you won't believe it."

We waited more.

And then, at about the time we expected, the gadget that was the Florida to Kilchurn portal jumped and buzzed for a moment then quit, like a warning. We all froze. I felt a bit shocked, I had been waiting, but here it was. Then it buzzed again and then an absolute disruption — the portal exploded with a storm. The day went from calm and cool and pretty to extremely horribly stormy. We were battered with winds that grew into a roar.

The Duke met my eyes — a silent goodbye.

Then Charlie and I rushed away with the wind behind us, shoving us toward the parking lot. At the safety of the truck we looked back, a cumulonimbus cloud rose above the dunes, roiling and storming.

Charlie yelled, "Do you see him?!"

"He's right there, by the..." I peered into the storm. "I don't see him anymore!"

We climbed into the truck. Winds buffeted the sides, a sand storm of debris in front of us, torrential rain splashing around, lightning striking the boardwalk. "I wish we were farther away!"

Lightning struck close. I shrieked and covered my head.

The truck rocked back and forth in the wind. "Is it going to tip?"

Charlie said, "Nah, no chance," but he had a white-knuckle grip on the steering wheel.

The storm lasted for about fifteen minutes.

Then as quickly as it came on it dissipated.

We had visibility again: the waves were still ferocious, but calming, the wind still gusting, but lessening. There was a shower of rain. And we could see the beach. It was empty. The Duke was gone. We walked out to the end of the decking to make sure all the stuff was gone.

I stood and looked out at the ocean, my arms crossed, my shoulders huddled under the wind.

Charlie kicked sand, making sure everything we brought was gone. Then he met me on the deck and put out his fist. "Our boy is back in the past."

We fist bumped.

"Yep." I exhaled. "I'm going to miss him."

"It's where he's supposed to be though, this is what's right."

"Yeah. Of course. He belongs there. I belong here."

He said, "Let's head home, I'll buy you a carnivorous treat in the Duke's honor."

Chapter 37 - the Duke

1670
NEAR LOCH AWE

I heard a grunt nearby, the sounds of a scuffle. I felt as if I was emergin' from underwater and felt a heavy weight upon m'chest.

My focus sharpened tae find a man on me, his dirk aimed at my chest, about tae plunge it down. I willed m'self — *Fight!*

I raised m'arms, blocked his blow, and wrestled for his dirk. A struggle that I was losin' as I wasna ready or capable — a sharp pain against m'arm. There was a blow against the man's head, he fell sideways and a long blade sliced through his chest. He was shoved tae the ground in a puddle of his spilled blood and the sword was yanked from his body.

Aenghus came fully intae focus, yelling, "We daena hae time for ye tae explain why ye are just layin' under a man who is tryin' tae kill ye, ye must be up!"

I suffered, but Aenghus was prowling around a second man, swords drawn. I clambered up and opened the bag as a third man rushed up behind Aenghus, tryin' tae wrestle his sword away, holding him down, as the second man lunged. I yanked the rifle free from the bag, flicked off the safety, aimed and fired, the gun kicking hard against my shoulder, before the man was about tae stab m'brother. My ears rang.

But I shot him in the head. He fell tae his knees and then slumped tae the side.

I aimed at the man holdin' my brother. "Let go of him, hands up, on yer knees."

Aenghus struggled tae free himself. The man said, "Ye winna shoot me, I hae yer brother."

"I daena like him much. He is nothin' but trouble for me and if I hae tae kill him tae kill ye, twill be a chance I am willin' tae take."

I glared at the man, holdin' the gun steady, aimed for his chest, but sweat rolled down m'cheek. I was achin' all over, weakened, this was my second jump. I had landed in 1560, had hidden in the woods until the following day, and then had ridden the storm here. I dinna hae the strength tae fight, and I wasna a good enough shot tae risk firing toward Aenghus. I lied, "But I winna shoot him, I am good enough tae fire a bullet right between yer eyes."

He watched me. I kept my hands steady though I wanted tae collapse.

We remained locked facing each other and then finally he shoved Aenghus away and dropped tae his knees.

"Hands on yer head!"

I passed the rifle tae Aenghus and dug in the man's coat pocket. I found a small scrap of paper in one and shoved it in my pocket, but I dinna find anything else tae explain why he was here.

My ears roared, my heart raced, I screamed intae his face, "What are ye doin' here?"

The man kept his eyes averted. "I am tae keep ye from havin' the Tempus Omegas."

"Who do ye work for?"

He shook his head.

My fury rose.

"Brother, check the dead men. Look for anything." Aenghus passed me the gun and went from man tae man rummaging through their pockets. He pulled out a scrap of paper and tossed it tae the ground and then found another piece of paper. They looked tae be covered with marks. I picked up one — the markings looked verra like the marks on our portals. Or my portals now that I possessed both of them.

"What are these markings?"

The stranger said, "The location and time we're supposed to get back tae collect our money."

My brother said, "Ye are a traitor tae the man who rules ye."

"He daena rule me, he paid me tae get yer devices, nae tae die." He spit on the ground.

"Where is he?"

"The year 1558."

I said, "We need tae keep this man alive he has much tae tell us, we will carry my gear tae the—"

The man lunged, his hands aimed for m'throat — I shot him through the chest.

My brother's brow went up. "Nor! Ye just, one moment ago, said tae keep him alive. Ye are a terrible commander."

I shook my head. "My brain said I wanted tae get information from him, but m'body was pained and m'mood wanted him dead." I nudged him with my foot.

He was dyin'. I dropped tae my knees and held him by the shirt. "How dost ye put the markings in the devices? How dost ye work it?"

Blood rushed from his mouth.

"Are there more men comin'?"

He convulsed, dying.

"Och." I shoved him back on the ground. "I dinna want him tae live anyway, he is traitorous. I canna trust a word he says."

"We ought tae gather our gear within the tree line and cross over tae search the woods for their equipment—"

A shot was fired from the other side of the burn. Birds were unsettled and flew up in the air over the woods.

My brother's horse was standing a few feet away along with

m'own. We jumped on our horses and galloped tae the tree line and looked back over the moor.

Aenghus said, "Now they hae done it, we will hae tae go over there and kill them."

"Aye, they are keepin' me from my portal layin' over there in the dirt. I hae two ammunition cans, I must hae those. And dost ye see the white chest out there? I hae food for ye, packed by Madame Livvy. Tis a gift for ye and I winna leave it for these bum-bunkles, they canna hae it. But we daena hae tae go over there."

"What is yer plan?"

I unpacked the binoculars, given tae me from Madame Livvy's Uncle Dan. It was difficult at first tae get it focused, but I adjusted it and then watched the distance.

"I am goin' tae shoot them from here."

I passed it tae m'brother who held it tae his eyes.

"Dost ye see through it?"

"I canna, what does it do?"

"Ye are pointin' it up tae the sky, point it toward the horizon. Dost ye see the area there? I saw birds rising from the trees, there is at least one more man sitting at the base of the largest fir."

I dismounted, pulled my rifle, set it on a boulder, and trained the scope on the woods. The storm had fully dissipated, the rain ceased, we continued watching, waiting.

My brother spoke, "This is a better plan than mine, I was goin' tae ride over and fight them."

"Aye, we daena want tae die, I want ye tae taste what's in the chest."

I looked through the scope on the rifle and saw a movement within the woods on the other side of the stream.

I pressed m'finger tae my lips.

We went verra quiet then, and I kent it was a waiting game.

A verra long time later a shadow left the far trees.

A man was creeping forward tae steal my things. There was a portal layin' there, glintin' in the sun. The portal that went back and forth tae Florida. I couldna let them use it, twould put Madame Livvy and her family in danger.

I aimed.

The man crept toward the box of food. I steadied m'heart and my shakin' hands and whispered tae m'brother, "Cover yer ears."

The man drew closer and closer and then I shot.

I caught him in the shoulder. He blew back and stumbled down tae his knees. I fired again and hit him in the back.

My brother started tae race toward the chest, but I held him back, "Wait, we must see if there are more."

We watched the far trees. But finally Aenghus said, "There arna more, brother, ye can tell, dost ye hear the birds?"

"I canna hear them over the sound of ringin'." I pressed my ear trying tae get it tae work once more.

He said, "Well, there are birds singin' over there."

I said, "Then we can retrieve m'things."

We raced tae the middle of the moor, I picked up the portal and put it in a small sack beside the other. Aenghus picked up the box of food. I slung a larger bag over my shoulder and we lugged it all tae the woods. Aenghus ran back over tae check the pockets of the newly dead man, grabbing a bag from around his shoulder, stuffing things in his own pockets, then he met me in the woods where we dropped it all tae the ground, and I sat on the chest tae catch my breath.

"Och, I hurt in every part of m'body, I daena ever want tae do any of this again."

He asked, "Speakin' of, where is the lass?"

He looked through what we had collected. "Ye gained another one of the devices."

I groaned and then complained, "Now I hae three! I dinna want a single one yet I am gainin' more — and by lass ye mean, Madame Livvy?"

"Aye, ye ken."

"Madame Livvy dinna come, we hae said our goodbyes." I picked up the three portals and placed them in a sack.

"Mam will be pleased, she has designs and yer new lass was ruining her plans."

"Mam needs tae mind her own business, I am a duke, I could send her tae live in Finlarig castle with our brother Malcolm."

Aenghus said, "She would weep at being sent away from us. She canna bear the thought of separating. She would much prefer Malcolm return so she can hae all her children under one roof."

"She would only find happiness if Malcolm returned without his wife. Och, the castle used tae ring with their bickerin'."

"Aye, twas many a day they were squabblin' like two hens — I suppose it would be cruel tae Malcolm tae send Mam tae bicker with his wife in that drafty castle."

"True, I suppose we will hae tae give her some duties here tae distract her from attemptin' tae rule my life."

Aenghus's horse stamped impatiently. "We ought tae head back tae the castle."

I straightened my back, stiff from the travel, my sight was dark after the brightness of the future. I unlatched the chest and gave him a glimpse of the interior. "I hae food and somethin' called vitamins for yer wife and our sister. A bag of coffee and some oranges. Aenghus, ye canna believe how many oranges Madame Livvy's grandfather grows."

Aenghus said, "Now that I hae seen inside the chest I want tae head tae the castle."

I latched the chest. "But first we ought tae ride across the plain and see if the men left any gear and weapons."

"Fine." He climbed ontae his horse. "If we are lucky they brought a cart."

I laughed and mounted Balach Mòr. "I canna believe it all culminated tae this point, four men dead in Barran Moor. We are goin' tae hae tae deal with these bodies."

"Aye, and all the portals, they are dangerous, brother. Men are willin' tae die tae gain control over them."

"Aye, this has been a warnin'. I fully understand the dangers now. I will hide them away and guard them. They winna be used, we winna need tae, we ought nae defy the natural order of time."

Aenghus and I rode from the trees and crossed the moor, picking a route, then wadin' our horses through the stream, and continuin' tae the woods on the other side. There we found some blankets and flasks, as well as two horses and a cart with two wheels tae put the load on. We returned tae our side with the cart and what we considered useful and then strapped our things tae the cart as well.

Aenghus said, "This is a great load, ye hae gained three of the devices, two more horses, a chest of food, a new gun, and even a cart. It looks as if ye hae different boots as well."

"Aye, they are verra warm. This rifle is verra good — it almost makes the near death worthwhile."

"I daena mind the storms when they bring us this largess. Is that the way of Madame Livvy's land, did they hae many of these death-dealing weapons?"

"Aye, I hae seen the New World, brother, and aye, tis full of weapons. The men there are so well-armed that they daena hae tae keep guard at night." The cart loaded, we hitched it tae m'horse.

"Och, then what do they do? Sleep like bairn? They must be weak if they daena hae tae guard."

I laughed as we mounted our horse and pullin' the cart full of spoils, began makin' our way through the woods toward Kilchurn castle. "Tis funny that ye would see so many weapons as weak! They had wealth and strength, Aenghus, they had more food than ye can envisage, whenever they choose tae eat, and they can ride much faster than our horses. Tis verra fun. They drove me in a carriage, they called a truck, with nae horses—"

"Nae horses! What was pullin' it?"

"Nothing! It careened so much I had tae vomit in the grass."

"Ugh, I haena vomited since the burnt livers that Auld Aymer cooked last Lughnasadh."

"I remember, they were terrible. This was called coak and a

blizzard. Twas all verra sweet." I grimaced and clutched my stomach just thinking about it.

"But I did enjoy the ride, and when I requested, Madame Livvy's brother drove the carriage-truck even faster, twas breathtaking."

Chapter 38 - Livvy

We were all out on the screened-in porch. I was curled up against my mom's side.

"You'll miss him, huh?"

I nodded. "Yeah, I really will. It's a little like having someone die, I think — he's gone, you know, he's completely gone. It was chilling how he disappeared from the beach."

Charlie said, "Not unlike when you disappeared and Lou was left lying in the sand. That was the worst few hours of my short life."

"Yeah, I suppose it was just like that."

Mom said, "I don't know how to advise you, or what to say. You've made friends with someone from over three hundred years ago. That's not how it's supposed to work."

Junior said, "No matter how you cut it, he's a dead man."

My face turned down in my frown.

He said, "Aw Livvy, you still doing that?"

"Aw, Uncle Junior, you still being a poopoo-head?"

"I'm sorry to be blunt, but sometimes blunt's the best thing. I mean that's why we have open casket funerals so you can get used to the idea, our eyes need to see it to tell our heart that it's true. To be blunt, you met him, but he was already long dead. He's long dead now."

Uncle Dan said, "He died before America was even a thing. That was so fucking long ago."

I frowned even more. "He didn't even know about the New World, not really."

Uncle Tim said, "Exactly. And think about it, you're lucky, he was probably full of outdated ideas."

Uncle Dan said, "He was probably very unenlightened. I would have loved to hear him expound on his thoughts on women."

I said, "Or maybe, and hear me out, maybe he was full of so many ideas, ancient and modern, that he was the most enlightened of all of us. He was a man who was called Your Grace and he has also seen the New World. He lived in medieval times and has tasted a Coke. He might be the most important mind of our time. Plus he's hot. Maybe he *likes* women and he, I don't know, respects them, hotly."

Uncle Tim said, "Hot damn, I forgot how fun it was to have Livvy here to argue about everything."

"I don't argue about *everything*."

My whole family laughed.

I said, "I just can't think about him being dead, it's heart-breaking, and to dismiss him as 'always' having been dead is infuriating. He was flesh and blood, living and breathing, we sat around the dinner table with him. He was here, not a feature of my imagination."

Mom smoothed my hair saying, soothingly, "Shhhhhh, he was definitely flesh and blood. He was not a feature of your imagination. Shhhhhh."

"Why are you shushing me?"

"I don't know why, this is not a normal thing. I don't know what to say."

Charlie said, "I've never seen you so bummed. When you broke up with Sammy you didn't seem to care."

"I cared, he just sucked, it's not hard to get over someone who's a dick. And that was years ago. I'm with Chris now."

"Yeah...." Mom said, "How's it going with him?"

"Fine, he... you know he's got his own thing he's dealing with, his work... I'm sure if he could have gotten away he would have. Our relationship is very normal, we are good roommates, it's not on us to get overly emotional."

I felt Mom's arm tense.

Charlie said, "Maybe a little emotion?"

"What do you know, got a girlfriend?"

"Nah, last girl I went out with was a train wreck."

"Overly emotional?"

"She was emotional all over the place."

"I grew up with three brothers, I learned to suppress."

Charlie said, "Except for your dumb pout."

I did my comic frown. "Don't be mean."

He and Uncle Tim laughed.

I comically frowned even more. "The duke thought it was funny."

Mom said, "You were with him long enough for him to see it?"

"We went through so much!"

"Did he see you cry?"

I nodded.

Lou said, "I don't believe it, I haven't seen you cry since you were six and you tripped when you were leading Dewdrop around the arena, you cried and your brothers mocked you for it and you haven't cried since, at least not in front of your old grandfather."

Mom said, "But you cried in front of Nor?"

"Yes, the situation was dire."

Birdie said, "You were vulnerable around him, this is important."

"It was important. Very important. I just miss him is all."

I saw a look pass between them all. Mom said, "I've never known you to be this upset about someone before."

"I don't know what's wrong with me... I have Chris and he's really great."

"Sure... he's just, honey, he's kind of boring."

"Boring can be nice, right? I mean, this was some death-defying bullshit. I barely survived. It's good to have a boring guy, it's normal." I stared off at the distance then said, "And it's right that the Duke's gone. But also I miss him. I don't know how to deal with all of it."

Lou said, "You're powerless. If you think about it it's a little like he joined the army and he's stationed in some far away place like Ryan."

"Yeah, except we can call Ryan every night if we need to."

Mom sighed. "Except I don't call him all the time because it's too stressful. He's serving, he does not want to hear about his mother's day to day worries or about the family's ranch, he has plenty to deal with already. Both your brothers were so worried when I told them you had disappeared during a storm chase and that Charlie was driving Lou to the hospital. There was nothing they could immediately do to help, so I try not to call too much, my job is just to answer the phone when they call, first ring."

"It's a lot like that, except no chance of phone calls."

Mom squeezed me around the shoulders. "It's the 'no chance of phone calls' that's the hardest part."

"And the never ever going to see him again... I guess you're right, I am in mourning."

Birdie said, "I for one don't like thinking of that nice young man as dead, but... one way Lou and I deal with the passing of our friends and relations is by reading the obituaries. Have you thought of doing that?"

I blinked. "I can't decide if that is a great idea or a heartbreakingly awful one."

Charlie said, "It's the truth. The truth is always a good thing. You find out when he died and how and then you at least have closure."

I blinked some more.

Birdie said, "I don't think there will be *that* kind of obituary, you'd be lucky to find any mention of him in the history of the world. It was the seventeenth century after all, written records were spotty."

I moaned. "He was a duke, he *must* have a record of his life, right? He was too important, there has to be one truth in the world, that people who are good and kind and important and make me laugh will end up in the history books."

Charlie got up, went in the house, and returned with his laptop covered in stickers. He placed it on the glass coffee table and sat down on the couch in front of it. "So... what's his full name?"

"The Duke of Awe, Nor... I think... he was a Campbell, I'm pretty sure."

Charlie said, "You barely know the guy."

"True."

He sighed as he clicked around on the keyboard.

Then he said, "Kilchurn castle, right?"

I nodded, my head against Mom's shoulder.

"I found him! Look, here's a Wikipedia page about the Dukes of Awe. There's a list of the children of the second duke: Including Normond... did he have a sister named Claray and two brothers, Aenghus and Malcolm?"

"Yes, I met Claray and Aenghus, I didn't meet Malcolm he was visiting another castle, but yeah, that's him."

Charlie said, "Weird, you met people that have a historical page in Wikipedia." He added, "But we found him. It looks like he was born in 1645."

Dad said, "That's what Nor said, 'Born in 1645.'"

Charlie closed the laptop.

I gave him a look. "Why'd ya stop looking?"

"Dead end, and not the way we hoped."

"What do you mean?"

"There's no link to his name, nothing more about him — look..." He opened the laptop and pushed the return key. "Nothing."

"No death? No history? No heirs?"

"Nope."

Lou said, "This is the exact opposite of closure."

"But his brother, Aenghus, has three sons. That's good."

"Well, that's shit." I felt like crying and a tear slid down my cheek. I fiddled with a piece of tissue. "So he doesn't have a wife? Kids? He's got no death?"

"Nothing, none of these names are clickable, but don't despair, I'll follow some of these other links." He worked for a bit, then said, "It seems like our man Nor disappears from history."

Birdie said, "This isn't some big mystery. He doesn't disappear. He's just got no records, someone just hasn't filled in the history yet. You know what? I have my Ancestry account. I'll go looking for him, and I will build up a tree around him. Don't you worry dear, the history is there, we just need to get it listed."

"Thank you Birdie, but it's still worrisome. It might be that he doesn't have it written down, but it also might be that he didn't make it home. What if he got lost? What if he's stuck in another time?"

Charlie's eyes went wide. "Shit, that could happen?"

Lou said, "I don't see why it wouldn't. The truth is, time travel could land you anywhere and without a support system: money, clothes, transport, food, you'd be screwed."

Junior said, "If you landed in dinosaur days and a dino ran up and ate you right as you woke up, that would be the end of it, you know?"

I said, sarcastically, "You know what, thanks for cheering me up." I stood, wanting to get the heck out of there.

My mom grabbed my wrist and pulled me back down. "I'm sorry sweetie, that was unfortunate, right Junior? You didn't mean it."

"Yeah, I didn't mean it, you know your uncle Junior, he's always gotta put his foot in it, most of the time it's charming, but sometimes it's a pain in the ass."

I rolled my eyes.

Birdie said, "*Most* of the time it's charming? The word 'most' is doing some fancy work in that sentence."

Mom said, "Our imagination is running away with us, Livvy, you just need to go back to mourning the end of your relationship with Nor, and thinking fondly on him. Tell us the best thing you did together?"

Charlie said, "Nothing nasty."

I said, "He told me 'Daena worry, Madame Livvy, I will get ye home,' and he meant it."

Mom said, "He said it with that low voice? I can see why it would be your favorite."

"The funniest thing he did was when he was trying to stomach the fries and Coke when Charlie picked us up, he was grimacing and retching, then he threw up on the side of the road — I mean it's not funny, but if you saw how important he was in the past... Everyone bows to him."

Lou said, "I saw him easily down a shot of whisky but it was Coke that got to him? That is funny."

I continued, "...and the most frightening thing that happened was these men tried to kill him in the castle Kilchurn in the year 1560 and I got sent from the castle with his horse and could hear him getting his ass kicked inside. It was scary, but his biggest thought was getting me out of there."

Lou said, "Question for you, Livvy, and we won't need to speak about it again. Was he responsible for the dead body that washed ashore on Amelia Island two days ago?"

Everyone looked at me.

Charlie said, "Wait, was that the reason for the police tape?"

I said, "Yes, but it was in self-defense. And yes, Charlie, the police tape was because of us."

Lou said, "I knew it, but I wanted to hear it straight from you. That bit of information doesn't leave this circle, got me?"

Everyone nodded.

Charlie said, "I am glad I didn't know it when we returned to the beach. And it's good you returned before I filed the missing persons report, huh? The beach might have been crawling with police."

I nodded. "I have no idea how I would have explained any of that."

Mom said, "So, Livvy, when do you need to go back to work?"

"I go back two days from now."

Mom sighed.

"What?"

"I just wish you didn't live so far away. I wish you would live closer to home, so I could see you more often. You don't even have to live here on the ranch, you could live in Tallahassee or Gainesville, you know, an easy drive. You could come for dinner."

"Mom, *this* again? I have a job. It was the literal only job I could find in my field. So, you know, I have a townhouse. I'm trying to make it work."

Charlie said, "You have a dumb job and you live eight hours away because you don't want to live nearby, that is a fact. Don't make excuses, you don't like us. It's clear."

Lou said, "Speak for yourself, she likes me fine. She just has an important meteorology job and it's the culmination of her hard work and her education and it's meaningful, or she wouldn't be so far away."

I gulped. "Dylan and Ryan don't live here, either."

Charlie said, "Dylan is getting his masters, he's planning to come back once he graduates, and I guarantee when Ryan gets out he'll move back here. He misses the horses."

Lou said, "We have plenty of room and enough work for the lot of you."

Charlie pretended to be scrolling on his laptop and casually said, "Speaking of riding, you rode a horse with the Duke? You don't ride much anymore, did you forget how?"

I said, "It was nice, it reminded me how much I miss Dewdrop."

"I'll saddle up Dusty for you tomorrow, he misses you."

"That would be great."

Mom said, "I don't mean to make you feel guilty, dear, I just want to remind you what you have — not everyone gets a whole family as awesome as us, all in one place. It's a blessing. You don't have to go out and seize the world by yourself, or be lonely—"

"I'm not lonely, I have Chris."

Mom said, "Far away doesn't have to be your aspirational goal. Chris is of course welcome too."

Junior said, "Speak for yourself, Joni, that boy wouldn't last a minute on this ranch."

Mom huffed.

Uncle Dan said, "Living away from family is a bullshit goal that the *man* wants you to buy into. They don't want you to have a family. They want you to be lonely so they can sell you stuff." He was holding a beer bottle and poking the air as he spoke. "It's the machine, man, it wants you alone, to clock into the system, to take your check and buy your doodads, and do it again the next day."

I joked, "You think my tiny little tv station in North Carolina is part of an oppressive patriarchal system? That I am a cog in the machine? I mean, yeah, it's kinda lame, I'm just an assistant, but one day I'll be the on-air weather person, you'll see."

My eyes went to the satellite radio. "Speaking of which, do you think there will be a storm tomorrow?"

Charlie shrugged. "I don't think so, it needs one of the gadgets, we checked the beach, they're all gone."

"When I leave for North Carolina, will you promise me you'll watch the weather station on Amelia Island?"

"Sure, I'll watch the data, I'll pay attention, but he's not coming back, right Livvy? He has a life, a family."

I nodded, "Yeah, and he's going to get married."

"You don't want to get in the middle of that."

"You're right, I don't. Now I'm going to bed, thanks for cheering me up, and I mean that non-sarcastically this time. It didn't work, but I appreciate that you tried. And Birdie, if you add Nor's info to ancestry.com, I have a photo for you."

"Oh that will stir the comment boards! How fun, show me."

I opened the photos app on my phone and turned it around to show her the one where I had my tongue out and he was laughing at me and we looked happy.

Birdie laughed. "Now *that* photo will create an absolute tizzy on the comment boards, I'll get reported for putting up a false record, but I'll do it anyway. They might suspect that's not really the Duke, but I will refuse to back down — I know the truth."

Mom said, "You both look happy, this is my dream for you, a great love story."

I sighed, looking down at the photo. "It's not a love story, it's just a photo of us together, oh, and I also took this one." I scrolled until I found a photo of the Duke leaning against a rail, looking out over our pasture, his kilt long, his modern shirt stretched across his shoulders. A bit of light on his hair.

Birdie said, "I like *that* one very much."

Lou took my phone, and gazed at the photo. He joked, "Ah yes, that is one fine pasture."

"Lou, it's not about the pasture, it's about the handsome duke!"

"You think he's handsome?" He teased, "I suppose if you like men in skirts. It's not my style though, I prefer a man who looks grizzled like Jeff Bridges in True Grit."

"You prefer a grizzled man?"

"Or a beautiful woman like Birdie."

"Aw, that's really nice."

Birdie said, "It's not nice, it's romantic, and also very hot."

Me, all the uncles, and Charlie groaned.

Uncle Dan said, "Can we not talk about how hot dad is, it's going to set me off romance all together."

Birdie laughed. "Speaking of which, it's long past time for you to get back out dating."

Chapter 39 - the Duke

1670
KILCHURN CASTLE

I had placed the devices in the lowest cell of the dungeons, inside a box, hidden from all. I locked the door and kept the key. From that day there were nae storms.

I kept the scraps of paper in my sporran and studied them, trying tae make sense of the markings. The papers that I took from the men looked much the same as the notations Livvy made, and after studyin' until m'eyes were sore, I looked away briefly and glanced back and noticed that a few of the forms looked much like numbers.

It was easier tae understand the list of markings once I associated them with numbers, and I would go down tae the cell with a flashlight that Madame Livvy's Uncle Tim had given me and lined the portals up and studied. I checked them against the notations on the papers tryin' tae make sense of them. I had grown comfortable handling them because they dinna move down here. Under the ground seemed tae be safe storage for these portals.

Then one day I found a pattern — a string of numbers that seemed tae match within the markings, repeated in one of the portals. I realized twas the string of numbers and shapes that meant: Barran Moor near Kilchurn castle.

The other string of numbers must hae meant the beach in

Florida, but I couldna be sure. I couldna figure out which of the numbers meant the year.

I put them intae the sack and placed it under a stone in the corner and went upstairs tae the Great Hall for yet another meal noddin' and smilin' while Mam and Madame Enid made decisions about m'life.

It had become verra clear that Mam was indeed attemptin' tae match us taegether. Madame Enid was in every room, always at m'left side.

The meals were long, the conversation, dull.

Mam had a deft hand at puttin' us in the same space.

Claray scowled and frowned through every meal and one afternoon after Madame Enid mentioned that Claray ought tae consider the match with the Earl of Dunfermline, Claray barged intae m'chamber later. "Brother! Ye canna marry me tae Dunfermline, he is awful!"

"I am not plannin' tae marry ye off tae Dunfermline, when did that happen? He inna even here!"

"He has gone back tae his castle, with intention tae return for my hand. It was a full conversation at dinner, and ye dinna even notice. They are conspirin' tae marry me and ye arna doin' anything tae stop it. Ye hae been home for three weeks and tis as if ye are asleep. Ye are neglectin' yer life."

I sighed and sat down. "That is a verra heavy charge, Claray. Hae I really been home for three weeks?"

"Yes! Ye do nothin' but ponder! I am tired of ye contemplatin' about all the wrong things. Our mother is making decisions while ye brood."

I said, "Everyone around me seems tae believe that if our mother decides something, twill be decided for all of us. I told ye, Claray, I dinna see the match as one that was—"

She frowned and flounced her way into a chair.

Aenghus walked in then. "What is happening? Claray, are ye harrassin' the Duke again?"

"Sister is full of fury as she believes that, although I hae told her that I daena intend tae match her with Dunfermline, I will do it anyway, against my word."

She said, "Because yer word inna good enough."

I scoffed. "How is my word nae good enough?"

"Because ye daena understand, brother, ye are in grief still and ye walk around here," she hunched over and lurched across the room draggin' a foot behind her. "Ye are all morose. 'Oh woe is me, I hae lost all I care about and now I just sit in my chamber and allow things tae happen tae me.'"

"That daena sound or look anything like me."

Aenghus laughed. "I daena ken, Nor, tis almost exactly like ye. If I dinna ken it was our sister I might hae been confused by it, thinking it was you I was watchin'."

I leaned on m'desk, crossed my arms with one boot over the other. M'new boots were verra fine. "Ye are both conspiring against me."

Claray said, "I am nae conspirin', Yer Grace, I am tellin' ye that tis time tae do the things that yer word is promisin'. Ye told me that I wouldna hae tae marry the auld vapor-monger, and yet he is still under the belief that he is goin' tae take me as his wife. I am better-suited tae be his bairn than his bride."

Aenghus said, "Ye are an auld maid. Ye need tae become a wife and hae a bairn afore ye grow too auld."

"Och nae, ye are the worst, brother!"

Aenghus said, "There are worse things than marryin' for advantage instead of love—"

She pouted. "There is nothing worse! Ye love yer wife; Nor loved his wife; Malcolm married for land and none of us can stand his wife; dost ye see the pattern? Am I nae tae enjoy the love of a good man, tis nae for me?" She huffed. "Well, I will tell ye, if ye marry me tae auld vapor-monger and *especially* if I am married tae him *not* because ye decided twas best but simply because ye were too saddened by yer state tae stop it as it was happening, I will make ye miserable."

I stood over her. "This is a threat, Claray? Ye are nae tae threaten me, *ever*!"

She raised her chin as she used tae do with our father. "Tis not the usual kind, Yer Grace — I only meant, if ye marry me tae auld Dunfermline I will leave and go tae live in his lands, verra far away and ye winna see me anymore. I winna be here tae keep ye company and tae make ye laugh and tae look after ye and I do feel so strongly that ye will miss me."

"Ye look after me? Last I kent ye were my younger sister, a tryin' young lass at that."

"This is what I mean! Ye daena even see it! Ye spend all yer time in yer chamber, a great deal of time considering things. Ye only go tae hunt when invited, ye only laugh when ye hae tae, ye go tae yer rooms when the music begins, ye never once dance with me, and ye are verra close tae marrying Madame Enid and I am the only person who is warnin' ye that tis coming. Ye are about tae allow it tae happen tae ye and ye will wake up one morn and ye will be married and forever from then, ye will wake up tae her face beside ye. She will be sayin', 'Aye, Yer Grace, would ye like me tae send yer sister away tae live with an auld goblin?'"

She crossed her arms and very funnily huffed so loudly that I had tae stifle a laugh. I asked Aenghus, "What say ye, brother?"

"Daena drag me intae it."

"Och, ye are dragged right intae the middle of it, do ye believe there is a truth tae what our sister says?"

"Aye, ye are morose and ye hae been since yer Mary and Eaun passed. I daena blame ye, but I do worry on ye, and I believe tis time tae become more yer past self. Ye do hae the tendency... tae allow things tae happen without dissent. We hae been discussing it and—"

"Ye and Claray are meetin' tae discuss my disposition?"

"Aye, because we are worried about ye."

Claray said, "When Madame Livvy was here twas the first time I saw ye behave like ye used tae, ye smiled and ye laughed, and ye acted as if ye wanted things for yerself. Twas verra nice tae see."

"Madame Livvy will not be here anymore. Tis useless tae speak on the concern as if it was something I may remedy." I tapped my fingers on the table. "Do ye ken, she inna even born yet? Her grandfather inna born yet, her house has yet tae be built, her ancestors haena moved there yet from the Old World. When she is born I will be long dead. There is nae remedy." I adjusted my feet and asked, "What do ye propose I do tae live up tae yer expectations of me, since ye seem tae speak on me so freely?"

Claray said, "I wish ye would just decide that ye winna marry Madame Enid. Tell Mam nae, and send her home. Then we can find another lass who is a better fit for ye. I want ye tae decide things and make them happen. Ye deserve tae be comfortable and tae be in love with yer wife. Tae hae a maiden who will make yer rooms pleasant and will rub yer temples when ye hae had a long day."

"Aenghus, what do ye think I ought tae do?"

"Ye should decide what ye want and make it happen. Else why are ye a duke if ye arna going tae command yer lands tae provide what ye want?"

I narrowed my eyes. "Good, I hae taken yer advisements and I will consider them, but I want ye tae ken that ye spoke tae me, Claray, in a way that is impermissible. Ye must practice holding yer tongue or I will hae so much trouble marrying ye off that I might hae tae resort tae auld vapor-vestibule."

Claray curtsied. "Aye, Yer Grace," then she started tae speak but then clamped her mouth shut, but then she looked pained and the words burst forth, "Just please nae auld vaporous-vaminy, Yer Grace."

She clamped her mouth shut again.

I chuckled and shook my head. "Ye are right, Claray, how can

I marry ye off and hae ye leave the castle? I would miss yer measured conversation and yer harmonious company."

I turned tae my brother. "And Aenghus, I appreciate all ye did tae help me with our recent difficulties. I was nae aware that I hadna planned a hunt in a long while... perhaps tomorrow ye will accompany me?"

"I would like that, Nor."

"Good, and Claray, ye daena get tae advise me on matters of the heart, I am the Duke. Ye are the younger sister of the Duke and ye must remember that ye arna tae boss me or threaten me, ye canna, tis verra poor form. Ye are a verra small amount of years in the world, so how are ye tae think ye ken what I need in a wife?"

"I am a woman, and I hae grown up with ye. I ken what will be good for ye."

I exhaled. "Well, ye daena get tae say it! Ye can ken it, but ye must keep it tae yerself. And however ye are married ye canna threaten tae leave me, tis heartless."

"Aye, Yer Grace."

I smiled. "And now ye must leave me tae ruminate, as I am in need of solace and nae more lectures."

They bowed out of the room.

That night a fine dinner was tae be served in the Great Hall. I hadna noticed a great deal of the workings of the household, as m'mother had been handling the meals, but I was told tae dress well, that the meal would be fine, and I discovered that it was Madame Enid and Mam, conferring taegether, who had planned a special feast.

I was dressed in m'best coat, a clean shirt, my hair tied back, my fine new boots.

Lacin' them up I wished I had brought some for m'brothers and a pair of fine boots such as I had seen Madame Livvy wear, for m'sister. Mam needed shoes also, as she often complained of her feet achin' from the cold, a chill that went 'through her bones.'

Chapter 40 - the Duke

1670

KILCHURN CASTLE

I descended the stair, entered the Great Hall, greeted the guests, and sat in my chair. Mam sat Madame Enid tae m'right, her father, Laird John Holborne, tae my left.

I tried tae think when was the last time I had dined without her beside me. I glanced up at m'sister, whose eyes were narrowed, watching me.

I inquired after Madame Enid's day.

She kept her eyes down. "Twas ordinary, Your Grace."

Laird Holborne began a long recounting of having gone on a hunt with some of the men of my castle. He looked comfortable, enjoying my largess, he had grown familiar with m'lands and at ease with the use of m'stables and armory.

I watched Madame Enid, as she remained demure while he told the tale.

Then I asked, "Do ye like tae ride, Madame Enid?"

She shook her head, her eyes cast down. "Nae, Your Grace, I prefer the arts of the home tae bein' outside the castle walls."

My brow drew down. "What arts of the home dost ye enjoy?"

"I daena like tae be idle. I am often at the loom and enjoy the quietude of church. I do like tae pray."

I nodded. "Those are verra fine qualities."

She smiled, a blush drawing up her cheek.

I raised my glass, "Here's tae the enjoyments of the home."

All raised their mugs except Enid who seemed too modest tae drink in front of me. I asked Laird Holborne, "Is yer wife as demure and acquiescent as Madame Enid?"

"Aye as wives ought tae be, demure and acquiescent and most importantly, silent." He raised his glass.

I raised mine along, so that all joined us in the toast.

I drank a swig and changed m'focus. "I hae a question for ye, Mam, if a young woman is ready tae be married and there is an eligible man who needs a wife, and they hae lands and titles that will be accentuated by their joining, does that mean they are suited for the bond?"

"Aye, Your Grace, that is all that needs be ken. If she is ready and he is eligible, and there is a purpose of it, then aye."

"What if they arna suited by mood or interest?"

Madame Enid blinked.

Lady Gail said, "I daena think that if there is a *reason* for the marriage that they *can* be unsuited."

"That is a verra curious thing tae say — ye and father were verra suited tae each other. I heard ye laugh a good deal. I heard ye advise him about policy. Were ye nae fitted for each other?"

She waved my words away. "If ye are bonded taegether in a marriage than ye will *become* fitted."

"Tae 'become fitted', I see. This is a verra good point." I said tae the whole table. "I do verra much like tae ride, I like tae go on a hunt, I like tae read about the world, and I enjoy travel. I hae a newfound taste for coffee." I turned tae Enid. "Ye say ye prefer the arts of the home, hae ye tried coffee, Madame Enid?"

"Never, Your Grace, I hae heard of it, but the minister tells me that it is a drink that comes from darkness and ought not be tasted by modest women."

I took a sip of m'whisky and surprised my mother with a question. "Lady Gail, hae ye been makin' arrangements tae marry Lady Claray tae Laird Dunfermline?"

Her eyes widened. "Where is yer mind this eve? Ye are conversing as if ye were uncovering intrigues. Aye, and I informed ye he was comin' tae visit next week. I hae nae kept it from ye. I am plannin' tae make an agreement, I am tryin' tae be of use tae ye: he has a great deal of land, Claray is from the house of Awe, it is a suitable match."

I scowled.

"Ye daena think it is a good match?"

"He is near forty, at least, and she, Claray, is less than half his age, for one."

"There are worse things."

"Well, I dinna want tae say it, but I believe he is tedious as well."

"Tedious!" She laughed. "That is the best of compliments. He is staid and quiet. He keeps tae himself, he—"

"He is the kind of man who would expect his wife tae be verra quiet and tae only speak when spoken tae, tae sit and be obedient, I hae seen him beat his horse because it was out of his control — is this a suitable match for Claray?"

Laird Holborne said, "This has gone past agreeable dinner conversation, but if a man is tae be a good husband he must keep a firm hand. Tis proper tae beat a horse or a wife if there is need of correction."

I raised my brow.

A glance at Claray and she had gone pale. She looked about tae speak but I shook my head.

She sat back, quieted.

I slammed the rest of m'whisky and called the server over tae bring more drinks.

I asked Madame Enid, "What dost ye think, Madame Enid, of this match for Lady Claray?"

"I wouldna want tae advise ye, Your Grace, ye will always ken best when it comes tae yer household."

"I hae heard though, that ye do hae an opinion on it. Please share it with me as I am makin' up my mind."

She asked, "May I speak freely, Your Grace?"

"I asked ye for yer thoughts."

"I believe twill be good for the family, as Laird Dunfermline's lands are near Edinburgh, and twill be good for Lady Claray as she is impetuous and unruly. She will need a husband with a firm hand."

I glanced over at Claray whose chin was trembling.

I nodded.

Madame Enid seemed tae think I was nodding in agreement.

She raised her eyes and allowed herself to gloat in her power, givin' me a true glimpse of her nature. "I do think that the match with the Earl of Dunfermline would be verra good for Lady Claray. She would be able tae move tae his castle, there she could see tae running her household, much as yer next wife will see tae running the household of Kilchurn." She looked around at the Great Hall. "I do see a great need for improvements."

I ignored the comment and asked, "What do ye think of the meal this evening, Madame Enid? Did ye find it overly bland? I thought it might need some more spice."

"Nae, I thought twas respectable, I daena want for spice, I believe it ruins the true taste. There was a gravy, but I found it too rich. Tae use gravy sparingly is tae walk in the Lord's grace."

"I disagree."

She turned her eyes back down. "My apologies, Your Grace, I should nae hae spoken out."

I looked at Mam, shaking my head.

I asked Madame Enid, "Ye mentioned Lady Claray would enjoy livin' near Edinburgh, but Lady Claray has told me she would rather remain here at Kilchurn, she is young though, she might change her mind, but would ye enjoy livin' near Edinburgh?"

"I would enjoy it, but I will live wherever my laird bids me."

I said, "I think Claray is growin' up tae be a fine woman, full of spirit. She has wit and she has advised me and been correct in the matter. I will nae see her married tae Dunfermline, she is nae tae be married for another year, at least, and when it happens I will be the one making the decision. I had a fine match with Mary, and I agreed tae the marriage of Laird Aenghus and Madame Ailsa — it has also been a fine match."

I raised my glass toward Aenghus and his wife. "I believe I hae a good history of arrangin' matches and so I will be in charge of finding Lady Claray a husband. Mam, with due respect, I ken ye want what is best for her, but from now on I am in charge of negotiations on her behalf, and I will decide who I will negotiate with."

Lady Gail said, "What if I hear of a match that I believe would be good? Am I supposed tae hold my tongue? I am much more likely tae ken of available prospects. I told ye many times that I was interested in a match between Lady Claray and the future Earl of Dunfermline, and ye wouldna hear me on it, ye were not payin' attention, and now, Your Grace, ye dismiss it, though it is a verra good match — he is in need of heirs!"

"I daena care if he is in need of salmon and I hae the only salmon stream in all of Scotland. I am tae turn over what is mine just because he needs it? He also needs a better manner, a good washin', and tae learn tae take a joke. He is frightfully stiff and unmercifully rude. But what ye say is true, I hae not given heed — I will going forward. If ye hear of a suitable *young* man for Claray, ye may mention him tae me. I will take it on advisement."

Laird Holborne said, "This is all well and good, Yer Grace, but ye winna learn what ye need tae ken unless ye invite him on a hunt: Does he hae a firm hand? Is he willing tae correct? Will he be the moral judge of his family and the arbiter of all punishments?"

"This is a verra good point, I will take each eligible man out on hunts and see how he treats his animals. *Then* I will make m'decision. But one more question, Laird Holborne, what dost ye think of mercy?"

"Mercy, for whom? Only a weak-willed man would shew mercy tae someone who requires correction. "

"For a member of yer family — does every misstep from the laird's rules require a correction?"

"If ye are running a proper household, then aye."

I exhaled. "Laird Holborne and Madame Enid, I believe I hae led ye along the wrong path. I ought tae hae been more forthright, I am not plannin' tae wed again. I am—"

Lady Gail said, "Nor! Ye canna make this decision without considering all—!"

"I hae given it a great deal of thought, Mam."

I addressed Laird Holborne and his daughter, "My deepest apologies that ye hae been called tae Kilchurn under the pretense of havin' us wedded, but as ye hae now learned, I would make a particularly bad match for ye, Madame Enid. I am weak-willed where it comes tae my family, I believe in mercy, and I think a satisfactory coupling ought tae be based in friendliness and comfortable shared interests rather than a union of titles and a promise tae keep each other in line. At the verra least I am proud of my Great Hall and daena believe it needs improvements. Dunfermline, however, has land, his castle is near Edinburgh, it wants for improvements, and he needs heirs. I believe a union between Madame Enid and Dunfermline might be the best course going forward."

Laird Holborne huffed and stood. "Madame Enid, we must retire, the night has grown unseemly." Then he seemed tae regret showing me disrespect and bowed, "My apologies, Your Grace..."

I stood. "Daena concern yerself with apologies, Laird Holborne. I wish ye safe travels and will send gifts on yer return tae Menstrie."

"Thank ye, Yer Grace." He bowed as they left the Great Hall.

I sat back in my chair, slammed another shot of whisky, and put down the glass.

Mam said, "I canna believe ye just made that decision with such haste!"

Aenghus laughed. "It wasna in haste, Mam, he has been slow as a rain puddle in the rut of a path."

She looked as if she might weep. "I look a fool!"

I stood and moved tae the seat beside her and patted the back of her hand. "M'apologies, Mam, I ken ye want the best for yer children, and we often frightfully disappoint ye."

"I simply want ye tae hae someone so ye arna so lonely. Yer father would hae wanted me tae see tae yer contentment."

"I ken, Mam. Ye worry on us, ye want what is best for us. Sometimes though we hae tae decide for ourselves."

"What if ye are wrong, Nor?"

"How can I be wrong? I am the Duke! I daena think tis possible for me tae be wrong."

She chuckled, dolefully, and I kent she was forgiving me for the distress. "Tis not possible for ye tae be wrong, Nor, but ye might not be *right*."

"I might not, Mam, tis true, but I hae considered it, and I hae acted. If twas not the right course, I will alter it. But while I head out on my path ye might say, 'Och, His Grace, the Duke, is verra wise in his dealings,' while ye are thinking tae yerself, 'Och, he is makin' a blunder.'"

"Tis how it must go? Ye could listen tae me from the first — ye could want tae find comfort and enjoyment, ye could remarry."

I squeezed her hand. "Aye, I could, but I need more time, Mam."

"Well then what am I tae do with myself if I am not tae match my children?"

I chuckled. "Ye could make the match between Enid and Dunfermline."

She looked off at the far wall. "They *would* be well-suited. The union of their lands would make a strong alliance and if I were the one tae set it up I would hae *influence*."

I patted her hand again. "That is the spirit, Mam. We will *all* be the better for encouraging the alliance well away from our lands."

I smiled down at Claray, who smiled back.

My head was swimming from the drink and the blunt conversation.

I stood. "I am goin' tae my room as it has been a long day — again my apologies, I do hope ye will all remain here and enjoy the rest of the meal."

Claray asked, "Yer Grace, the musician has begun tae play, ye winna dance?"

"Nae, Lady Claray, I must change m'mind a wee bit at a time, I canna be so changeable that I can become joyous just because ye tell me tae be."

Chapter 41 - Livvy

2012
NORTH CAROLINA

Chris threw his arms around me as soon as I stepped out of the car. "I was so worried about you!" He was handsome in that Frat Boy kind of way — short cut hair, shirt and jeans, pair of Nikes. Every outfit he put on looked exactly like every other outfit he owned.

I hugged him, and inhaled. He smelled good, I had missed his cologne. Then I went around to the trunk and pulled out my suitcase. "It was crazy." I wheeled my luggage behind me up to the front stoop of our townhouse "But I told you about it."

"It sounds *really* crazy."

The television was on, the PlayStation humming. "You playing World of Warcraft?"

"Hell yeah, you want to play?"

"Nah, just got home, want to take stock..."

He sat down on the couch a few inches away from his controller. "I got some beer to celebrate that you're home."

I went into the kitchen and opened the fridge, I had been gone for a week, it was basically empty except for the milk carton that was... I unscrewed the top and sniffed. *Yep, so bad.* There would be no coffee in the morning unless I went to the store first.

I popped open a beer and returned to the living room.

He was already playing the game. "Hey, can you get me a beer too?"

"Sure." I got him a beer and placed it on the coffee table in front of him. And then I stood there and drank, kinda watching him play, blinking the tears from my eyes.

He was twisting and turning the controller, his eyes on the screen. "You go back to work tomorrow?"

"Yeah." I drained the end of my beer. "I need to run to the store to get some groceries."

"Hey, will you grab coffee? We ran out."

"Sure, yeah."

I cried in the car on the way to the store.

It was suddenly so clear to me — we had been happy once, content, but we had slid so far away from that into really low expectations and I totally wondered how in the hell I had gotten myself into this mess.

I couldn't believe I had stopped kissing the Duke for him.

I decided for the hundredth time that I would break up with him. But like always, I could never just do it. I promised myself I would do it the next day when he got home from work, or Friday night at dinner, and then Saturday morning over coffee — but all those moments passed by without doing it, because it was either too hard to bring up or he would do something mildly, *barely,* kind, and I would talk myself out of it.

Like the day he called me from the convenience store on the way home to check if I needed anything.

And afterwards I looked at the phone thinking, *aw, that was nice.*

But it was the bare fucking minimum of what a human does for the person they love.

Plus we had terrible sexual timing — he stayed up late. A lot. More and more. He barely ever touched me.

I was twenty-five and my partner was uninterested in me.

I was grateful, because as the weeks progressed I didn't *want* him to touch me, at all. I made excuses, I planned things, I got up early in the morning to go on a run. I went to bed early and pretended to be asleep when he joined me.

But finally, three weeks after I got home, I did it.

It was not a plan, it was out of fury.

I drove home one day and it was pouring down rain and he had parked in my spot: the one closest to the front door.

I sat in the car with the rain coming down, thinking about the Duke and how he would have worried about me. How he would have made sure I was okay. He might have teased me about things, but he wanted the best for me. He would *never* take my parking spot for himself. A spot that was established mine because I usually brought in the groceries, so I got the closer spot. It was the closest thing Chris had to chivalry.

Except today.

Today I had a bag of groceries, a bunch of files from work, no raincoat, and I was wearing suede shoes.

My anger rose as I stared up at the house, a blue light flickering from the window.

His damn games.

I called him.

"I'm outside... It's raining a lot."

"Hell yeah, buckets."

"You're in my space."

"It was pouring down, did you pick up groceries?"

"Yeah. Yeah I did."

A pause, but not a listening pause, it was a paying attention to the game pause. By now I knew the difference. "You coming in?"

"I think I'll have to wait until the rain calms down..."

"All right, see you in a bit."

He hung up.

I banged the heels of my hands down on the steering wheel, *fuck you, fuck you, fuck you*. And then I jumped out of the car.

I slammed the car door, raced through the rain, and got out my key to unlock the door, because yeah, it was locked. I barged in, like a wet rat, totally drenched, chest *heaving* in fury.

I said, evenly, "I want to break up."

He looked up from his game confused.

I plowed on. "I want to break up, I want you to move out. I will take over the lease. You will go stay with Mike till you figure something out. I want you out right fucking now."

"What the hell Liv, what are you talking about?"

I wrung out a strand of my hair.

"I'm being as plain and direct as I can be. We are over. I want you to pack up your stuff and go. If packing up will take you longer than thirty minutes then I want you to go and come back for your stuff later."

"This is ridiculous. Is this because I parked in your spot?"

I gestured to the front door. I gestured to him, incredulously. I gestured at myself. I gestured back at the front door and then I waved my hands around in the air.

He put down the controller. "What are you fucking doing?"

"I'm telling you that it's *every*thing. But yes, if that makes the most sense to you, if you are that confused, yes, yes indeed, Chris, I want you out of here because you parked in my space. When you ask Mike to let you sleep on his couch, you be sure to tell him that I kicked you out over a parking space. Tell him you were blameless, tell him I was totally unreasonable."

He stood up, crossed to the tv, and began unhooking the PlayStation wires. "You *are* unreasonable, and absolutely mental." He angrily wrapped the cords up and stacked the controller on them.

I barged down the hall, and started stuffing his clothes into a duffel bag. I didn't even fucking care about helping, if it got him out of here sooner, then I would pack it all.

I shoved clothes and shoes in the bag and zipped it across the top. Then I went into the bathroom and shoved all his toiletries into a makeup bag and zipped it up. I lugged it all down the hall where he was standing, glowering.

"You have laundry, you can come back for it, call me, and I'll let you know when it's gone through the full cycle."

I put out my hand.

"What?"

"I want your key."

"Fucking A, Liv, do you hear yourself? You're unhinged."

"Absolutely. See, I have a failing, I let shit go, because I'm really nice, and I go nice nice nice, and then I fucking snap. It's a failing, really, I see it. A truly nice person would let someone know where the line is — so they wouldn't cross it, but here we are."

"Are you saying I crossed some kind of line? I didn't do fucking anything. I'm just home from work, relaxing, playing a video game."

"Exactly. The line you crossed is so far back, that I can't even remember you stepping over it, but you've been across it for a long time."

"Name one thing, Liv, one thing that I've done to you."

"You didn't drive down to Florida when I went missing."

"What the fuck — why would I?"

"Because you've been there, a lot, you know them, Lou was in the hospital. You could have driven down and been worried about me, but you didn't. It never even crossed your mind."

"You came back!"

"Yeah, you're right, I did, it's all moot. So you know what, let's chalk it all up to you parking in my spot. *That's* why."

"I'm not going to come running back when you call. When you're done with this crazy carrying on, I'm gone. This is *my* line."

"I'm glad you have principles. Good. See you later, bye."

He said, "You're fucking infuriating." He ripped open the front door. There was a torrential downpour. He grabbed his raincoat off the rack and wrapped it around his PlayStation and rushed out to his car and placed it in the front seat, then he ran back up the steps and grabbed his duffel and toiletries bags and rushed them down the steps, tossed them in the back of his SUV, slammed that door, yanked open his driver's door, climbed in, and drove off.

Leaving me with a full view as he drove away, because of course he left the front door wide open.

I closed it, leaning against it and bursting into tears.

I had been dating him and living with him for years.

It was terribly sad to have broken up.

But the crazy part was that though I cried it was less about Chris, truly, and more about missing Nor. That I felt unloved because I had lost the Duke and... it had been three weeks. I cried some more.

I knew that I had said goodbye and I knew it was for forever.

And it made sense.

He was the kind of guy who needed me to call him 'Your Grace.'

He was from the seventeenth century.

None of it made sense... but...

He could come.

He could come and see me, if he wanted to... if he missed me. The storms had been regular, but now they weren't. And day after day had passed, week after week, and life was moving on.

If I had had a portal I would have traveled to see him by now.

I was weak.

I was smitten.

I was, if I was totally honest, kinda a stalker.

Or I would be if I could be.

I would have time jumped, as awful as it was, as painful, just to have been lying in the dirt with him standing above me asking, "Are ye all right, Madame Livvy?"

Just to have him say, "Och nae, why hae ye come all this way?"

But it wasn't on me to go see him because I didn't have one of the portals.

He had two and he didn't come to see me.

Weeks passed, probably months in his time, and he was fine.

He was probably married by now.

~

Three more weeks and the break up with Chris was final.

He had gotten all his things. We had arranged the lease.

We were over.

Now I was living alone.

I had been pretty solitary, because he had been such a lump, but now there wasn't even an irritating lump on the couch anymore. There was no one here.

It wasn't that I didn't like living alone, it was just that it got kinda lonely.

Another three weeks passed while I adjusted.

I cooked, I watched tv, and work was lame. I aspired to be a meteorologist, but mostly I got coffee and worked on my 'project,' taking twenty years of local weather data and entering it into the database so we could look at trends, which now went back to 2004. I was typing all day.

Some of the notes were handwritten, I had to decipher what it all meant.

It was very boring.

I had grown away from my friends, I lived far away from my family. My job was boring. Why the hell was I in North Carolina anyway? Was this being an adult? Did it mean being alone a lot of the time?

It was Friday night, I worked late. I bought a bottle of wine and turned on a movie. Drank too much, lay in bed, scrolled through Facebook. Googled: Should I get a dog?

Around 11 pm I called Charlie. "Hey."

"Hey, dumdum, I'm headed to bed, why you calling so late?"

"Because I'm buzzed up and bored."

"I got chores in the morning, Lou wants help, gotta go to sleep." He yawned.

"There haven't been any storms?"

"Of course not, you would know, first thing."

I fluffed my pillow and flipped onto my side. "Do you think I'll ever see him again?"

There was a long pause. "I'm not sure how to answer that — no, you can't go see him, you don't have one of the gadgets, and he's probably not going to come here. It's complicated, right? He's a duke, that's a pretty big deal, I gather. What's he doing here? *Nothing.* He's not going to subject himself to that. Men want to be successful. Men don't want to go to a place where they don't know anything, where they throw up on the side of the highway. That's the truth."

I sipped from a glass of wine dribbling it down my cheek. I dabbed it off with a tissue. "So what you're saying is no. You're mean."

"He's a dead man from hundreds of years ago. He doesn't even have a social media presence. You're better off not thinking about him."

"I miss him."

"Yeah, he was cool, there was something about him, direct and old fashioned, handsome and mysterious, that we all liked, and the kilt. Do you think I would look cool in one?"

"I don't know, it's kinda hard to pull off a wool kilt in Florida, I think. It's likely to seem ironic. He was authentic, you know?"

"Yeah I know, when you coming home again?"

"I don't know, like next month?"

"You're ridiculous."

"I know, g'night."

"G'night." I hung up the phone and tossed it to the side.

And flipped to my other side. I turned on an episode of Friends that I had watched five times already. I sipped my wine and didn't notice when I was scrolling through Wikipedia again, looking for any trace of Nor.

Chapter 42 - the Duke

1670

NEAR LOCH AWE

Aenghus and I rode out tae hunt pheasant the following day.

We had our fowling pieces, and I carried my rifle. Aenghus was pleased that we were going on the hunt and he was in a verra good mood about it. We were ridin' in the north woods, along the River Strae, just after the sun had come up, when he said, "So, brother, ye hae had an evenin' where ye spoke the truth and ended upsettin' everyone at the table."

"Except Claray."

"Aye, except Claray."

"And yer wife, I spoke highly of her, raised m'glass."

"She is still upset, she thinks ye were inconsiderate tae our guests."

I scoffed, and directed Balach Mòr around a boulder in the path. "How am I tae be considerate tae guests who are guests only because they hae been invited by our mother, who ought not hae a say in the matter, tae move intae my castle and take over the runnin' of it? Ye heard Madame Enid, she wanted tae send Claray away!"

"I did hear it, I couldna believe she said it direct as she did, she ought tae hae hidden her scheme. It shows she lacks the wit necessary tae connive as she did. If she would hae listened tae the members of the household she would hae learned: one does not tell the Duke that Claray is disobedient, even if she is."

I pushed a thin limb away as we rode under some trees. "It is not that I think ye are wrong on Claray, but tis that I think the solution is incorrect. Claray has a big heart, she does well too often speak her mind, but with a look from me she bit her tongue. She will be a fine woman once she is old enough tae marry. She will need a husband who can manage her with a look and not a 'firm hand' as they kept saying. Ye ken, MacLean has a firm hand with his wife and bairns and the castle was full of their wailin' until father handled *him*. A title is only as strong as the strength of the laird and his men and strength is best quiet than loud. I winna hae wailing and beggin' for mercy in my household."

Aenghus said, "I remember MacLean's family well, it was a mercy on all of us that father solved it. So in yer speech last eve ye set a match between Madame Enid and Laird Dunfermline?"

"I am quite proud of it."

"Mam has already sent a messenger."

"Dear God, she is relentless."

"Madame Enid and Laird Holborne are packing this morn, they will be gone by the time we are returned.

"That is for the best."

We came tae a wide field, where we sat upon a boulder and had a breakfast of boiled eggs and a hunk of bread. Aenghus said, "How many times hae we sat here enjoyin' a breakfast?"

"Many a morn."

The sun was risin' the cool night air replaced by warmth, the dew dryin' upon the stalks of grass.

I said, "Did ye ken that hundreds of years from now, in the New World, they still eat the lowly chicken egg when they wake in the morn?"

"Do they now? Do they sit upon a rock while eating it, with their horses near?"

"Nae, they daena, they hae a table right inside the kitchen and Livvy and I cooked on the stove and then we stood there and ate, leanin' on the table. Twas a verra interestin' ritual, though the food was much the same." I chewed the egg and swallowed. "They like a great deal of sweetness, they want tae ruin the food with it."

"Ye had a fine time when ye visited the New World."

"Aye, she had an easy smile about her, did ye notice it?"

"I did, and she believed ye tae be witty. I found it bewilderin' that she looked upon ye as if ye were wise and charming. She found ye pleasing, Your Grace; there is nae understanding some people."

"Ye think? She probably found me tae be verra auld fashioned." I scanned the horizon, and added, "I do miss her."

"She was a fine lass." He cut his eyes at me and teased, "She had ample broad hips, she will make someone a fine wife."

I scowled. "That is a terrible thing tae say."

"What dost ye want me tae say tae ye? She is verra far away and she has wide hips and an easy laugh, but she is gone now. Ye gave her up, and so she inna yers tae think upon, wide hips or nae."

"I dinna give her up, she was never mine tae hae."

He looked at me askance. "Madame Livvy looked upon ye as if ye were all she wanted. She thought ye had, as Ailsa would say tae me, pleasin' knees.'"

"Och, that is what ladies like?"

"Ye ken it, tis the most basic truth of ladies. If ye shew them yer knee they feel verra inclined tae accept ye tae bed. My Ailsa also likes the look of m'hand, she will hold it and feel verra desirous about it. She will also remark upon m'shoulder."

"Ye are verra forthcoming on yer wife. She has just had a bairn. I think ye are readyin' yerself tae make another."

He laughed. "Tis true, but we arna here tae talk about m'wife or yer Madame Livvy, of the broad hips and the fine, easy smile.

She is never goin' tae be here again. Ye will hae tae become familiar with some other fair lassie."

I said, "What are ye about?"

"Nothing."

"Ye are about *something*. Ye keep mentioning how I am never goin' tae see her again."

"Tis true, ye said so yerself."

"Aye, I canna, tis not the natural order of things. She lives there, I live here."

"Absolutely, tis God's plan. Ye canna go against it, even if she is verra fine and makes ye feel pleased simply tae hae her around, ye canna."

I nodded, narrowing my eyes.

He crunched the bread crust and drank a sip of whisky, while I listened tae the birds sing.

Then he said, wiping his lap with a napkin. "Unless..."

My eyes went wide. "Unless *what*, Aenghus, ye hae become insufferable, almost as bad as Claray when she has an idea in her head."

"Ye are telling me I hae an idea like a young lass? This is yer way of insulting me, and when ye insult me tis tae cause me tae be quiet, but I winna quiet. I am goin' tae finish my idea... *Unless*... is a lead off from what I said earlier."

"I ken, I can follow ye, I am nae dim. *What?*"

"I wonder, is the travelin' through time a part of God's plan? He is the only plan, ye ken."

"Unless it is the work of the devil, or mischievous fae."

He waved his hand. "I daena believe a bonny lass like Madame Livvy could be the work of the devil. She has a handsome breast, tis too handsome for mischief."

"Och ye are rambling now, the devil is *precisely* goin' tae make a handsome breast the work of his diabolical schemes, tis exactly what we are warned about. Are ye not payin' attention in sermon? And, brother, when ye first met Madame Livvy, ye accused her of witchcraft, here ye are as if that were not even a possibility. Tis not a possibility, mind ye, but tis surprising that ye are so altered in yer opinion of her."

He grinned. "She won me over. She charmed Ailsa, and Claray adored her. And ye... how should I describe yer face when she was around?" His expression became slack-jawed and he batted his eyelids.

I exhaled, pretending tae be irritated. "All of this is pointless. She is gone, whether she was the work of God or nae, she is an impossibility."

"Unless..." He grinned more. "What if God wants ye tae see Madame Livvy again?"

"If ye had ever used the portals tae move through time ye would never suggest it so freely. Time travel feels as if twill kill ye, and ye canna be sure ye will mind the death."

Aenghus shrugged. "Ye mentioned it was awful. I feel like, tae put yer head upon that breast, ye might find yerself more courageous."

"Ye and Claray hae crossed all the lines of appropriate discussion with me, I hope ye ken."

"Aye, I ken, we hae pushed ye past yer good humor, but and I say this with all due respect, Yer Grace, yer humor has been verra thin, and what if Mistress Livvy is the one who can bring yer good humor back?"

The hunt took us through the woods and down tae the river's edge. We found a good many birds and had them strung up on the back of our horses.

Aenghus held up a hand tae still us and pointed. We watched as a deer moved through the trees.

He said, "Close enough tae kill."

"Aye, but this day is for the birds, we will come out next week for the deer."

"There will be a hunt with ye, next week? Och, ye are an altered man."

We kept quiet and I was deep in thought, but then as we turned tae head home, I asked, "Dost ye think she is fine?"

"I ken it."

"What dost ye think, Aenghus, of my opinion about wives — would ye prefer a woman who keeps her eyes cast down?"

"I do verra much like when Ailsa defers tae my judgments."

"But she daena always, I hae heard her speak her mind."

"Aye, ye are right in it brother, sometimes she speaks her mind, other times she is demure, I think she is the right amount of both."

"That's what I think... my Mary was like that."

"Your Mary was just right, and Madame Livvy was nae like that, she was verra direct, ye would hae had a challenging time with her, she would hae argued with ye, she would hae spoken her mind, but she would also hae been a favorable companion for ye—"

"Och nae, ye are on it again, Aenghus, we are men out on a hunt and ye are going tae talk about marryin' me off the whole time? Ye are as hare-brained as a giggling kitchen lass."

He laughed. "Aye, ye are right, I will cease tellin' ye tae find a wife — perhaps ye need a harlot, we could take a trip tae Edinburgh."

"Nae brother, ye ken I winna."

"Fine, I will stop tryin' tae distract ye."

"Ye ought not distract me, with the recent dangers."

"There haena been a danger in a time, ye call it recent but we hae seen weeks pass, perhaps it's settled."

"I hae three portals that are worth a great deal tae a man, one Johnne Cambell, who kens how tae find me. We must remain on guard."

Chapter 43 - the Duke

1670
KILCHURN CASTLE

I saw movement on the path farther ahead.

I held up a hand, drawing Aenghus tae a halt. There was a man ridin' toward the castle.

I glanced at Aenghus and we wordlessly followed, but as we gained on him he sped up. I yelled, "Hold up! Who are ye?"

But the stranger continued riding — we made chase.

Aenghus broke off following a different path, meaning tae overtake him.

I gained upon the stranger, alongside, my rifle readied. "Stop! I will shoot ye!"

The man veered from our path as Aenghus caught up and blocked the route. The stranger attempted tae pull a gun — I fired.

My horse reared dangerously.

The stranger slumped over, then slid from his horse tae the ground.

Aenghus and I dismounted and I lunged on him and yelled in his dyin' face, "Who are ye?" something I was having tae ask verra regularly.

He just grinned, blood spreading in a puddle around him.

"Tell me what ye are doing!"

I dug through his coat pocket, finding a folded paper, unfolded it and read:

Jamie Munro, 1610 - 5757...
Ludan Campbell, 1629 - 5607...
Gospatric Campbell, 1582 - 5640...
Duke Nor, 1670 - 5027...
Olivia Larson, Lou-Moo ranch, Florida 2012 - 3029...

Each name and year had a long string of numbers after. The first three on the list had lines crossed through them.

"Why is m'name upon yer list?"

He dinna answer.

"Who charged ye tae do the work? Who has given ye the list?"

I felt desperate for answers, but Aenghus stopped me with a hand on m'shoulder. "He has passed, Nor, ye winna get answers from him."

"Och nae, why dost the man hae her name on this page — what is he about?"

"He has yer name upon it as well."

"Aye, but he has lost, his blood is spilled out around him."

Angus said, "It looks as though he has three men he has bested already. Tis a good thing ye went on the hunt or we might not hae found him in the woods."

"Aye, if he had gotten tae the castle... I would hae still killed him, but it might hae ruined the evening meal and I am famished."

I shoved the stranger's paper intae m'sporran, put his gun intae m'bags, then I went tae his horse and searched through his things, finding a velvet sack, with an insignia with the letter C in the middle and the year 2270. I loosened the gold rope cinching the top and rolled out two more portals.

"Och nae! I daena want one and now I hae five!"

"What do the numbers mean beside the years?"

"They are the locations — a time traveler has ordered him tae hunt down this list of names and so I ask again... why does he hae Madame Livvy's name on his list?" I met Aenghus's eyes. "Dost ye think she is safe?"

"I daena ken, how would ye ken? She canna get a message tae ye."

I groaned and packed the portals intae one of my sacks.

"We need tae return tae the castle." I mounted my horse.

We rode fast and once we were through the gates had them closed. We alerted my guardsmen tae be vigilant. We accounted for all visitors, and made sure our household was safe, then declared the castle clear.

But I was already packing tae go.

I had decided.

I couldna spend another minute worryin' if she were alive and protected. I had tae ken.

I packed m'gear in a bag. "Ye must guard well, Aenghus, I am sorry tae leave ye with this danger afoot, but I hae tae go see—"

I had a heavy heart beat, a worry that had settled in m'stomach. *What if she wasna safe?*

"I ken, ye hae tae check on Madame Livvy, I will watch over the castle."

"I will take the portals with me, I daena ken if they can be tracked, but I daena like the idea of ye havin' tae be in charge of all of them."

"That is good, I daena want them. I am convinced they are a dark evil."

"I am convinced as well, yet I must ride one tae find out if she is all right."

. . .

I rushed down the stone steps tae the dungeons and tied various sacks filled with my portals tae my belt, leavin' out the one that was set for Florida, I put that one in m'pocket.

Then I rushed back up the stair and out tae the courtyard where Aenghus joined me. A guard would follow us. We rode up the causeway, intae the woods, and then tae Barran Moor.

There, Aenghus said, "Ye want me tae wait with ye?"

"Nae, ye ought tae get the guard back tae the castle, tis growing dark." I passed him the rifle. "Keep this with ye."

He smiled. "I was hopin' ye would give it tae me eventually." He raised it tae his shoulder and aimed. "This is much better than our flintlocks."

"Aye, they are... and tell Claray and Mam that I will return, I just had tae go see tae something."

He joked, "Mam will be relieved, she is irritated with the sight of ye."

"Ye might tell Lady Gail tae forgive me, tell her I am riskin' my life tae keep her safe and that she ought tae pray for me."

"Aye, I will. Godspeed, Nor, I hope ye find Madame Livvy well."

He turned and rode away leading my horse, leavin' me standing in the moor. I pulled the portal from m'pocket and looked it over. I placed it on the ground, crouched beside it, and nudged it with m'finger. *Och nae, it wouldna move...*

I pulled the scraps of paper I had collected from m'pocket and looked them over. There was one that had the list of markings and numbers that matched. I kent this was the portal that went tae Florida, and that it had, in the past, turned on at the same time of the day, but that time of day had already passed.

I sat back on m'heels. *Would I hae tae wait for tomorrow?*

But I felt sure that men shouldna hae tae wait.

I was impatient and I couldna think of a reason why I would need tae wait. I had a powerful portal, *why couldna I use it?*

I picked it up and considered it: the markings, the form of it. There was a ridge around the middle, like a ring. Two of the portals had the ring, three did nae. I picked at the ring with my nail. With effort I would be able tae pull it off.

I speculated whether that was a good idea, *would I break it?*

Holding the portal, I noticed a give, as if it might extend like a telescope, or come apart altogether when held a certain way. In case, I pulled all my gear and bags intae my lap. I said tae m'self, what m'brothers and I often said tae one another, our battle cry — *Le misneach! Cruachan!* It meant *With Courage!* and the name of the mountain that rose above our Campbell lands. Tae yell it was tae persuade ourselves tae be brave enough tae accomplish what needed tae be done.

I had five portals. I was a time traveler. Time travel was not for the timid.

Not knowin' whether she lived or died was tormenting.

I was at the mercy of things out of m'control: chased by men, attacked by strangers who had me on a list. I was spied upon.

I had these portals without wantin' them. This was much like being inside of a game without having decided tae play.

I pushed on the device, causing the middle tae twist.

I felt the shock of pain up my hand. I dropped the portal tae the ground, but in my head I yelled, *Le misneach! Cruachan!* I grabbed it up, and turned it along the middle. The metal felt liquid, it grabbed m'wrists and dragged me from m'form. Pain shot up m'arms and spread tae my heart and mind. It felt as if I were torn from m'limbs and—

Chapter 44 - Livvy

2012
NORTH CAROLINA

I was pouring cereal into a bowl and staring out the window at a bird in the feeder. I was in pajamas and trying to figure out what I would do with myself this weekend. I scrolled through my Insta.

The phone rang — Charlie.

My heart raced. He never called me, ever, and definitely not at 8 am on Saturday morning.

I answered, and he uttered one word: "Storm."

"Really? A storm? How do you know it's one of our storms?"

"Because the radar says the day is clear. But the weather station has a storm over the south end of the island, high intensity, out of nowhere, exact same location. Lou, Mom, and I are driving over now."

I glanced at the kitchen clock. "It'll take you about two hours—"

"Yep and then we shall see, right?'

"Then you find him and—"

"We don't know if it's him, Livvy, we have no idea. We're just, we're going to check."

"Thank you." I glanced around the room looking for my keys.

I was wearing pajamas and a robe. I needed a shower. I needed fifteen minutes, but then I would get in the car. "I'm on my way."

"You don't have to, it's—"

"I'm coming, I'll be at the ranch in six and a half hours, seven tops. Either you'll have... *someone*, or you'll have a story to tell me, or... you know, but I'm coming. Call me when you know anything."

I jumped in the shower, and took the fastest shower in the world. I scooped my stuff into a suitcase, pushed toiletries into a bag. Grabbed my toothbrush and my phone cords, and ran out to the car.

Chapter 45 - the Duke

2012

AMELIA ISLAND

I woke up with a start: rain sprinklin', the storm lessening, clouds clearing. I scrambled tae my feet and hustled tae a low tree where I collapsed against its trunk. I stared out at the beach in a daze, every part of m'body ached.

I kent there was a piece of equipment that Lou had strapped tae the deck, but I dinna ken what tae do with it.

Now that I was here I wasna certain what tae do next.

I wondered if I ought tae go tae the house.

Usin' the tree I pulled m'self up, aching, and trudged up the boardwalk. I climbed the steps tae the house and copied the manner that Madame Livvy had used tae open the door.

I entered and relieved m'self in the bathroom and drew a glass of water from the tap in the kitchen. I had arrived at the limit of m'knowledge.

I stood, drinking from the glass, looking down at the yellow object on the table wondering how tae get the voices tae come through it. I sat on the settee and picked it up and listened. There was a hum. *How would I get Madame Livvy's voice tae come through?*

I would need tae walk tae the ranch.

I wasna sure of the route but I kent the direction was west. I would ask for guidance from fellow travelers and walk along the road until I found it.

Chapter 46 - Livvy

2012

ON HER WAY TO FLORIDA

Charlie called: "I'm there now."

"What's going on, is anyone there?"

"No, no one, but we're walking out to the beach now. Where are you?"

"I'm in Georgia, making good time."

I heard his feet thudding on the boards of the deck. "We're in the sand. Wait, I see footprints, a man's footprints, boots. No one wears boots to the beach."

I said, "He's there, you just... is he in the house?"

He said, "It looks empty, we'll go look."

"You have to find him, he might be... I don't know, he might be walking... he doesn't know how to get anywhere. He has to be there." My heart was racing. I was so freaking excited.

He said, "Mom is looking through the windows, we don't — we don't see anyone inside. Look I'll call you back..." He hung up.

I turned on my blinker to pass the car in front of me, I felt like I was in a slow-motion rescue and — the Duke was here! He had come!

I pressed the gas to go even faster.

Chapter 47 - the Duke

2012

HEADED TO LOU-MOO RANCH

I was walkin' down the road when a truck pulled up beside me.

The window rolled down and inside there were Charlie, and Lou, with Madame Joni in the backseat.

"Och aye, are ye here, Charlie?"

"Hell yeah, I came to get you."

Madame Joni opened the back door of the truck.

"Tis a good thing as I was comin' tae the ranch and I dinna ken how tae get there."

"It would have taken you a few days on foot."

I climbed in the truck and closed the door. "Where is Madame Livvy? She is safe?"

"She's going to meet us at the ranch."

Charlie passed me a black rectangle shaped apparatus.

I looked at it blankly. "I daena ken...?"

"Say hi into it."

I leaned forward and said the word, "High."

I heard, faintly, Madame Livvy's voice.

Charlie laughed and began tae drive the truck.

Joni took the black thing up from m'lap and pressed it tae my ear. "Talk."

238

"Hello?!" I yelled.

Madame Livvy's voice came tae me as if it were disembodied. "Nor! I'm driving, I will see you soon."

I yelled, "Good, I will see ye! Are ye all right?"

"I'm great, I'm so glad you're here!"

Charlie drove us around a circle in the road, my stomach lurched.

I closed my eyes tight and clutched my stomach.

Joni said, "Are you okay, Nor, are you carsick?"

I nodded.

Charlie said, "Nor, want to get in the front seat?"

"Aye, but promise we will go fast?"

"Hell yeah, with the windows down."

He pulled the truck tae the side of the road and Lou got out tae trade. I climbed from the truck and got in the front seat.

Livvy's voice from the apparatus. "Got your seatbelt on?"

I strapped on the belt as Charlie drove us back ontae the road, speedin' up. "Aye, I do now." I leaned m'head intae the wind comin' through the open window.

She said, "Let me talk to Mom."

Joni moved the apparatus tae her own ear and said, "Yeah, he's better... we'll be home in about two hours. You'll be there soon after?" There was a pause, then she said, "Alright hon, see you then."

She passed the apparatus tae Charlie.

A few minutes later the truck was goin' much faster.

Charlie grinned at me. "Want to go even faster?"

"Och aye, as fast as we can." I relaxed and put my hands out flat instead of bunched intae fists. I asked, "Did ye bring weapons?"

Charlie said, "Yeah."

Lou asked, "Why, did something happen?"

"I saw the name of Livvy and yer ranch on a list in a dead man's pocket."

Charlie said, "How did a dead man get a list?"

Lou said, "He wasn't dead when he got the list, boy, pay attention."

Charlie met m'eyes in the mirror near his face. "Did you kill him?"

"Aye."

Madame Joni said, "Dear God, I mean, good, but also what happened to the world? A couple of months ago my kids went storm chasing with my father and now it's just all upside down."

When we arrived at the ranch I asked Lou, "Do you have a place to hide these devices?" I placed the sacks out on the porch.

Lou said, "I have a couple of safes and some good hiding places, we ought tae divide them up, it'll be more secure."

"Aye, that is a good idea." I began tae describe them, "There is this one — tis mine, tis known that I hae it—"

"By who?"

"By a real arse."

Lou nodded.

I said, "This one comes and goes from Florida."

"Then we ought to secure it by itself."

"Aye, keep that one apart because the arse daena ken I hae it."

"Ah, it's your secret weapon, it's good to have one of those."

"If it can be underground, tis preferred."

"I can put it down in the root cellar."

I pointed. "This one is from the first group of men I killed. They were hunting the machines, I think."

"That one ought tae be secured by itself then, in case someone comes looking for it."

"I hate tae think it, Master Lou, I wouldna want tae bring danger tae yer family."

"We're protected, Nor, don't worry about it too much."

I nodded. "And these two were from the mercenary with the list."

Charlie said, "Shit, that is a lot of dead men."

"Aye." Tae Charlie I asked, "How long until Madame Livvy arrives?"

He looked at the black apparatus. "It looks like another hour. Why not come in and get a drink, some food?"

"Nae, I think I will wait here for her arrival."

Lou lifted them up, "Alright, I'm going to go secure some weird gizmos all over the ranch. Want to come, Charlie?"

"Yep, there ought to be a second person who knows where they are." They left the porch.

I leaned against a column, and stared at the large oak in the front yard, and waited.

Chapter 48 - Livvy

2012
LOU-MOO RANCH

I pulled in under the archway across the ranch road, typed the code into the pad, and drove through the gate. I drove up the long drive, but jerked to a stop because the Duke was running down the steps to meet me.

I threw the car door open, jumped out, and ran, meeting him at the tree where he swept me up in his arms. I threw my arms around him and buried my face in that warm spot between his shoulder and his neck. He lifted me, so my toes left the ground, and I held on, tight. He held on tighter.

He said, his mouth below my ear, in my hair, pressed against my neck. "Are ye all right, Madame Livvy? I was worried on ye, are ye well?"

I said, "Yes, I'm okay, I just... I really missed you."

He said, "I missed ye as well. I... I daena want tae leave ye again."

"I don't want you to leave."

We were talking into the space right beside our ears, during the golden hour, the last glow of sunset, setting the world in a subdued shimmer around us. Sunset has a feeling — there is a 'before' the sun going down and an 'after' with the night. But in the middle there is a pause, a hang-time, where the wind stops, the light flashes, the world seems to slow, and especially this night — where we had a clash of time, grabbing each other and holding on. The world would keep turning, but we were going to hold on through it, and in a world ablaze, our feelings matched the moment of the setting sun.

I imagined how we must have looked, standing, holding, embracing, completely still, our moment between lost and found, gone and returned, released and now held.

I glanced over his shoulder to see my family on the porch watching. He dropped my feet tae the ground and put his hands on my cheeks. "I was frightened for ye, there was a man, a list, with yer name upon it. Has anyone come for ye, tae scare ye?'

I shook my head, looking up in his eyes, "No one, I wasn't frightened."

"Good." The corner of his mouth went up. "Now I feel chagrined for havin' rushed here so insistently."

I put my hands on his. "What was your plan?"

"I dinna hae a plan, I just came. I couldna not come, I had tae."

"Thankfully Charlie was watching for storms."

"Aye he likely saved m'life." He waved his hand at the porch. "Thank ye, Master Charlie for savin' me from walkin' across Florida."

Everyone laughed.

Charlie said, "Have you seen an alligator yet, Duke? Not thinking you would enjoy the sight."

"What, pray tell, is an alligator?"

More laughter from the porch.

The Duke looked into my eyes, "Do ye still belong tae the man named Chris?"

"I told you, I never belonged to—"

A smile went up in his mouth. "Ye ken what I mean."

"I left him, I didn't... I told him we were done, yeah, I'm alone now."

"Aye, that is..."

"Are you getting married to Enid?"

"I was never getting married tae—"

"You know what I mean."

"It was explained tae me that I was makin' a mistake by allowing Lady Gail tae arrange my marriage." He added, "In m'defense I was in mourning, but I hae used that excuse a great deal, too often, one might say. This is something I hae learned, that it is time tae move forward intae m'future."

His eyes softened. "May I kiss ye, Madame Livvy?"

"Yes."

His lips pressed against mine. I exhaled with the swoony pleasure of it. My tongue against his... tastes and nibbles and licks as our breathing sped up.

Lou said, "Well now, there they go, they're kissing, we ought to go in the house and get away from all this romance or Birdie is going to get ideas."

My family — my mom and dad and grandparents and uncles and brother left the porch.

And the Duke and I stood in the golden light and kissed and kissed. Then he moved his lips to my ear and breathed in and out. His arms around me. He was so tall I arched back, my arms up around his neck, my fingers looped in his hair.

"I was given a lecture, Madame Livvy, from Claray and Aenghus, and they hae told me tae be more decisive, tae fight for what I want, but this is a world full of strangeness — time will always keep us apart. I daena understand it, but I ken I want ye, and this will seem abrupt, but it has been deeply considered."

He pulled away and ran his hand through his hair. He straightened his coat and he lowered himself to his bare knees, the bottom hem of his kilt brushing the ground.

"Uh oh," I said, not because I was upset by it, but it seemed big.

I glanced up to see my family through the main window, watching out, Mom rushed back out to the porch. "Livvy? What is happening?"

I called up. "I think something hugely meaningful."

The rest of my family filed back out to the porch to watch.

The Duke said, "Aye, this is verra meaningful."

He clutched my hands and kissed the back of one. "Madame Livvy, I daena understand how we hae come tae find each other through time, we hae all these years between us, and I hae nae answers on the big important questions about how this all works. There must be rules tae the games afoot, but what are they? I am lost, but I ken when I am with ye I am found."

Tears streamed down my cheeks. "I feel found too."

He pressed my hand to his cheek. "It makes nae sense tae love ye, but I do... and so it must be the work of God tae hae brought us taegether, else why are we—"

"So good together."

"Aye, we are verra good together."

He looked up in my eyes. "We ought not fight it — Madame Livvy, will ye become m'wife?"

"Yes!" I leaned down, steadied his gorgeous face between my hands and kissed his lips. "Yes, I will marry you." I hugged him, "Want to get up off your knees, my love?"

He grinned up at me. "Ye called me yer love."

"Is that better than 'Your Grace'?"

"Twas the one I was hopin' for all along."

"I don't think you loved me from day one, I kind of think you thought I was an unmanageable pain in your ass, and perhaps a bit of a witch."

"Tis true, but remember when ye sat behind me in the door? Twas then that I knew I would love ye."

I grinned. "Brought together because of a rat."

He said, "That was more than one rat."

"And we are going to get married? We are going to live here and live there and—?"

"As ye said, we will figure it out."

"Then yes, absolutely yes, yes, my love."

"Hae ye considered—"

I pressed my finger to his lips. "We, my love, don't need to consider anything, or think it through, or decide. You love me, I love you. The world went crazy and we are surfing a wave of unreality—"

"What does that mean?"

"That the world made sense and now it doesn't, so how are we to consider the future or decide anything when we don't know what will happen next?"

"That is true."

"I mean a fire-breathing dragon could show up on the lawn and I would not be surprised."

"Ye wouldna? I think if he breathed fire upon ye ye would be verra surprised."

He rose, using my hand to help pull him up, and brushed off his knees. "Och nae, I hae pins." He stamped his feet to get the blood flow back to them. "But dragons daena exist?"

"They don't exist, that's one thing in the world that still rings true."

"So far."

I cocked my head to the side. "So, Your Grace, are you going to marry me?"

"I plan tae marry ye so so so hard." He grinned. "Did I do it correctly?"

"Yes, everything about this was perfect."

He put his arms around me and lifted me up again. "Madame Livvy! I am goin' tae marry ye!"

I giggled merrily, then whispered, "I think we ought to tell my folks." We both turned to the porch where all my family was standing. My mom wiped her eyes.

I said, "Guess what, family? I'm going to marry the Duke."

Birdie said, "You will be a duchess!"

My eyes wide, I said, "Wait... what?"

Everyone laughed.

Mom said, "At the risk of being the voice of reason, have you thought this through?"

I grinned. "Not at all, that's the best part." I shrugged. "I love him, and he loves me, that's all we need to know."

Chapter 49 - Livvy

We had a big meal, out on the porch since it was cool outside, Nor asking about security and everyone explaining how cameras worked, until he had a pained expression and we assured him that all was well. He asked, "How many men are on the lands?"

Lou said, "Well, Nor, there's me and Junior, Tim and Dan, Dave and Charlie right now. We have three ranch hands that live with their families down on the south acres."

"So we hae ten men tae guard the ranch?" His eyes swept the darkness.

I put my head on his shoulder. "Our fences are electrified, our gates have codes, we have cameras at every corner."

He nodded and patted the back of my hand, and soon the dinner, the meatloaf and potatoes that were Birdie's specialty, was eaten and then the plates cleared, and everyone scurried away to do their own thing so we could talk together. Nor and I sat on the porch swing and put our hands together between us on the seat.

Our chair swinging back and forth and back and forth. I said, "You're doing better. You look more comfortable."

"Och, I am. The day started with a hunt, and then I had tae kill a man, but then I traveled through time, and now I am goin'

248

tae marry a beautiful lass in a far away land, I rode verra fast in a truck, and her family has riches, the union of our families will strengthen us all."

"That is a *lot*."

"Aye, it has been verra much, most of it good." He kissed my head. "Tis hard tae keep m'eyes from waterin' though. I am thankful tis dark."

"You must be exhausted."

"Aye, but I daena want tae miss anything from this endless and verra good day."

The porch was screened in, the woods around us buzzed with night sounds, the bugs and owls that had been here long before me.

I looked down at his hand, bunched and thick and strong, entwined in mine.

"Did you know...?" I got out my phone and pulled up my timer. "That there was a man, named Amos Dolbears, who figured out if you take the number of cricket chirps in fifteen seconds... like now, listen...count the chirps." I set the timer for fifteen seconds.

We both listened and sort of pretended to count, but the crickets sounded like one long buzz.

The timer went off and I guessed, "Maybe thirty-five? I don't know, we need a better way to count them, but now — we add forty to that number, thirty-five plus forty is seventy-five. That is the temperature tonight! Except..." I looked at my phone. "It's actually 73 degrees Fahrenheit. We were very close, but the point is that we can tell the temperature by counting a cricket's chirps."

"The world is a miracle."

His eyes swept the lawn, the horse pen and stables beyond, the tree line surrounding us. He said, "I feel a little unmoored, as if I daena ken enough tae keep m'self and those I love from harm." He brought up my hand and kissed it. "I usually hae an army around me and brothers."

"I never met your second brother."

"Aye, Malcolm, he has gone tae stay at Finlarig. He daena like tae fight much, he is better suited tae oversee our lands. He is verra good at negotiatin' with the farmers."

"He sounds like my brother Dylan. He's in college right now, studying agriculture."

He nodded. "Aye, they do sound alike. It pains me that Malcolm daena live nearby, but I always hae Aenghus, he will never leave m'side, and he is good protection. We fight differently, he likes tae brawl. I never liked tae fight much. I am trained, but I like tae consider the plan first. He will run headlong intae a fight if I daena hold him back first."

"It sounds like you work well together."

"Aye we do, and I am fortunate, my brothers and I each hae strengths and they daena want the title, och, I canna tell ye how difficult it can be when younger brothers want yer title. Tis verra complicated."

"It seemed like you have a really good relationship with Aenghus."

"Daena get me wrong, I hae tae beat him verra regularly."

I laughed. "Now you sound like my older brother, Ryan, he's off at war right now."

"And who are ye at war with?"

"Well, he's fighting for the United States, that's this land and—"

"I thought this land was Florida?"

"This state is Florida, within the United States, and right now Ryan's stationed in Europe. He's not fighting, not really, though it's dangerous, it could turn."

"Aye a battle can turn at any time."

His fingers stroked the back of my hand.

"And so you are strategizing, worried about danger, and concerned that you don't have your brothers to back you up—?"

"And my full guard and the army that I can raise if needed..."

"Well, you have Lou Muller, he's a storm chaser and a cattle

250

rancher. You've got my uncles and you have Charlie. Charlie is my brother who will run headlong into a fight. Ryan too."

"Aye, I could see it in Charlie the minute I met him."

"And they are all armed, and all the women on the ranch, we can all shoot and ride and... you know, I think we'll be fine."

He said, "Aye, I am sure we will be. We are goin' tae be married on the morrow?"

"On the morrow. You said a lot of really sweet things to me earlier."

"Because I deeply like ye, I am trying tae win ye tae m'side."

"Won."

He teased, "Ye were verra easy, ye agreed afore I made m'case."

"You had more to say? Okay, continue, make your case."

"I hae gained more portals, Livvy, I now hae five—"

I looked up at his face. "You have five now? How in the world do you have five?"

"Aye, a great deal has happened and without even trying I am amassing a fortune in portals that I daena ken how tae use."

"When you learn how, you will be very powerful."

"Or I will be dead from the misadventure. I daena mean tae make light of it, but it does seem tae come close tae killin' me. I hae been closer tae death than ever before."

"Thank you for coming all this way, I know it's painful."

"Yer welcome, Madame Livvy ye are worth it."

"Are you saying you would live here, with me?"

"Aye, if tis required..."

The porch swing went back and forth as I considered. "That is not required. We have been given the ability to time travel, it sucks horribly to do it, it's awful, but I would never ask you to give up your family. We will figure it out."

"Aye, I agree, would ye like tae walk out tae the stables?"

"Sure." I grabbed a lantern for the walk and we strolled through the back fields to the horse arena.

I stopped at the chicken coop. "I love it at night, listen... there are so many birds in there, just all sleeping."

We paused listening to the coo of the birds. Then we continued on to the stables and inside I turned on the low light near the baseboards. Junior had installed it so we wouldn't trip, but it was low so it wouldn't interfere with the horses' sleep. He doted on them.

Nor asked, "Which one is yers?"

"Well, you heard already that I had a majestic horse named Dewdrop."

"Ye dinna tell me how he passed?"

"He broke his leg." My face drew down.

Nor said, "Och, ye hae yer face fallen."

"I'm sorry, I get upset thinking about him, we grew up together. I didn't want to replace him, but Lou wouldn't sit with that anymore, he bought me Dusty." Dusty snuffled at me when he realized I was speaking about him. I stroked his muzzle. "This is Dusty, he's a sweetheart, and I love him, it's just complicated, because I don't live here anymore."

I leaned against the rail and Dusty nestled his nuzzle against my cheek and the three of us were very close. Nor stroked his hands down his neck and looked directly into Dusty's eye. "He's a good horse. I hae never met a woman who owned her own horse, this is a new thing."

"Dusty represents me very well."

We walked back to the house.

∼

Nor paused on the porch. "I daena want tae go inside, I feel at peace out here, tis calm."

"You want to sit on the swing for a little longer?"

We sat on the swing. I curled up under his arm. We entwined our fingers together.

I said, "I'm nervous."

"I am as well."

"We're going to be mixing two families. This is big, you know?"

"I do, tis verra momentous."

"I feel like we ought to be talking stuff out, making decisions, and coming to agreements, like a treaty or something."

"Usually a marriage requires a great deal of negotiation, but perhaps we can accept that this is momentous, and sometimes a verra big thing requires us tae be quiet upon it. Sometimes the best treaties are decided from two families travelin' tae the same place, a neutral location, and gatherin' around a hearth and they daena even hae tae talk about the issue at hand. There is the act of sittin' down and havin' an ale taegether that is enough. We learn that we like tae share a hearth with someone by sittin' beside them. I hae learned that I like tae share a hearth with ye, Madame Livvy."

"I don't want to go to separate bedrooms, and I know you want to be watchful — can we sit and enjoy the quiet night?"

"Aye, I would like that."

His strong legs rocked us gently in the swing and we cuddled occasionally saying things like, "You know who would love a swing like this? Your sister," and "Do you like this beer? It's my favorite," and, "have you ever been outside of Scotland?"

"I hae traveled tae England."

"How did you go?"

"By ship, from Glasgow, tae London."

"How long did it take?"

Until, after a while in the night, in the quiet pauses, we fell asleep.

Chapter 50 - Livvy

2012
LOU-MOO RANCH

Birdie stood in front of us. "You can have a bedroom! You don't have to sleep on the porch like an old ornery dog! You're a duke, a guest!"

Nor stretched and rolled his neck. "Och, Madame Birdie, twas my choice. Ye canna be angry with Madame Livvy, she relented because I asked."

"You didn't want a bed — the night before your wedding?"

Charlie walked up just then. "Birdie, I think the bed is more important on the wedding night." She laughed, spun up the dish towel she was carrying, and smacked him on the ass.

He said, "Whoa! Birdie is feisty this morning!"

Lou came out. "It's too early for everyone to be out on the — what is happening? We're all camping like heathens? Is that what this has come to? We have a five-bedroom house and we're going to live on the lawn?"

I said, "Lou, we were talking and decided to fall asleep during it — it's not a reflection on the interior of the house at all."

"Good, because the inside is where the feast is happening. Pastor Gil will be here this afternoon to marry you off. I convinced him to do it without a license, it took a donation. You

are promising not to defraud the government with any enti-
tlements."

Nor looked confused.

"Don't worry about it, you're not marrying me for US citi-
zenship."

"Again I hae nae idea what ye are talking on, but thank ye for
arranging the pastor."

We ate a big breakfast and then went for a ride.

Nor and I rode side by side around the property, up and down the
old familiar trails. I said, "You know what is bothersome about
this?"

"What?"

"I did really like your arms around me while we rode the same
horse."

He grinned. "Ye liked that? Even when I was asleep on yer
back?"

"That part was scary, I was so glad the horse knew where
to go."

We made it to the wetlands at the south edge of our land, a
large pond, and farther down at the water's edge, two alligators
basking in the sun.

Our horses side by side, I cut my eyes in their direction. "See
that, Your Grace? Dragons among us."

"The logs over there?" He looked and blinked. "Och nae, hae
they legs?"

"They have legs, yes, we named them George and Betsy,
because they are the original settlers around here. I don't know if
they're the same ones, but there are always two down there, they
all get the same name."

His eyes wide he asked, "Do they breathe flame?"

"Nope, but if they get roaring mad they holler and I swear I've
seen smoke come out of their mouths."

He said, "Dear God, m'maiden lives amongst monsters. I question all I knew about the world. What dost they eat?"

"Small animals. They like chicken if they can get it. Oh, and they run really fast."

He feigned his eyes going even wider and drove his horse around to the other side of mine.

I laughed. "You're putting your future wife between you and the monster?"

"I am not from here, ye ken their names. Ye will need tae be the one who talks them out of eatin' me."

I leaned from my horse toward him, and he leaned toward me and we kissed, then we pressed our faces together for the briefest of moments, a linger, then we pulled away. We swung our horses around and went back up the trail toward my house.

I said, "That, right there."

He said, "What dost ye mean, Livvy?"

"You knew that I meant for you to kiss me, and you leaned in and did it, and I just want to tell you, I love you, and this is one of the reasons why."

Chapter 51 - Livvy

2012

LOU-MOO RANCH

It was a Sunday afternoon wedding.

Right after breakfast we had gone through Mom and Birdie's closet and the rack in the attic, but found nothing suitable, so Mom drove to Lake City to the dress store while we were out riding.

She returned with a beautiful simple white dress, tea length, with a low scoop neck, that fit me really well. She also bought me a pair of white shoes and had rented a tuxedo for Nor.

Nor and I separated to get dressed. He would be helped by Charlie and Lou. I was helped by my Mom. Birdie was there for conversation and support.

As Mom pulled up the zipper on my dress, Birdie asked, "Will you be quitting your job?"

I said, "I don't know, will I be...? Oh man, that is... I mean, yes, I will be quitting my job, oh god, Mom, what am I doing?"

Her eyes narrowed. "You know what you're doing, right? You're getting married, honey, this is not to be entered into lightly."

I adjusted the front of my dress and checked my cleavage in the mirror, then exhaled. "I know that, I know that I am marrying the du— I mean, Nor. I get that, it makes sense. I one-hundred-percent know that I will do that. But, what's freaking me out is that when I'm with him I am already in the world of him. But I still have to close out my other world. It's like having two realities."

Mom said, "Most mothers consider it a red flag when their daughters give up *every*thing for a man."

"Yeah, I get that, but it's not really like that, not as dire, or maybe it's more dire, I don't know. It's like choosing to jump into the ball pit at the trampoline park, and I'm ready for that, but I forgot I have a popsicle in my hand that I have to put down first."

"Popsicles are not allowed in the ball pit, we learned *why* the hard way."

"That we did. So, what I'm saying is I'm not going to let the popsicle interrupt the decision to jump. I'm going to toss it away. If I say and do things that make that look like I'm not thinking it through I want you to know I am."

Birdie said, "He is very easy on the eyes and he absolutely adores you—"

Mom said, "But what do you really have in common?"

"Mom, he makes me laugh. I don't know if you know how hard that is to find. You and dad laugh together. Nor thinks I'm funny, he likes me, he just... I know you don't really know what he was willing to give up for me, a large swath of land in Scotland, a crazy amount. It's in the seventeenth century, but still. I just think those things... we are rare in that we are good together. We worked as a team right off the bat. It's pretty unheard of in relationships."

"What will you do for money, where will you live?"

"We have a time travel device. Actually, we have five. I figure I should be able to figure out at least three ways to turn that into money or real estate. Also, we will live here and there. These are not the things that will make or break a relationship."

"I don't know, family is pretty important."

I put my hands on both sides of her face. "My last relationship put a wedge through us pretty good—"

Birdie said, "I didn't really understand what happened there."

"He was an ass, I hid it from you, Birdie. I made excuses for him. I stayed away. I let it go on too long. That's what happened. But if you want the short answer, he parked in my parking space."

Mom said, "Well, you know what they say, if a relationship breaks up over a tiny dumb reason then it must have been really shitty, pardon my French."

"That's because he and I were not compatible. We started out great, we had common interests, we went to the same college, had the same kind of upbringing, went to the same church. But we weren't compatible in the *right* things. Like making each other laugh. Or willing to put down the Playstation controller for a conversation. Or wanting to help each other survive a castle battle."

They laughed.

I put out my arms. "What do you think?"

Birdie dabbed at her eyes. "I think you are beautiful. I think the Duke will fall to his sexy knees in front of you and swear his undying love."

"He already did that, you saw."

I sat in the chair and my mom brushed out my hair. She said, "I think he cannot help but love you, you are the bright future that awaits."

"And he is my solid foundation, the past holding me up, kind of like ancestors." I put some primer on my skin, and rubbed it in. "You know what he did today?"

Birdie said, "Tell me, I want to know about all the romance. It's the best part."

"We were out riding and I did this..." I mimicked leaning out and tilting up my chin. "And he rode close and kissed me, and not just a peck, it was an 'I wanted to kiss you desperately' kind of kiss."

Birdie fanned herself.

I brushed mascara on my lashes. "Keep in mind we have known each other for such a small amount of time, but that's all it takes, a tilt and a lean. I don't know. I kind of think that's all I need in life."

Mom said, "Well, this all sounds really important. I know you're fond of him and when I see him look at you... boy howdy, he has a smolder in his eyes."

Birdie said, "When they were asleep on the porch this morning, he had his hand sweetly wrapped around hers though his neck was all cricked up." She bent her head to the side. "He was loving and selfless. Seeing that was enough for me."

"For me too. There are worse reasons to marry someone." I smeared a bit of pale pink on my lips. And I dabbed on a bit of gold-flaked highlights on my cheeks.

"Now?"

"Perfect."

My brown hair was piled up, held with rhinestone pins, my simple white dress looked great, natural makeup, perfume sprayed all over me. I stood back so they could look me over.

Mom clapped.

I said, "Guess what? I'm getting married."

Birdie said, "*Finally.*"

Chapter 52 - the Duke

2012
LOU-MOO RANCH

My chin was freshly shaved. I was covered in a cloud of fragrances. I was wearin' a new shirt, a crisp white with pressed folds down the front and pale buttons. M'usual scarf at the throat had been exchanged for a bow. I had a new coat, a rental, because I was told by Lou that the coat I had arrived with was too filthy for a groom and m'shoulders were too broad tae borrow one of theirs.

I wore a flower in m'lapel. I was wearin' my kilt but Lou lent me a nicer belt, in black leather, so that it wouldna look like I had 'been tae the rodeo.' Whatever that meant. Charlie had leant me a cream for m'hair tae push it back from m'face.

I tied the ends taegether with a small string, and all approved.

The rest of her family wore gray coats, what they called their 'church clothes,' and all looked verra dignified.

I was called down tae what was called the formal livin' room, following the sound of Birdie's voice.

Birdie smiled broadly when I walked in. "Look at you! Perfection! Livvy will cry when she sees you!" She held my arms out tae see the full effect.

"I hope I winna bring her tae tears. Is that the usual way of it?"

"Of course it's the way! It's emotional! It's hugely significant, it's...." She looked as if she might weep right there.

"Och nae, Madame Birdie, are ye goin' tae cry as well?" I put my arm around her as Lou entered with a stranger behind him.

"Birdie, are you crying? Are you crying on the Duke's rent-a-tux? You're the head of the women, if you start sobbing, they're all going to go."

She waved her arms around. "Oh, we are all already going, there are already tears flowing."

I was introduced to Pastor Gil, and we shook hands.

"So you're a duke? Truly?"

"Aye, I am the Duke of Awe."

"Wow, that is interesting. Marrying into Lou's family, here in Florida. What an interesting..."

Lou said, "Now, Pastor Gil, maybe we don't need to tell everyone in the whole of North Central Florida that we have a duke marrying into the family."

Pastor Gil said, "Not everyone, but Lou, I already told Marsha and Tunsten, last night."

Birdie said, "That does it, all of the county already knows. And we missed church this morning, it's likely they were *all* talking about it."

Pastor said, "It's exciting, I don't know why it would need to be hidden. We need some good news now and again, and your Livvy getting married is some of the best news we've had in a long while. How did she even meet a duke?"

He directed the last tae Lou but looked at me at the end so I answered, "We met in Scotland."

"Well now, that is exciting. She is a lucky girl."

"I am a verra fortunate man." I raised my eyes to the door as Madame Livvy appeared. She was beautiful.

"Pardon me," I said tae the pastor and strode across the room.

I took both of her hands in mine. "Ye are a vision, Madame Livvy."

"You are too, Your Grace."

I pulled her tae my chest and we held each other at the side of the room.

She whispered, "Are you nervous?"

"Aye, but that is the moment, nae the marriage. I feel clear upon the marriage."

Birdie sat down at the piano and began tae play.

Madame Livvy hugged me tighter then let go and brushed off the front of my coat. She straightened my coat shoulders and then tugged the arms down m'wrists.

"Ye are fussin' with me."

A tear slid down her cheek. "We must be set to rights, Mom is going to take so many photos."

I gently wiped her tear away with my thumb.

"If ye are going tae remember it as a happy day ye might not want tae be weepin' throughout it."

Madame Joni passed Livvy a tissue. She wiped her face and fanned her cheeks, then cocked her head. "You're right, let's practice, because our last photo was ridiculous, show me how you plan to smile — this is me." She crossed her eyes and stuck her tongue out. "I have it down, now you."

I smiled at her, then jutted out m'tongue.

"Perfect, a perfect smile."

I laughed. "I daena think that is true."

"Let's do this thing, Your Grace."

We walked over to the end of the room where the pastor stood waiting.

Livvy held my arm, our hands clasped. Her family stood around us.

The pastor began tae speak.

Twas verra different from m'first wedding, and I kent I wasna supposed tae think on that day as twas the past. I had been verra young, and she had been verra bonny, she was also sweet and affectionate. She had been a good wife, contented in our life, in our castle, she had become a mother verra quickly and only lived a year after.

I sniffed.

Livvy glanced at m'face.

I dinna mean tae feel solemn, but there was a difference tae a second marriage. As a widower, I kent I had stood here before. I had pledged m'oath before God and had meant tae keep it, yet here I was doing it once more. I had loved m'first wife, but it had been verra innocent and simple compared tae how I felt for Madame Livvy, a love that was more complicated, newer, and though I had loved her for a shorter time, there was a feeling as if this new marriage would be more profound. I felt guilt for comparing the two and solemn for the act of remarrying. I held a great deal of affection for m'new wife, and somehow all those feelings combined and added tae the importance of the day.

I exhaled.

And looked down on her face, her head bowed, her lashes on her high dazzling cheeks with flecks of golden light upon them.

Pastor Gil said, "Heavenly Father, we ask your blessing upon Olivia and upon Normond, knowing that you have created them for a purpose, and we're confident that your will for them will contain triumphs as they walk together in your name. We ask that you bless them and keep them. In your name we pray," and there was a long time where we had our heads bowed as we listened, our fingers remained entwined. There was a tremble tae her arm beside mine.

He continued, "We hold marriage up as a sacred union between two people who are committed to loving one another and spending the rest of their lives together, faithful to each other, and to their journey together..."

I glanced at her, and she glanced at me... *our journey was meant tae be different than others.*

He continued, "...marriage is a serious institution. It requires deep commitment, faith and trust, and patience..." I pulled her hand in front of me and held it in both of m'own.

He said, "...the Apostle Paul provides us with a description of the love a marriage needs... love is patient, love is kind..." I raised her hand to my lips and kissed her knuckle.

"Normond, do you take Olivia to be your lawfully wedded wife from this day forward — to have and to hold, in good times and bad, for richer or for poorer, in sickness and in health; will you love, honor, and cherish her for as long as you both shall live?"

"Aye, I do."

"Olivia, do you take Normond to be your lawfully wedded husband from this day forward... will you love, honor, and cherish him for as long as you both shall live?"

Livvy's voice was tremulous when she said, "I do."

He said, "Normond, please repeat after—"

Birdie exclaimed, "I forgot the rings! Dear me! Hold on, I'm coming right back!"

We watched her charge from the room.

Olivia and I were made tae stand looking at each other, holding hands between us, looking intae each other's eyes, a comforting of each other.

Birdie rushed back. "I meant to show you these earlier to make sure they were all right, Livvy, they were your great-grandparents' rings, I have had them in my jewelry box since forever." She pulled the lid off a small box, inside were two simple gold bands.

Livvy's eyes misted. "They're perfect."

"I never thought anyone would want them, I guessed that modern women would want a whole ta-doo, but here we are." She passed the smaller band tae me.

I repeated after Pastor Gil, "Olivia, with this ring I thee wed, and I do promise tae love, honor, and cherish ye, in good times and bad times, for richer or poorer, in sickness and in health, until death do us part."

I slid the ring upon her finger. Twas a perfect fit.

Pastor Gil said, "Olivia, please repeat..."

Livvy slid the ring on my finger. "I can't believe it fits you!"

Birdie said, "My father was a big man. I had hope."

Livvy cocked her head, and considered, "I think I forgot what I was supposed to say, but..." She exhaled and looked down at the ring on my hand. Then she looked up and met my eyes. "With this ring, Normond, I thee wed, and I do so much promise to love, honor, and cherish you, in good times and bad, for richer or poorer, in sickness and health, until death do us part."

Pastor Gil said, "Normond and Olivia, having proclaimed your love for, and commitment to, one another in the sight of Almighty God and these witnesses, it is my pleasure to pronounce you married. Normond, you may now kiss your bride."

And Livvy rose up on her toes and I put m'arms around her and we kissed.

Chapter 53 - Livvy

2012
LOU-MOO RANCH

My family was ecstatic. I loved how Charlie was like, 'yep, they're married now,' but the older folks who had walked into the room with us, had watched the moment, and were now standing in the exact same places all acted as if it was the most amazing thing they had ever seen. 'So surprising! Wonderful! Amazing!'

Lou clapped Nor on the back. "It is a pleasure to have you in the family, son."

Dad and Junior shook his hand. "Nor, very pleased." Uncle Tim and Uncle Dan shook Nor's hand while Junior's girlfriend hugged me, and Uncle Tim's date shook all of our hands.

Birdie hugged Nor. "I am so happy, you both look wonderful together," and Mom drew him away, held his hands, and said something quiet and serious to him, they remained talking for a long time.

I was hugged by everyone, laughing and chatting. Charlie was making jokes about how surprising it was that I was married at all because who would ever really want me.

"Which," I retorted, "is rich coming from you."

We hugged again.

. . .

Soon enough, the solemn dignified wedding was replaced by a celebration. The pastor went home. Dad opened a bottle of champagne and filled glasses, and we stood drinking as some of the guests bustled around pulling a cheese and meat tray from the fridge. We stood around the kitchen island with a big tray of antipasto, drinking champagne and laughing.

Birdie and Lou sparred and bickered with each other and gently teased, my dad and Uncle Tim started a round of Bottle Toss. Charlie joined in, adding Toss the Tinfoil Ball into the Trash Can game, where your partner had to step on the pedal for the trash can lid at just the right time.

Nor and I watched the games and then he put his arm around me, pulled me close, and kissed the top of my head.

I said, "Is this whole scene totally unreal?"

"Aye." He waved his arm around. "All of this makes no sense except tis verra alike the game of Chippy we played in Scotland — tis interestin' that the world is so much the same, while bein' in every way different."

Birdie said, "Point at a thing and we will tell you what it is."

He pointed at the refrigerator. "I hae surmised what it does, but I daena understand it."

"That's a fridge, it keeps food cold, through electricity which is energy."

"Energy makes almost everything work, it's like the wood in the fire, fuel in the truck, the heat of the sun."

Dad said, "Everything you see that has a cord is using electricity."

"So ye use a flame tae make the food cold?"

"Something like that."

Nor pointed at the trash can, "This also makes nae sense."

Lou passed me the tinfoil ball. "Looks like it's your turn."

My family watched while I said, "Okay, so you're going to stand here. You step down on this pedal, and the lid comes up, and we have to time it so that it eats this ball when I toss it. Ready?"

"I get tae test?"

Charlie said, "Hell no, no tests."

Nor said, "Since I hae never seen one in m'life?"

Lou said, "You can have three tests."

Nor stepped on the foot, raising the lid and then lifted it two more times watching it lift, and really concentrating. He took his foot off. "Ready."

"No pressure, but as newlyweds, the whole fate of our marriage rests on how *good* we are at doing this."

Nor laughed.

I stood on the line and wound up. I felt his eyes on me, intense. I tossed.

He stepped.

The lid popped open for the ball, a clean shot direct into the middle. It closed with a thwack.

Everyone cheered.

Lou said, "I think that there was beginner's luck, it's his first time with a trash can, they have to go again cause I don't believe it."

I grinned, another tinfoil ball in my hand. "Ready, Your Grace?"

Nor said, "Aye, Lady Livvy."

I tossed. He watched my arm move, intently, then pressed with his foot and the lid swallowed up the ball, perfectly. Everyone cheered again.

I was handed a third ball.

I joked and twisted around, throwing it behind my back. He pushed the foot down, and tilted the top to make up for my poor toss, the ball went in.

More cheering, I jumped around like I had won the Olympics, and threw my arms around his neck.

We ate and drank some more, then Dad said, I have a gift for these kids too." He pushed two boxes forward. "Now I can't remember which is which."

Mom said, "The big box has Livvy's in it."

"Oh, right," he switched the boxes around. "This is from your ancestors on my side of the family, Livvy. As you know my grandfather had a collection, there's one for each of my kids, but the one for women is small and plain so, this larger one is for your husband."

I opened my box, a velvet lined chest with a gold lock, inside was a small gold pocket watch on a delicate chain. I clutched it to my chest. "Thank you, Dad, I have always loved it."

Nor lifted the top off the other box. Inside was a larger pocket watch, gold, engraved with an intricate pattern. On the back were the initials: DL.

Dad said, "Those are my great uncle's initials. This watch is from 1869, it's very old." He got nervous then and shifted his weight. "I um... didn't mean anything by that."

Nor looked down on the watch. "Nae, ye are correct, tis verra auld."

I pointed. "See the dial there? That's showing night and day, and this right here is a calendar dial."

Dad said, "I figured that would be useful."

"Aye, thank ye, Master Dave, it means a great deal that ye would bestow it upon me, tis an exquisite clock and I will take care of it." Nor bent his head to cover his emotions while he clipped the chain of the watch to his sporran.

Birdie asked, "When did you lose your father, Nor?"

"He died about um... three years ago... the year 1667."

Birdie said, "The loss might be centuries ago, but in your heart it's been three years, that's all that matters."

"He was a good man, and a strong duke. I was verra young when I took over the runnin' of our lands."

"That must be a great deal for a young man to take on his shoulders."

Nor nodded. "He saw me married, tae m'first wife, but he missed m'son being born..."

"And remind me, when did they pass, dear?"

"Two years ago, a fever swept through the castle. M'son was a wee bairn, just learnin' tae race 'round the castle."

Birdie patted the back of his hand as he leaned on the kitchen island.

"This is a lot of grief for a man, with such an easy smile."

"Tis yer Livvy, she has brought joy intae my heart again. She has been a gift from God and I daena intend tae ever take it lightly. I will spend m'life in gratitude."

I said, "Nor, you don't have to spend your life in gratitude, you just need to laugh with me."

"As long as my heart beats, Madame Livvy, it will be a beat of love, and in the rhythm beneath, ye will ken, I am saying thank ye for saving my life."

Everyone said, "Aw."

I curled up in his arms, and he kissed the top of my head.

Chapter 54 - the Duke

2012
LOU-MOO RANCH

I followed Livvy up the steps tae the guest room. We were both quiet. She had moved her things tae the bathroom, so when I went in tae relieve m'self there was a toothbrush and paste and soaps and shampoos added tae the ones that had been there when I had visited last.

There was a bag on the counter full of potions and cremes.

I looked through it and carried a thin tube out tae the bedroom where she was takin' off her shoes. "What is this?"

"That is my lipstick. See...?"

I followed her tae the bathroom where she stood in front of the mirror, opened the tube and drew it slowly across her lips.

The way it tugged against her lips was verra... I ran my hand through my hair.

"You like when my lips are colored?"

"Aye, but tis nae the color, as much as tis the watchin' of it bein' applied — can ye show me once more?"

She drew it along her lips even slower than before. "What do you think?"

I chuckled. "I canna put it tae words. I like it, we might need tae go tae our bed faster than this."

She laughed and raised her hair. "Unzip me?" She tapped her finger on the tab.

I fiddled with it then drew it down verra slowly a long descent, tae bare her back. I said, "Stay like this," and drew my fingers down her skin tae the top of her undergarments where I hooked my finger under the band and rubbed it back and forth.

She wriggled under the sensation.

"Ye like it when I touch ye here?"

She moaned as my fingers trailed up her back.

"I believe I will like it when you touch me everywhere."

I could see her in the mirror as I put my arms around her and kissed her neck, the scent in her hair of lavender, the musk of perfume behind her ear, a bit of rose there as well.

Chapter 55 - Livvy

2012

LOU-MOO RANCH

I led him through the room to the bed and looked down on it while he pulled my shoulder straps down my arms, tantalizingly slowly, but then, nervous, I stopped his hand mid-descent.

He said, "Nae?"

"I'm so freaking nervous. Maybe all of this was a big mistake."

"What, Livvy, marryin' me?"

I stared down at the bed. "No, not really that, but this whole, this is really big, and I'm trying to be hot and attractive for you, but this is where my confidence goes bye-bye." I gulped.

He trailed a finger down my shoulder.

"Ye might think our whole marriage is a mistake because ye are frightened of our marital bed?" He chuckled. "I daena think ye can back out now."

"It's not funny."

"I dinna mean tae make light of it, Livvy, I love ye. I wanted tae marry ye, and now we're expected tae consummate it. Ye canna be afeared of me, we're doin' it taegether, and what are ye talkin' on, yer confidence?"

"You're going to see me naked, what if you don't…?"

He froze. "Daena what...? Ye think I might nae like yer body? Ye are verra confused about how yer husband feels about ye. And what of my own body? I am filthy, hae ye heard or smelt my flatulence? I think if ye are standing afore me, willin' tae take the pure white dress off yer body and give me a glimpse of ye, och, these are m'dreams come true. Ye are the beauty, there inna a time in which I am not a beast."

"You know that story?"

"What story?" He drew close and took me in his arms and kissed up my throat to my jaw. He breathed in my ear. I lost myself in his hands sliding up and down my skin, his kisses on my throat.

"Ye daena hae tae be nervous of me, Livvy, ye ought nae be, ye ought tae hae mercy on me."

"Mercy — how come?"

"Because ye hae wedded me, many long hours ago—"

"Like three."

"I hae had tae be so patient, and ye hae sweetly kissed me..." He sucked on my neck and breathed on my cheek.

"But I had tae wait and I hae wanted tae see ye under yer clothes since the moment I laid eyes upon ye, it has been centuries."

"Oh my, I guess it really has." His hand pressed up my side and around to my back.

He kissed me, urgently. "Aye, centuries I hae waited, and now we are in a bedroom and I am allowed tae do it, as I hae married ye, tis with God's approval, and yer father's blessing, and Lou's permission—"

"Dear me, you'll make me lose my sexy mood by talking about the permission of my patriarchy, did you ask Mom's permission as well?"

He grinned. "Aye, I hae her permission, they are all in agreement, tis the whole point of the ceremony, ye ken. Tis for the family tae hear that we are going tae bed each other in a few hours. Tis tradition, but och nae, it has been a long time since I first

275

wanted tae, and now... a verra long time has passed, that is why I beg of ye tae hae mercy on me."

I pulled the strap of my dress down on one side, clearing my right breast.

His chest heaved with an intake of his breath.

"Can I see both, Madame Livvy?"

I held up the other side and said, "Just one, until you take off something."

He ran his hands through his hair, pulled his coat off and folded it over the back of the chair, then he untied his tie and tossed it onto the desk.

He nodded.

I let the second strap drop down so that both breasts were exposed.

He reached out and I took a step back. "More of yours."

He unbuttoned his shirt, his eyes on me, but then pulled his eyes away as if it were a struggle, took the shirt off, and lay it over the back of the chair. He unclasped the sporran and the gold pocket watch and strode across the room to place them on the desk. He sat in the chair, alternately looking back at me, and working on his boot laces.

I turned off all the lights except for one low one, dimmed, near the bed.

He tugged his boots off, peeled his socks off, shoved them in the boots, and placed them side by side under the desk.

"I am learning so much about you."

He said, "Next — more Madame Livvy."

I cheated and holding the dress at my waist pulled up the hem of my skirt and pulled my panties off and tossed them to the side.

"Madame Livvy, this is causin' me discomfort."

"Would you like to see me?"

"Aye, I really would. The moonlight upon ye from the window. I would like it verra—"

I dropped the dress to the ground.

He breathed in and out. His eyes traveling up and down my body.

He mumbled something like, *och she is m'wife...?*

"It's only fair for you to drop your skirt too," I grinned at him, teasing.

He worked his belt a little frantically and then whipped it away and his kilt dropped to the ground.

He smiled. He was fully erect and a truly glorious man in his hot erect fullness. I took in a deep staggering breath, *och he is m'husband?*

I backed up to the bed, sat down, pulled up the covers, and tunneled under them to my side. I patted beside me as he followed, crawling under the covers. He embraced me, then rolled over onto me, his wide shoulders covering me, his shoulders and biceps bunched, his muscles taut. He placed his big forearms beside my ears, his lips centered above mine, a bit of perspiration on his lip, a wetness there, and then a deep kiss, a taste and a nibble, and more tongue-searching deepness. The scent of him, a musky cologne, under it the smell of his skin. It was intense having him this close, on me, heavy, pressing in all the best ways.

His mouth pressed to my skin, he inhaled. "I love the way ye smell."

You do?

"Aye, ye smell of yer ranch."

This is good?

Aye, tis sunlight and a warm breeze, of heat and grass, and always a bit of flower, here, at the nape of yer... He kissed along my throat.

I wrapped my hands around his and we kissed deeply, focused on our mouths and the pressure of him on me, panting, close to beginning, struggling against our desire, our passion, taking it slowly although it was becoming desperate.

He pulled his hand away and clutched my chin to center another kiss, and then he bowed his head and peeled his chest away, to look down at my breasts as his hand stroked down my neck, across my chest and around. He stroked my breasts and fondled and played there and then stroked down my stomach and his fingers played between my legs as I arched up to meet him and he ran his hand around the back of my thigh and pulled it up to his waist and put his mouth on my jaw and pushed inside of me, a lovely desperate fantastic sigh of relief that we had made it there.

We stilled for a moment, marking the meaning of it, our breaths caught — this was our first, and it was intense, our temples pressed against each other, a long deep lingering... *I love you — I ken, I love ye too.*

I looked up at him, out of my mind with desire, my finger trailed up and pushed his hair from his forehead and then I arched up, raised my hips and he entered me again and again and oh so much again. I met him at a peak, as he climaxed and collapsed down on me with a groan.

"Wow."

He nestled his face deep against my neck in my hair.

"That was amazing."

His voice was low and deep. "Ye liked it?"

"I liked it so much."

He breathed deeply. "I am relieved, I wondered if the mechanics of it had changed in yer time, perhaps I had tae learn yet *again* something new."

I pulled away to look at his face. "Really? No, no, this is something that will always be the same."

"Good, because I do rather think the act is perfected, and we ought tae enjoy ourselves doing it."

"Whenever we want because we are married now."

He rolled to the side and put out an arm and I lay tucked on his chest.

"That was intense, everything about you is intense." I raised my head. "In case you didn't notice I think you're great, I'm a huge fan, Your Grace."

"I love it when ye call me that, ye ought tae do it when I am beddin' ye next time, though it might cause an unfortunate rapidity."

"We can test it, does it make you faster or slower? We have a whole lifetime and, actually, we have more than a lifetime. We have years of making love, we can practice, we can experiment, we can test what we like. This is going to be great. I should have married you centuries ago."

"This is what I think as well."

"This time I was kind of speechless I think, if I said anything, it was disconnected from my brain. It was the sight of you, hooo boy, your big D — your wife likes."

He chuckled. "My big D?"

"Your... you know?"

"My cock? Ye are goin' tae call it the Big D? I am verra fond of ye saying these things tae me, ye are a bonny wife."

"Do I have all the, you know, the things you like in all the right ways in the good sizes and shapes? What I'm saying is your bonny wife wants more compliments."

He raised his head and put his hand on my breast. "All yer parts are in the perfect places, dost ye see this breast, Madame Livvy? When I saw the top of it, heaving with yer breath, in the yellow dress, back in the year 1560, I thought, 'Och, underneath the cloth must be glorious.'" He tweaked my nipple, until I giggled. "And now the cloth has been pulled away — Lo! Look upon them! They are perfect mounds for m'mouth or m'hands, m'fingers can trace my thoughts and ideas upon them. There is a place for m'head tae lay upon. Think of the bairns they will feed!"

I giggled more.

He continued on, "And then this, this is the pinnacle of yer shape and form." He pressed his thumb into my belly button. "This wee divot here. I am rarely allowed a glimpse of one but now..." He squiggled down the bed and pressed his lips to my navel. "I ought tae write poetry tae it, tis majestic."

"Wait until you see bathing suits. You'll literally swoon." I rolled onto my side, his face pressed to my belly, and held on around his head, wrapped around him. His arm under me, my thigh over him. It was wonderful and... and... "I will never get to sleep. For one it's early, like nine o'clock. I don't think you will like tv."

"The blue box yer family stares at in the night?"

"Yes, you are not ready for that. In any way. Want to know how I fall asleep usually? Reading. Want me to read you a book?"

"Aye, I think so as long as ye daena dress in any way. I wouldna be able tae bear it."

"It's a deal. Except I have to put on something to go to the bookcase." I pressed my finger to his lips, "No protesting, this is going to be good for us, I will make it quick."

I got up, plucked his shirt off the back of the chair and pulled it on. I peeked out of the door of the guest room right and left and then crept down the hall to my bedroom.

There I looked over my old bookshelf, trying to decide what book he would love. I considered *The Lion, the Witch and the Wardrobe,* but thought that the fantasy aspects might confuse him, so I grabbed *Little House in the Big Woods* by Laura Ingalls. I crept back to our bedroom.

"Got it!" I put the book on the desk and took off the shirt.

He said, "Och, I daena think I breathed the entire time ye were clothed."

I folded the shirt over the chair, crossed to the bed, and climbed in.

"That was frightening?"

"Aye, I thought my heart would break."

"We are going to have trouble tomorrow when I have to dress for breakfast." I fluffed the pillow under me, leaning on the headboard.

He tucked his head to my breast.

I opened the book and read,

"Once upon a time, sixty years ago— "

"Sixty years ago?"

"More like a hundred and sixty years ago now."

"'Tis much like time travel."

"...*The great, dark trees of the Big Woods stood all around the house, and beyond them were other trees and beyond them were more trees....*"

I read to him about the wild animals that lived all around the cabin, like wolves and muskrats and otters and bears and foxes and deer.

"It sounds much like Scotland, but Pa ought tae build a castle."

"It does, and yes he should." I kissed his head. "Want me to keep reading?"

"Aye."

I read, until a while later his hand began to travel up and down my side and for a moment he was driving me back to excitement and his fingers stroked my breast, my breath caught, and I couldn't read anymore.

He whispered, "Ye stopped reading."

"You, Your Grace, stopped listening."

"Och, 'Your Grace'. Ye are drivin' me tae distraction, Madame Livvy..." He grabbed my legs and pulled me down from my berm of pillows, and climbed on me again, "How can I concentrate, my bonny wife?" He kissed my throat and my cheek and my mouth... "When yer lovely voice is vibratin' my loins?"

I grinned up at him.

"My voice is vibrating your loins?"

"Och aye," he playfully growled in my ear. "Ye are makin' me a wild animal," and we made love again.

Finished, satiated, done, exhausted, climaxed, and through, I spooned against his stomach, wrapped in his arms, his hands wrapping mine. The book lying face down in front of us, the last thing I said before falling asleep was, "I love you, Nor."

"I love ye as well, Livvy. I am in gratitude that I found ye on that fateful day in the moor."

Chapter 56 - the Duke

2012
LOU-MOO RANCH

There was a noise. Twas different, out of place. I woke from a sound sleep with a start. My body tensed, listening — what was it?

Livvy mumbled, "What, did you have a nightmare?"

"Nae, I heard something."

In the darkness, her voice, "What did you hear?"

I listened.

"There, did ye hear it?" I climbed from bed, pulled on my kilt, and strapped on my belt.

"No. I don't..."

"Daena turn on lights, stay verra quiet. Will ye let Lou ken? There is a sound, I am going tae check."

I pulled on my socks and stuffed my feet intae m'boots. A quick cursory tie at m'ankles. "Livvy?"

She had fallen back tae sleep. "Livvy, love, there is someone outside."

"Oh," she sat upright, "Oh. Yeah,"

I pulled a shirt over my head.

She said, "I will go wake up and... I'm sure it's nothing, probably just..."

I stilled, listening. "Tell yer grandfather tae arm himself, call yer father."

Chapter 57 - the Duke

2012
LOU-MOO RANCH

I rushed down the stairs, grabbed m'sword from the hall, and rushed out ontae the porch. A man stood in the yard, he was holdin' Livvy's Uncle Junior with a gun tae Junior's head. He had six guards around him, they had guns pointing toward the house.

I glanced to the right, Charlie was on the porch, his hands up in the air.

Och nae.

I asked, "Who are ye?"

"Maybe you don't recognize me. Johnne Cambell? We met centuries ago..."

"Twas a couple of months ago, ye look altered as if ye hae allowed many years tae pass."

Johnne Cambell was clean shaven, wearing a suit with medals on his chest, clean cut. Shiny boots. His weapon looked new and verra dangerous.

He growled, "Put up yer hands."

I tossed down my sword and raised my hands.

"Why are ye holdin' this man, nothing good comes from it."

The door opened behind me.

From the corner of my eye I saw Lou. "Who, and — what the hell is going on?"

Johnne said, "Put down yer gun, old man."

"You're on my property, you have no right, asshole!"

Johnne grabbed Junior tighter, the gun pressed tae his temple. "I will shoot him if ye daena put down yer weapons! Tell everyone to come out. Unarmed!" He said loudly so the people inside the house could hear, "Did you hear me? Step from the shadows! Come out with yer hands—"

Charlie said, "You leave all of them out of this!"

Lou said, "You already have my son, you have men with their guns trained on me, you don't need the women to come out."

Johnne said, "Everyone! Now!"

I said, "Let Junior go, Johnne. This is between us. We need tae let Charlie and Lou return tae the house and ye and I can talk this out. Nae one need be hurt."

Johnne laughed, vindictively. "The unarmed man with his hands in the air, surrounded by his new family, wants tae negotiate?"

He brought the butt of his gun down on Junior's head, hard.

Lou yelled, "Watch what you are doing! Don't hurt him!"

Junior slumped over to the side. Johnne kept his gun trained on him and shrugged. "There is a man, right now, with a gun pointed out the window at me — tell him, Nor, that I have guns aimed at yer family down here on the porch. Tell him to come out with his hands up."

I said, "Livvy, did ye hear?"

Her voice behind me, "Yes."

"Tell yer father tae come down, tell him we daena want any trouble."

The screened door behind me slammed. "Ye arna going tae cause trouble, are ye, Johnne? Ye hae just come tae talk, ye and I are going tae hae a conversation." I stepped down the porch steps, slowly, tae the lawn.

"Wonder how I found you, Nor?"

"Did cross m'mind."

"Your wedding has been noted, congratulations, by the way."

Junior, beside his feet, groaned.

I asked, "What dost ye want?"

"I want ye tae return my Tempus Omegas."

"I only hae one."

He grinned maliciously. "Even with guns aimed at yer family ye will lie — come now, Yer Grace, you have more than one of my instruments. I know ye do."

"I daena—"

He drew back his foot and kicked Junior, hard. "Ye hae stolen two, Nor, I want them back!"

"They are mine, I hae gained them. They belong tae me now. Ye hae tae be more reasonable, Johnne, ye hae soldiers on Lou's land ye—"

"I am being reasonable, if ye daena return my Tempus Omegas yer new family will die. This is a trade ye are willing tae make?"

Lou said, "This is outrageous! Dave, call the sheriff, tell him to come down to the ranch—"

Johnne fired his gun. Junior coiled intae a ball.

A shriek went up from the porch.

"I missed!" Johnne laughed. "Now, the question ye ought tae ask yerself, Lou, is, 'Will I miss the next time?' And even if you call the sheriff, it will take them too long. I'm impatient, we ought to solve this now."

He said tae me, "Get on yer knees."

I exhaled and then dropped down on my knees. "Ye might make a duke kneel, but it daena mean ye win."

Johnne grinned, then he lunged and punched me.

Och. I grabbed my face, there was blood on my hands.

He laughed holdin' his arms up, as if victorious.

His men laughed, but I scrambled up and charged, my shoulder at his midsection, I plowed intae him, knocking him back, and I had his gun.

I stood over him with the gun at his face.

His men all stepped forward, I perceived about five guns aimed at me. I was assuredly a dead man.

Livvy's voice, "Nor! Please don't!"

Blood dripped down my nose, and splashed ontae Johnne's shirt.

He grinned. "What are ye goin' tae do, Nor? Die in a blaze of glory, riddled with bullets, or are ye going tae cooperate?"

He and I locked eyes. "Put down the gun, Nor, I canna hold m'men back for much longer, Billy, tae yer left, has a temper and he daena listen well."

I held the gun for a moment longer then lowered it tae the ground.

He climbed tae his feet, dusted his pants, and laughed again, a malicious laugh. "Yer face is bloody. Get back on yer knees." I lowered myself down.

He wrestled my arms behind my back and bound my arms behind me.

Lou yelled, "You can't just waltz onto my property and kidnap someone in our family, this is the US of A!"

He said, "Lou, stop yer yellin' and go get me the Tempus Omegas Nor stole from me. *Now*." He commanded three of the men, "Follow him."

They marched up the steps, Lou yelling, "This is outrageous, I don't give you permission to be inside my house!"

A soldier aimed at Lou. "Hands up."

Lou said, "Shit, this is absolutely a degradation of every damn thing this country stands for."

"I'm not from this country. I daena care what ye stand for, m'men are going tae accompany ye inside while ye get my things."

I heard the screen door slam and then we were quiet, waiting for Lou and the men to return. I prayed that Lou knew which portals tae give him. Mine and the one that came from the group of men on the moor.

For some reason Johnne dinna ken about the other two portals I had gained from the mercenary with the kill list.

And he still dinna seem tae ken about Livvy's portal.

I asked, "What is yer goal here?"

"I changed my mind on ye. I thought ye would be helpful, but I discovered that ye are dangerous. And now ye hae another of my Tempus Omegas and I winna stand for ye taking what is mine."

I sneered. "I found them — they are not yers."

"Oh, they are certainly mine, without a doubt, all of them. I won them in a battle at—"

"Ye plundered them."

"Nae, twas a battle—"

I said, "I gained mine in a battle as well. How come they arna mine?"

"Because they belong tae—"

"Ye dinna invent them?"

"Nae—"

"Then they arna yers, I think I will hold ontae mine until the real owners arrive."

He chuckled. "They are all dead, Duke. Their blood spilled in the dirt of Scotland the day they arrived, I was a member of their welcome party. We killed all but one, took their Tempus Omegas, and kept one man alive long enough tae teach us how tae use them."

The screened porch door opened again. Lou's voice, "I have them."

"Bring them here."

I said, "If ye hurt a hair on his head I will kill ye."

I heard Lou's footsteps moving toward us. He held out a sack. Johnne snatched it away and looked inside. "Good, thank ye, Lou. See, that wasna so hard."

I exhaled with relief.

Johnne began tae tuck the sack intae his belt, but then he met my eyes. His brow went up. He paused and seemed to consider, then he dropped the sack tae the ground, got out a flashlight, and shined it down into it. He moved the portals around.

Then he shone the light intae my eyes. I flinched.

"How do ye set these tae come tae Florida?"

Och nae.

"Answer me, Yer Grace, how did ye get here?"

"I twisted it."

He chuckled. "Aye, but first ye...?"

I shook m'head.

"Who do ye want me tae kill first while ye decide tae give me the third Tempus Omega?"

"Nae one."

Johnne said, "Lou, what do ye think? While ye decide whether or not tae give it back, would ye like me tae kill the Duke?" He put his gun tae my forehead.

Livvy cried out from the porch, "No! Please don't!"

Lou said, "What do you want? What is it you're asking for?"

"There's a third Tempus Omega here, I want it."

Lou said, "If it will get you off my lawn, I'll get it for you. Just don't shoot anyone."

"Depends on how fast ye go."

Lou hustled around the back of the house, Johnne sent a couple of his men tae follow him.

He kept the barrel of his gun against my head. I silently prayed as we waited.

A few minutes later Lou returned with another sack. He passed it tae Johnne, who pointed his flashlight down and said, "Now see, tis always better tae be truthful."

He waved his gun at Lou. "Ye can return tae the porch."

Lou muttered, "Not without these boys, this is a goddamn travesty."

Livvy called from the porch, "You have what you want, let us have Nor and Junior — we'll do whatever you want."

He aimed his gun at her, she stopped talking.

"Hear that, Duke? Your new wife is begging me nicely. She is verra sweet."

"Ye best shut up about m'wife."

He laughed and said, "Ye are dismissed, Junior, go with yer father, get up tae the porch. Nor is goin' tae go with me."

Junior lumbered up, and Lou helped him tae the steps.

Johnne tucked the sack in his belt and then lifted me by my arm.

"Where are ye takin' me?"

The soldiers marched closer, surroundin' us, an arm on each shoulder, formin' a tight circle.

Lou yelled, "Where are you taking him? I demand an answer!"

"Honestly Lou what good will it do ye tae know? Seriously, you're enraged, demanding answers? This is an argument between time travelers. I am a king from the future, this is a duke from the past. We have a disagreement — why would either of us answer tae you?"

"You'll goddamn answer to me because I have property rights and you're a goddamned psychopath on my ranch."

Johnne laughed. "You're a funny man, Lou Muller."

"You need to unhand him and get the hell off my property!"

I said, "Daena hurt him, promise me — daena hurt anyone here."

"I wouldna dream of it, none of these people are worth the trouble."

I caught sight of Livvy's face, she looked terrified, held by her mother. I yelled, "Daena be frightened, Livvy! I will find my way back tae ye!"

One of the men shoved my head down.

Johnne laughed, "Find yer way back? In all of time, through the whole world, somehow ye'll find yer way back? I think that's unlikely." He laughed. "Now shut up, so I can think."

I clamped my mouth shut. I realized I needed tae pay attention. Johnne pulled a portal from his pocket and used a flashlight tae shine down on it. His dinna hae the band around it. He changed one row of the markings then beamed the flashlight directly intae my eyes. "What are ye lookin' at?"

"Naething, just it looks like ye put in the wrong number. Ye ought tae be careful. Ye daena want tae end up in the wrong place."

Johnne shined the light back on the portal, looking over the numbers, his mouth moving as he recited. He said, "Nae, this is right."

"Good, ye canna be too careful, tis always best tae check again."

Johnne said, "Fuck you." Then he called out tae his men, "Gun formation, go, no go?"

A man called back, "Gun, go."

He called out, "Rear formation, go, no go?"

A man called back, "Rear, go."

He said, "Turn and in," as he twisted the portal between us. The men in unison yelled, "All in!"

And without even a word goodbye I was ripped from Livvy's life, without any idea where I was headed.

Chapter 58 - Livvy

2012

LOU-MOO RANCH

The storm built overhead and we were pushed back from the screen of the porch by the violent gusts, our arms up to protect our faces. Birdie escaped through the door into the house, followed by a few others, but I wouldn't leave the porch. I clung to the wall trying to see what was happening in the night out on the lawn in the middle of a gale, lightning flashing, thunder rumbling, the wind whipping.

Then, after about twenty minutes, the lightning stopped. The wind died down.

There was some sprinkling rain and after that, a clear night, puddles in the grass.

Lou ran out on the lawn looking up at the sky. "What the *hell* was that?"

I burst into tears.

Charlie said, "That, Lou, was one of those storms, in our yard."

"It came right the hell up out of that damn device!"

Charlie said, "That's what we've been telling you."

My mom cut the zip ties off Junior's wrists. He held his head. "That psychopath rang my bell."

Birdie ran for the first aid kit.

Lou said, "So what you're saying is that maniac just marched in here, scared the *hell* out of my horses, and now he's kidnapped my grandson-in-law? Where the heck is the sheriff?"

Everyone was so frightened and confused I think they forgot I was there. I think they forgot in the drama that I was experiencing the bulk of it. We were all dealing with a lot it just... "Where did he go?"

My mom said, "Aw honey," and came over and folded me up in her arms. She smoothed my hair.

Lou barged up the steps to the house, grabbed his rifle, and said, "This will *not* stand." He stamped back down the steps headed to the driveway.

Charlie said, "Where you going, Lou?"

"I'm going to go check the fencing, want to come? Grab a gun."

A moment later he and Charlie, Uncle Tim and Uncle Dan, spun the truck out of the driveway, across the lawn to the fields.

Dad said, "I hope they find them."

"Dad, they won't, they're gone, this is how it goes — they time jumped. I have no idea where or when, it's... diabolical."

Junior sat on the porch swing, an icepack on his forehead. "That guy was such a dick." He peeled up the edge of the ice pack. "Who was he?"

"Some guy named Johnne, same last name as Nor, but I don't think they're related. At least not in any meaningful way."

Mom said, "Same last name as you now, too."

"Jeez, I just got married a few hours ago, and now he's gone." We all watched out over the land.

A bit later the truck returned and slid on gravel as it pulled to a stop. The doors opened, they all ran up the steps to join us on the porch.

Lou said, "Nothing, literal zip zilch."

Uncle Tim said, "So like, what the hell is going on?"

I said, "That guy visited Nor's castle a while back, he knew Nor had one of the time travel gadgets, and he threatened Nor and wanted him to do his bidding. I guess now he figured out that Nor has collected more of them, five in all, so that asshole has come here—"

Lou said, "On *my* property, threatening *my* family, stealing from *my* safe — but I only gave him three, Lil Livvy, that means ya got two left. That's a good thing."

I said, "I don't know how to use them though, and they're dangerous as hell."

Lou said, "Still good, in war it's definitely better to have two than none, it's the prime rule of weapons."

Charlie said, "That might be the rule, but did you see that storm come out of it? It's freaking extreme power, I can think of plenty of things that having two might be worse than having zero. Nuclear warhead in a basement closet for one. I don't want one, definitely don't want two. What's something else? Sharks in your bathtub, hungry sharks, one would be bad enough, two would make getting ready for work real shitty."

Lou said, "I get your point, Charlie, but Livvy's got two of the gizmos, you ought to let her have the win."

"And he doesn't know you have them. That is a win," said Junior from the couch. "I'm glad you kept them, never hand over your spoils of war. Them's yours."

Lou said, "Here's a downside though—"

I groaned.

Lou said, "You got to be realistic, Livvy, you got to think this all through. There are wins, there are downsides, you gotta look at them all with clear eyes. Nor told me that his two extra gizmos came from the dead man with the kill list. That asshole out on my lawn didn't know about them, that's good, but I hate to say it, the takeaway, Livvy, is there's someone else out there."

I gulped.

Junior said, "Yep, that's the takeaway. And those gizmos are powerful, when I was getting my ass kicked by that guy, hog-tied and head beat in, I figured out how bad he wanted them. We gotta step up security."

Junior added, "And Livvy, you ought to learn how to work these machines."

I looked over at the family portrait, the one taken last Christmas framed on the wall, thinking about how I had put my family in danger. "Yeah, but how...? We need to rescue him."

Charlie said, "We don't know where or when he is, we don't know how to rescue him, you have to learn to work the portals."

I gulped. "There's no instruction book, I'll have to test and test and test some more, right?" I shivered. "Ugh, it really hurts, I hate the thought."

Junior said, "I think it's your only option."

Lou said, "You gotta work the problem."

But they didn't need to tell me, I was already thinking it through, I needed to look at my drawings of the markings...

Mom yawned. "We can't do anything now, we are all exhausted, we need to sleep."

Charlie yawned so much it looked like his face might break.

I said, "Yeah, everyone go to bed, I'm going to sit with this, do some thinking, try to come up with some tests."

They hugged me one by one and then they went up to their rooms. My parents opted to stay here in the main house out of precaution.

As Lou slowly went around turning off lights, he said, "I'm sorry Lil Livvy that happened to you on your wedding night. That is a real shit show, but this is the kind of thing that will make you even stronger."

I flexed my bicep. "I'm a freaking strongman at this point."

"Yes you are." He ruffled my hair and kissed the top of my

head and then, gripping the railing, my grandfather climbed the stairs.

I stood in the darkened living room staring out the glass doors at the night.

It felt unreal how an hour ago my husband had been out there bleeding and being taken away by that horrible man and now the world was empty of him.

He had been a part of it. Now, it wasn't just that he had gone somewhere else in the world: he was gone from the world, at least this time of it.

I sighed and then I yawned.

I got a tall glass and poured cold water into it from the door of the refrigerator, remembering explaining the fridge to Nor just hours ago. So much of the world he had no idea about. We had been really close to a new adventure, together...

I finished the water and climbed the stair to the guest room. I sat on the bed. Looking around the room. Nor's sporran was in here.

I looked through it and found some papers. I unfolded them and saw one, my handwriting, my notes from the portals, and more I didn't recognize. One had my name and my family's ranch listed on it and numbers. And some scraps with markings. There was also the photo of us, it looked worn, as if he had looked at it often.

I took the papers, carried his sporran, and put it all on the bed beside me, the papers spread out so I could look them over, with the Little House book beside me. I climbed under the covers and felt exhaustion roll over me like a wave.

I needed to figure all this out.

I would need to run tests.

I would probably need to drive to Amelia Island and put the portal in the sand and wait for it to turn on.

This was a lot.

I would have to be brave.

And then what?

This was the brick wall I kept coming to, there was no getting past it, I had no real solution. How would I rescue Nor? *How?*

With a patch of moonlight on my hands, looking at the gold band on my finger, I fell asleep.

Chapter 59 -the Duke

~

?

?

I woke up with a sharp intake of air. The pain intense, all around me dark, I was on my side, on the ground, *get up get up get up* — my wrists were bound. I struggled tae stand, lookin' up tae see two verra bright lights bearing down upon me, a loud blaring horn. I was in the road — *och nae* — a large truck passed with a rush of buffeting wind. I stumbled back, lost m'footin' on a decline and got m'ankle twisted in somethin', and fell, then rolled down a hill tae a shallow pool at the bottom. Close tae m'face, a discarded cup; a piece of plastic wrapped around my leg.

The water smelled a bitter stench.

I lumbered up, soppin' wet and injured and my eyes swept the landscape. More of the horseless carriages sped by on the road above me. I was in a ditch. I couldna determine my direction in the world.

Behind me a low chuckle.

I turned tae make out, Johnne, standin' behind me.

"Where are we?"

"Somewhere tae prove tae ye, Yer Grace, that ye are but a wee subject and I am the laird. Ye keep yer title at m'discretion, dost ye understand?"

"Nae, I daena understand, explain it."

He backhanded me.

"Och!" I was blinded by pain. I opened and closed my mouth a few times tae make sure it would work later. It would be verra sore.

"I own ye, I am the ruler of the future and ye could hae lived yer whole life without me knowing about ye, but ye had tae go and steal *my* Tempus Omegas, yer designs on the future end here. I hae taken yer devices. Ye are grounded, nae more time travel."

Blood pooled in my mouth, I spit on the ground beside my feet. "What dost ye mean — I am not tae see m'wife, tae go tae Scotland, tae my ancestral home, my lands?"

"Ye will go wherever the hell I tell ye tae go."

I tilted my head back tae keep the blood from spilling in my eyes.

"What am I tae do?"

"Anything I want ye tae do."

Chapter 60 - Livvy

2012
AMELIA ISLAND

Lou, Junior, Charlie, and I drove to Amelia Island. Charlie and I had a plan: we were going to jump forward in time — one day.

We hoped.

I had been looking at the markings for two days, puttering around the house, feeling sorry for myself, wearing pajamas, hoping that Nor would surprise us by coming home.

He didn't.

But I came up with an 'idea' of what the markings meant.

My family had been listening to me conjecture and guess and speculate, but beyond theory, I had to jump to prove I was right. Or wrong.

Test and test and test some more.

Charlie was coming with me because he had badgered me, finally convincing me because, as he pointed out, "Who are you talking to when you're stuck in a field somewhere and can't figure out how to get back? You think out loud, you need me."

This was a good point.

Charlie and I had survival food. Weapons. Money. Phones.

The other portal was in a safe at the ranch, well guarded.

We had driven to Amelia island, Charlie and I had one portal laying in the sand in front of us.

Lou and Junior were standing above us on the boardwalk. Lou had all his storm-chasing equipment out, to get as much data from the storm as he could collect. He said, "So, you'll be back here tomorrow?"

I said, "Yep. Tomorrow."

Junior joked, "May 18, 2013."

I said, "Not funny, it's 2012, don't confuse me."

Charlie said, "I would think knowing what time it is would be the *most* crucial part of time travel."

"Yes... and..." I nudged the portal with my toe. "Having it turn on."

Lou looked up. "What did you say, Lil Livvy?"

"Nothing, just grumbling about it turning on. I guess we have to wait for the storm."

Lou put his hands on his hips. "I got the distinct impression you twisted that thing to turn it on. That's what Nor said, he didn't tell you?"

I asked, "When did you hear that?"

He wiped his sweaty brow with his forearm. "I guess he mentioned it when he was talking to that asshat on the ranch the other night."

"Oh." I crouched and looked closely at the portal. "That would have been useful."

Charlie said, "Or maybe not, you wouldn't have wanted to twist it accidentally in the ranch kitchen."

I nodded, but I wasn't really listening. I was concentrating. There was a twist, a tiny hairline slice — *could it be the way to activate it?* The markings were right, I checked one more time. They were the markings that meant Florida. The markings I thought meant 'the next day.'

So freaking much could go wrong.

Literally everything.

I looked up at Charlie. "Want to look over the numbers again?"

"Nah — I've looked over and over, it's good."

Lou picked up his worn spiral bound notebook covered in his blue-ink scrawl, ever since I had started 'working the problem' he had been keeping notes — he waved it and lumbered down the steps to the sand, put it down beside the portal, and checked the markings against his notes.

Charlie said, "Lou, you don't trust us?"

"Trust doesn't play into it, you always need someone to look over your shoulder, gotta check twice, time travel once." He declared, "Those numbers are as good as they get," and climbed back up the steps to the boardwalk.

I said, "All right, here we go, we're going to test this and figure out the rules of this insane game. So far I've got 'don't touch an active portal.'"

Junior said, "Yet here we are, about to do exactly that."

"Ever since I touched that first one months ago, nothing I do makes sense. Except one thing..."

"And that is...?"

"Marrying Nor."

I picked it up, stood, and stretched my stiff back. "Got our stuff?"

"Check."

"Hold my arm. Lou and Junior, get back." They both jogged away down the boardwalk to the truck.

I looked my brother in the eyes. "Ready? This really sucks, you got this? Ready to be brave?"

"Hell yeah, just go, stop drawing it out."

"Test number one."

I twisted the portal.

≈

The end.

Thank You

There will be more chapters in Nor and Livvy's story.

If you need help getting through the pauses before the next books, there is a Facebook group here: Kaitlyn and the Highlander for this whole world of Scottish time travel.

I would love it if you would join my Substack, here: Diana Knightley's Stories

Thank you for taking the time to read this book. The world is full of entertainment and I appreciate that you chose to spend some time with Nor and Livvy. I fell in love with the Duke when I was writing his story, and I hope you fell in love a little bit, too.

As you all know, reviews are the best social proof a book can have, and I would greatly appreciate your review on this book.

Next book:

Acknowledgments

Thank you so much David Sutton for your abundant notes and helping me wrangle this story in your busiest time. Helping me with weapons, character motivations, and helping me come up with a way for Nor to experience the world that separated him from Magnus. You gave me notes on every single page for which I am so grateful. I'm glad you liked Livvy, me too. And you took my emergency messages about mistakes and plot holes. You're such a good sounding board for these stories, helping me keep them real.

Thank you so much for your help.

~

And thank you so much Cynthia Tyler, for your bountiful notes, for reading through twice, fast, as I was in panic mode. I appreciate your expertise on menu planning, your help with the historical bits, and so. Much. More. And your great eye on the proofing... we were a hundred pages in this time before you found the wrong form of 'to lay' and 'to lie'. I'm calling that a win (though it's not a game but I'm so glad you're on my side.) And for your last minute emergency chapter look-over, thank you!

~

Thank you to Kristen Schoenmann De Haan for your notes, you had me adding and removing, and I so appreciate your notes about what you loved, and for still being here after so many books, thank you thank you thank you!

~

Thank you to Jessica Fox. Your notes had me furiously rewriting at the end, and thank you for telling me what you loved. You always find things no one else does. I appreciate you still reading after all these years, all these books.

~

And thank you to Jackie and Angelique for being admins of the big and growing Kaitlyn and the Highlander FB group. 8K members! Your energy and positivity and humor and spirit, your calm demeanor when we need it, all the things you do and say and bring to the conversation fill me with gratitude.

You've blown me away with so many things. So many awesome things. Your enthusiasm is freaking amazing.

And for helping with notes, thoughts, being my sounding board. Thank you.

~

Which brings me to a huge thank you to every single member of the FB group, Kaitlyn and the Highlander. If I could thank you individually I would, I do try. Thank you for every day, in every way, sharing your thoughts, joys, and loves with me. It's so amazing, thank you. You inspire me to try harder.

~

And for going beyond the ordinary and posting, commenting, contributing, and adding to discussions, thank you to:

Mariposa Flatts, Linda Rose Lynch, Tina Rox, Lori Balise,

Susan O'Neill Mottin, Anna Fay, Dianna Schmidt, Marcia Coonie Christensen, Dev Daniel, Kathleen Fullerton, Debra Walter, Nadeen Lough, Bev Burns, Dawn Underferth, Liz MacGregor, Christine Todd Champeaux, Patricia Howard Burke, Jennifer DeWitt, Cynthia Tyler, Anna Spain, Madeline Benjamin Gonzalez, Sharon Crowder, Thủy Purdy, Veronica Martinez, April Bochantin, Patricia Ashby Davis, Crislee Anderson Moreno, Kathy Ann Harper, Mitzy Roberts, Reney Lorditch, Retha Russell Martin, Kathy Janette Brown Murray, Hamsa Healing, Azucena Uctum, Carolann Hunt, Tonja Degroff, Colette Dullighan, Shannon McNamara Sellstrom, Sherrie Simpson Clark, Michelle Lynn Cochran, Lisa Hogan Sanabria, Alison Caudle, Linda Jensen, Diane M Porter, Amanda Ralph Thomas, Julie Chavez, Kathleen McCue, Jennifer Goerke, Leisha Israel, Elizabeth Pazzini Henry, Ginger Duke, Christina Holbrook Wagoner, Cindy Savage-King, Lillian Llewellyn, Elizabeth Govos-dian-Higgins, Christine Cornelison, Ellen McManus, Cindy Straniero, Enza Ciaccia, Joann Splonskowski, Harley Moore, Margot Schellhas, Carol Wossidlo Leslie, Lillian Silverstone, Jackie Briggs, David Sutton, Cheryl Rushing, Francie Meza, Marilyn Rossow, Sonia Nuñez Estenoz, Nancy Josey Massengill, Antionette Jordan, Diane Cawlfield, Sandra Martens, Sherri Hartis Hudson, Thunda Quinn, Denise Carpentier Sillon, Kalynne Connell, JD Figueroa Diaz, Liz Leotsakos, Christine Ann, Marie Smith, Kim Curtner-larson, Helen Tenn Karlton, Trista Strait, Diane McGroarty McGowan, Sylvia Guasch, Ashley Justice, Helen Ramsey, Therese Stigsll, Julie Lemire, Victoria Girard, Sharon Rigo Carr, Jan Werner, Deborah Carleton, Karin Coll, and Amanda Louise Murdoch.

~

When I am writing and I get to a spot that needs research, I go to Facebook, ask, and my loyal readers step up to help. You come up with so many new and clever ideas... I am forever ever ever grateful.

~

I asked:

What does Livvy have in her purse?

So many great answers, but I used Rebecca Meyer's almost verbatim:

Tampons and pads are a must (you never know when they will be necessary), a red rain poncho, a bright orange safety whistle attached to her keys that grandpa gave her after their first storm chase when she was 10 (she got lost due to the rain and wind and he couldn't find her for hours), a tin of Altoids cause you never know when you'll get the chance to brush your teeth during an intense chase, there's a ton of rubber bands in the bottom of her bag because she always puts them in there and then forgets about them, a dog eared copy of the farmers almanac that she carries around with her everywhere, her phone charger with a car charging port because sometimes she has to sleep in the car during chases, her Swiss Army knife that her parents gave her on her 15th birthday, a bag of lint with a strike starter that she carries in case she has to make a fire somewhere (her grandfather showed her this hack once), the earring that she dropped in there after losing its mate while out with her girlfriends on her 21st birthday, her pocket Kestrel 3000 Weather Meter, her phone, and a small roll of fishing line she picked up after combing the beach after the last hurricane she got to witness. At the very bottom is some crumpled cvs receipts for the travel size lotion, shampoo, conditioner, and lip balm she always forgets to refill.

Thank you for the great list!

~

And I asked for names for characters, here were some of my choices:

Ailsa was named by Hanna Pulver

Dave and Joni were named by Joann Splonkowski

Enid was named by Christine Ann

Birdie was named by Kellie Savage Davis

Ryan Larson was named by Brittany Hill to honor a US soldier who was KIA serving in Afghanistan in 2011.

Thank you to everyone who gave me names to use!

∼

Thank you to *Kevin Dowdee* for being there for me in the real world as I submerge into this world to write these stories of Magnus and Kaitlyn. I appreciate you so much.

Thank you to my kids, *Ean, Gwynnie, Fiona,* and *Isobel,* for listening to me go on and on about these characters, advising me whenever you can, and accepting them as real parts of our lives. I love you.

Some thoughts and research...

Characters:

Nor Campbell, the Duke of Awe. Born in 1645. Lives at Kilchurn castle.

Olivia Larson, Born in 1988. Grew up on Lou-Moo Ranch.

They got married on Sunday, May 13, 2012

Malcolm, Nor's brother

Aenghus, Nor's youngest brother

Claray, Nor's little sister

Ailsa, Aenghus's wife

Ian, Aenghus's son

Nor's first wife, *Mary,* and son, *Eaun,* deceased.

Lady Gail. Called Mam. Nor's mother

Lou Muller, Livvy's maternal grandfather

Birdie, Livvy's maternal grandmother

Joni, Livvy's mom

Dave Larson, Livvy's dad

Dylan and *Ryan,* Livvy's older brothers

Charlie, Livvy's younger brother

Livvy's uncles on her mother's side: *Junior, Tim, Dan.*

Johnne Cambell. Sigh, not this dude again. The Original Gangster, finder of the portals.

(Lady Mairead from the other series is not a fan of this dude.)

~

Some **Scottish and Gaelic words** that appear within the book series:

dinna ken - didn't know

tae - to

winna - won't or will not

daena - don't

tis - it is or there is. This is most often a contraction 'tis, but it looked messy and hard to read on the page so I removed the apostrophe. For Magnus it's not a contraction, it's a word.

och nae - Oh no.

ken, kent, kens - know, knew, knows

Coisich! - command to walk

Ben - mountain

Burn - stream

Alba - Scotland

beinn eireachdail - magnificent mountain

Le misneach! Roar of courage. Twas our battle cry. It meant we ought tae be brave tae accomplish what needed tae be done.

~

Locations:

Fernandina Beach on Amelia Island, Florida, present day.

Lou-Moo Ranch. Near Live Oak, Florida.

Kilchurn Castle - Nor's home. On an island at the northeastern end of Loch Awe. In the region Argyll.

Finlarig castle is on Loch Tay.

~

True things that happened:

Old Graybeard, Sir Colin, and his son, Black Duncan of the Seven Castles, were the builders of Kilchurn and Finlarig castles.

The Kaitlyn and the Highlander series

❦

Books in the Campbell Sons series...

Why would I, a successful woman, bring a date to a funeral like a psychopath?

Because Finch Mac, the deliciously hot, Scottish, bearded, tattooed, incredibly famous rock star, who was once the love of my life... will be there.

And it's to signal — that I have totally moved on.

But... at some point in the last six years I went from righteous fury to... something that might involve second chances and happy endings.

Because while Finch Mac is dealing with his son, a world tour, and a custody battle,

I've been learning about forgiveness and the kind of love that rises above the past.

We were so lost until we found each other.

I left my husband because he's a great big cheater, but decided to go *alone* on our big, long hike in the-middle-of-nowhere anyway. Destroyed. Wrecked. I wandered into a pub and found... Liam Campbell, hot, Scottish, a former-rugby star, now turned owner of a small-town pub and hotel.

And he found me.

My dear old dad left me this failing pub, this run down motel and now m'days are spent worrying on money and how tae no'die of boredom in this wee town.

And then Blakely walked intae the pub, needing help.

The moment I lay eyes on her I knew she would be the love of m'life.

And that's where our story begins...

About me, Diana Knightley

I write about heroes and tragedies and magical whisperings and always forever happily ever afters.

I love that scene where the two are desperate to be together but can't be because of war or apocalyptic-stuff or (scientifically sound!) time-jumping and he is begging the universe with a plead in his heart and she is distraught (yet still strong) and somehow — through kisses and steam and hope and heaps and piles of true love, they manage to come out on the other side.

My couples so far include Beckett and Luna, who battle their fear to search for each other during an apocalypse of rising waters.

Liam and Blakely, who find each other at the edge of a trail leading to big life changes.

Karrie and Finch Mac, who find forgiveness and a second chance at true love.

Hayley and Fraoch, Quentin and Beaty, Zach and Emma, and James and Sophie who have all taken their relationships from side story in Kaitlyn and the Highlander to love story in their own rights.

Magnus and Kaitlyn, who find themselves traveling through time to build a marriage and a family together.

And now Nor and Livvy, who found each other by accident, but love happened and they brought together two big families.

I write under two pen names, this one here, Diana Knightley, and another one, H. D. Knightley, where I write books for Young Adults. (They are still romantic and fun and sometimes steamy though because love is grand at any age.)

DianaKnightley.com
Diana@dianaknightley.com
Substack: Diana Knightley's Stories

A post-apocalyptic love story by
Diana Knightley

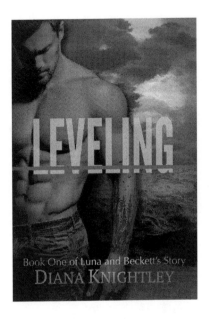

Can he see to the depths of her mystery before it's too late?

The oceans cover everything, the apocalypse is behind them. Before them is just water, leveling. And in the middle — they find each other.

On a desolate, military-run Outpost, Beckett is waiting.

Then Luna bumps her paddleboard up to the glass windows and disrupts his everything.

And soon Beckett has something and someone to live for. Finally. But their survival depends on discovering what she's hiding, what she won't tell him.

Because some things are too painful to speak out loud.

With the clock ticking, the water rising, and the storms growing, hang on while Beckett and Luna desperately try to rescue each other in Leveling, the epic, steamy, and suspenseful first book of the trilogy, Luna's Story:

Leveling: Book One of Luna's Story

Under: Book Two of Luna's Story

Deep: Book Three of Luna's Story

Also by H. D. Knightley
(My YA pen name)

  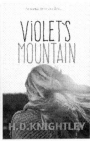 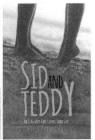

Bright (Book One of The Estelle Series)

Beyond (Book Two of The Estelle Series)

Belief (Book Three of The Estelle Series)

Fly; The Light Princess Retold

Violet's Mountain

Sid and Teddy

Made in United States
Troutdale, OR
10/23/2024